THE CATS' BRIDGE

HERMANN SUDERMANN

The Cats' Bridge

THE CATS' BRIDGE

HERMANN SUDERMANN

TRANSLATED FROM THE GERMAN

A FRONTISPIECE AND A BIOGRAPHICAL SKETCH

Fredonia Books
Amsterdam, The Netherlands

The Cats' Bridge

by
Hermann Sudermann

ISBN: 1-4101-0452-4

Fredonia Books
Amsterdam, The Netherlands
http://www.fredoniabooks.com

CONTENTS

Contents

LIFE OF SUDERMANN

NO indication of what the stars had decreed for Hermann Sudermann was to be read from the circumstances of his youth. Like the majority of Germany's *literati*, he springs from the middle class, differing, however, from the aforesaid majority in that his father was unassociated with any of the learned or artistic professions, or even with governmental service, but was a substantial brewer of Matziken, in eastern Prussia, where the future author of "The Cats' Bridge" was born on the 30th of September, 1857. Of Jewish origin, he from an early age showed the Hebrew's pertinacious industry and wise valuation of knowledge. It was at the Elbing high school that he was first given systematic instruction, though by reason of his father's bankruptcy he was obliged to leave school at the age of fourteen, when he became articled to a chemist. But the elder Sudermann recouped his losses, so that the son was able to resume school at Tilsit, matriculating for the University of Königsberg in 1875, and subsequently enrolling at Berlin University,

5

there devoting much time to the study of the best
English authors.

We find no hint that, so far, young Sudermann
had ever projected any work whatever for publi-
cation; neither did his career as tutor in private
families, begun after completion of the academic
course at Berlin, show forth tendencies of this
nature. Yet a change occurred upon his engagement to teach the children of the well-known
writer Hans Hopfen, for it was at least under
Hopfen's influence, if not through his actual suggestion, that Sudermann at last conceived the possibility of making a name for himself in the realm
of written romance.

The pessimistic tone of Sudermann's earliest attempts—his dramatic aspirations took rise at a later
date—may have been partly due to his acquaint-
ance with the grim philosophy of Schopenhauer and
the sombre tales of De Maupassant. As for Niet-
zsche's destructive doctrines regarding the "Super-
man," he knew them by heart. And there were
now other examples pricking at his awakened
ambition: Zola had already earned celebrity, Tol-
stoy's position was established, Ibsen had founded a
new school. Continual contact with these and other
master minds worked upon Sudermann's growing
capacity for description and psychic analysis, so
that after bringing out his "Twilight Tales"—the
advent of which passed almost unnoticed—he (in

1887) could present to the German public the notable novel "Dame Care." "Brother and Sister," which was printed two years later, was still pronounced under the tutelage of De Maupassant's spirit by the critics, who only with the appearance of "The Cats' Bridge," in 1890, began to admit there had come into the literary arena a man sufficiently original to erect his own standard.

An auspicious reception awaited his first dramatic effort in the following year, when "Honor" was produced. A drama directed against the tyranny of social and moral conventions, much of the success of this piece was due to the considerable divergence of opinion it evoked, some heralding the dawn of a light of the first magnitude, others declaring the *technique* of the play false to sound artistic tenets. Sudermann's stage experiments were, in any case, generally acknowledged to benefit "Iolanthe's Wedding" (1892) and "Once Upon a Time" (1894), through the kindlier sympathy, the broader knowledge of human nature, displayed in these romances—in some other respects pronounced inferior to "Dame Care" and "The Cats' Bridge." With the representation of "Sodom's End" the author took undisputed place in the forefront of contemporary German dramaturgy, while his reputation as a writer for the stage spread all over the world through "Home," better known in America as "Magda," the name of the heroine, whose impersonation has attracted the greatest histrionic talents—to wit, those of Bernhardt and Duse. When the impending performance of "Fires of St. John" was announced in 1899, a recrudescence of feeling against Sudermann was signalized, clearly traceable to anti-Semitic agitations. The play was read by the public censor and put under ban; but the Emperor William, being appealed to, himself perused the drama in question, terming it "a devoutly sublime work," when the piece was successfully produced, though not without the accompaniment of severely acrimonious discussion. If in the new century nothing of importance has issued from Sudermann's pen but the tragedy of "Long Live Life," this author's international fame, both as novelist and playwright, is now a commonplace fact.

In private life, Herr Sudermann is a person of varied social interests. His wife, formerly Klara Lauckner, whom he married in 1891, is locally known as a writer, while Herr Sudermann—who at one time edited the "Reichsblatt"—is a member of the Journalists' Club and a leading spirit of that lively organization, combining social amenity with intellectual distinction, the Berlin Club.

THE CATS' BRIDGE

CHAPTER I

PEACE was signed, and the world, which for so long had been the great Corsican's plaything, came to itself again. It came to itself, bruised and mangled, bleeding from a thousand wounds, and studded with battle-fields like a body with festering sores. Yet, in the rebound from bondage to freedom, men did not realize that there was anything very pitiable in their condition. The ground from which their wheat sprang, they reflected, would bear all the richer fruit from being soaked in blood, and if bullets and bayonets had thinned their ranks, there was now more elbow-room for those who were left.

The yawning gaps in the seething human caldron gave a man space to breathe in. One great chorus of rejoicing from the Rock of Gibraltar to the North Cape ascended heavenward. Bells in every steeple were set in motion, and from every altar and from every humble hearth arose prayers of thanksgiving. Mourners hid their diminished heads, for the burst of victorious song drowned their lamentations, and the earth absorbed their tears as indifferently as it had sucked in the blood of their fallen.

In glorious May weather the peace of Paris was concluded. Lilies bloomed once more out of lakes of blood, and from the obscurity of lumber-rooms the blood-saturated banner of the *fleur-de-lis* was dragged forth into the light of day. The Bourbons crept from their hiding-places, whither they had been driven by fear of Robespierre's knife. They rubbed their eyes and forthwith began to reign. They had forgotten nothing and learned nothing, except a new catchword from Talleyrand's *en tout cas* vocabulary, *i. e.*, Legitimacy. The rest of the world was too busily engaged in wreathing laurels to crown the conquerors, and filling up bumpers to drink their health in, to pay any attention to this farce of Bourbon government. All eyes were turned in a fever of expectancy toward the West, whence were to come the conquering heroes, the laurel-crowned warriors who had been willing to sacrifice their lives for the honor of wife and child, for justice, and for the sacred soil of their fatherland. They had been under the fire of the Corsican demon, the oppressor whom they in their turn had hunted and run to earth, till at last he lay in shackles at their feet.

When the victors began the homeward march,

The Cats' Bridge

the German oaks were bursting into leaf, soon to
be laughingly plundered of their young green foliage. On they came in swarms, first, joyous and
light-hearted, the pride and flower of the Fatherland, the sons of the wealthy, who, as volunteer
riflemen, with their own horses and their own
arms, had gone forth to the war of Liberation.
Their progress through Germany was one magnificent ovation. Wherever they came, their path
was strewn with roses, the most beautiful of
maidens longed for the honor of winning their
love, and the most costly wines flowed like water.
Behind them followed a stream of Cossacks, riding over the German fields with a loose rein. A
year before, when they had galloped like a troop
of furies in the rear of the hunted remnant of the
Grande Armée, the whole country had greeted
them as saviors of Germany. Public receptions
had been organized in their honor, hymns composed in their praise, and all sorts of blue-eyed
German sentiment lavishly poured out on the un-
washed Tartar horde. To-day, too, they were con-
scientiously fêted, but the gaze of all true-hearted
Germans was directed with intensest longing beyond them, looking for those who were still to
come, of whom they seemed but the heralding
shadows.

And at last these came, the men of the people,
who had taken all their capital, their bare lives,

11

in their hand, and gone forth to offer it up for the Fatherland. They advanced with a sound as of bursting trumpets, half hidden by dense columns of dust.

Not exalted and splendid beings as they had often been painted in the imagination of the "stay-at-homes," with a halo of diamonds flashing round their heads, and a cloak flung proudly like a toga round their shoulders. No; they were faded and haggard, tired as overdriven horses, covered with vermin, filthy, and in rags; their beards matted with sweat and dust. This was the plight in which they came home. Some were so emaciated and ghastly pale that they looked as if they could hardly drag one weary foot after the other; others wore a greedy, brutalized expression, and the reflection of the lurid glare of war seemed yet to linger in their sunken, hollow eyes. They held their knotty fists still clenched in the habitual cramp of murderous lust. Only here and there shone tears of pure, inspired emotion; only here and there hands were folded on the butt end of muskets in reverent, grateful prayer. But all were welcome, and none were too coarse and hardened by their work of blood and revenge to find balm in the tears and kisses of their loved ones, and to greet with hope the dawn of purer times. Of course it could not be expected that passions which had been lashed into such abnormal and furious activity

The Cats' Bridge

would all at once calm down and slumber again. The hand that has wielded a sword needs time before it can accustom itself to the plow and scythe, and not every man knows how to forget immediately the wild license of the camp in the hallowed atmosphere of home.

Every peace is followed by a period of delirium. It was thus in Germany in anno '14. That year, from which to this generation nothing has descended but the echo of a unison of pæans, swelling organ-strains, and clash of bells, was in reality more remarkable for tyranny and crime than any year before or since. More especially was this the case in districts where before the war the overweening arrogance and cruelty of the French occupier had been most heavily felt. Here the beast was let loose in man. The senses of those who stayed at home had been so inflamed by the scent of blood from distant battle-fields, and the smoke of burning villages, that they conjured up before their mental eyes scenes of horror and devastation at which they had not been present. Many thirsted for vengeance on secret wrongs, on acts of cowardice and treachery as yet unexpiated. After all, it seemed as if the awakened fervor of patriotism, the flowing streams of freshly spilled blood, could not suffice even now to wipe out the memory of the shame and humiliation of previous years.

13

The Cats' Bridge

No one had any suspicion, then, that the Corsican vulture, set fast in his island cage, was already beginning to sharpen his iron beak, preparatory to gnawing through its bars, and that before his final capture thousands of veins were yet to be opened and drained of their blood.

The Cats' Bridge

CHAPTER II

ONE August day in this memorable year a party of young men were gathered together in the parlor of a large country house.

The oak table round which they were seated presented a goodly array of tankards, and short, bulky bottles containing corn brandy. Their faces, flushed with alcohol and enthusiasm, were almost entirely concealed from view by the dense clouds of smoke they puffed from their huge pipes.

They were defenders of their country only lately returned home, and were reveling in reminiscences of the war. There was that distinct family likeness among them which equality in birth, breeding, and education often stamps on men between whom there exists no tie of blood-relationship.

Warfare had coarsened their honest, healthy countenances, and left its mark there in many a disfiguring scar and gash. Two or three still wore their arms in slings, and evidently none of them had as yet made up their minds to lay aside the black, frogged military coat to which they had become so proudly accustomed. For the most part they were well-to-do yeomen belonging to the vil-

The Cats' Bridge

lage of Heide and its outlying hamlets, and though
their homes were scattered they were united in a
strong bond of neighborly friendship. Some still
lived on their fathers' patrimony, others had come
into their own estate. It had never been their lot
to experience the pinch of poverty, to till the soil
and follow the plow, and so they had remained unaffected by the great changes Stein's new code a
few years before had brought about in the position
of the peasantry. In the spring, when the King's
appeal to his subjects had resounded through the
land, they could afford to leave their crops and,
like the sons of the nobility, hurry with their own
arms and their own horses to enlist in the ranks
of the volunteer riflemen.

Only one member of the little group apparently
belonged to another station in life. He occupied
the one easy-chair the house boasted, an ungainly
piece of upholstery, much the worse for wear.

His face was pale, somewhat sallow in coloring.
The features were refined and delicately chiseled.
The brown, melancholy eyes were shaded by long
black lashes, which when he looked down cast a
heavy fringe of shadow on his thin cheeks.
Though he must certainly have been the youngest
of them all, having hardly completed his twenty-
second year, he looked like a man who had long
ago ceased to take any pleasure in the mere frivol-
ities of life.

The Cats' Bridge

On his smooth, square brow were lines that denoted energy and defiance, and in the blue hollows round his eyes lay traces of a past sorrow. He wore a gray overcoat that seemed too narrow across the shoulders and beneath it a woolen shirt finely tucked, and ornamented with a row of mother-of-pearl buttons. The only military thing about him was the forage-cap bearing the badge of the First Reserve, which he had pushed to the back of his head, to prevent the hard edge pressing on the scarcely healed wound which made a lurid streak on his forehead, close to where the dark hair clustered in heavy masses.

He was the cynosure of all eyes. Every one waited anxiously for him to take the lead in conversation. Next to him, on his right, sat a muscular youth, not much older than himself, who regarded him with unceasing and tender solicitude. To all appearances he was the host. There was a patch of white plaster on one of his temples, but his round jovial face beamed radiantly nevertheless out of its frame of unkempt fair hair that hung about his neck and throat in wildest confusion.

"I say, lieutenant, you are positively drinking nothing," he exclaimed, pushing the bottle nearer him. "Because you aren't used to our beer, and still less used to our brandy, there's no reason why you should be shy of swilling that red stuff of which we have plenty to spare. We aren't rich, as you know, but if you stopped here till Doomsday we could supply you every day with a bottle like that. Couldn't we, lads?"

The others assented, and pressed round him eagerly to clink their mugs and liquor glasses against his cracked wine glass.

A ray of gratitude and pleasure illumined momentarily the sad, pale face.

"I knew," he said—"I knew that if I came here you'd make me feel at home. Otherwise I should have gone on my way."

"That would have been kind of you, I must say," cried the host—"what did we enter into our covenant of blood for, and swear to be true till death after our first battle, don't you remember? In the church at—where was it? I never can pronounce the name of the cursed hole!"

"The hole was Dannigkow," answered the young stranger addressed as "lieutenant."

"Ah, yes, that's it;" the host went on. "And do you imagine we went through that little ceremony with the sole purpose of letting you avoid us in future? Was it for that we chose you for our commanding officer; and blindly followed you into the thickest of the fight? No, Baumgart, there's no cement like blood and powder. So the devil take it, man, you must promise to stay with us a bit, now we've got you—"

The Cats' Bridge

"Don't talk nonsense, old fellow, it is impossible," the lieutenant replied, and blew thoughtfully on the purple mirror of his wine. But his friend was not to be silenced.

"You needn't be frightened," he continued, "that we shall plague you with curious questions. From the first we got into the way of looking on you as a sort of mystery. When we others used to lie by the bivouac fire and talk of our homes and parents, our sweethearts and sisters, your lips were resolutely sealed as they are now. And if one of us plucked up courage to ask you where you came from, and what you had been before the war, you always got up and walked away. We gave up questioning you at last, and thought to ourselves, 'He has gone through a furnace, maybe, that has spoiled his life, and what concern is that of ours?' You were a good comrade, all of us can testify to that, and what is more, the most fearless, the bravest—ah, well, the fact is, that you had only to tell one of us to cut off his right hand, and he'd have done it without a murmur. Isn't it true, lads?"

An exclamation of assent went round the table.

"For mercy's sake, say no more," said the young lieutenant. "I don't know which way to look because of all this undeserved praise."

"Wait, I've more to say yet," the master of the house insisted on continuing. "Once we were really almost angry with you. You know why that was. During the armistice, shortly before we joined forces with the Lithuanians under Platen and Bülow, you were in the guard-room one evening, when you suddenly made a clean breast of it and announced that you must go away. You said, 'Don't ask me the reason, lads. But believe me, I can't help myself. The First Reserve wants officers. I know it is not much of an honor to leave the riflemen for the Reserve; but I'm going to do it, all the same.' Those were your very words, weren't they, Baumgart?"

The lieutenant nodded, and a bitter smile played round his lips.

"Tears were in your eyes as you spoke, otherwise one or the other of us would have asked you if that was all the thanks we were to get for the confidence we had placed in you, to be deserted just then—just when we longed to show those Platen fellows what baiting the French really meant— We let you go without raising an objection, but our hearts bled— Afterward we heard nothing of you, no news in reply to all our inquiries; but I can tell you this much, we never ceased to talk of you every night for months. We racked our brains to think what had taken you away; speculated on where you were gone, and the like, till the men who joined later and had not known you got sick of it, and implored us to give up talking about you, and to consign you to the Reserve refuse-heap once for all. So you see how we pined for you; and now, after two days, you actually propose to turn your back on us again! It's a long journey from the Marne to the Vistula, and a solitary one to walk, and your wounds still smarting. Stay and take a good rest, and relate at your leisure what your adventures with the reservist graybeards really were, and how you came to be taken prisoner . . . it must have been a strange accident that betrayed *you* into captivity?"

He glanced down with ingenuous pride at the iron cross which dangled between the froggings of his coat. It had been bestowed on him in reward for the intrepidity with which he had hewn his way out of a nest of French Hussars and regained his liberty.

The lieutenant's breast was bare of ornament. At the end of the campaign, when a shower of decorations had rained down on the victorious warriors, he had not been present to receive his share. A painful sensation of being passed in the race, almost akin to shame, swept over him. He pushed his cap further on to his brow, and drew himself erect in his chair, as if its fusty cushions threatened to suffocate him.

"Thank you," he said, "for your kind intentions, but I must go to Königsberg directly to report myself to the Commandant."

The Cats' Bridge

"I'm afraid you'll have some difficulty in finding him there," put in a curly-headed young man with twinkling dark eyes, who wore his right arm in a black sling.

"Don't you know that directly it came back the reserve forces were disbanded?"

"Even the staff is broken up," remarked another.

"Then I must try my luck with the Commissioner-General," replied Lieutenant Baumgart. "I have more reason, perhaps, than any one else to be extra careful that my discharge papers are in good order. At least, I fancy so. I don't want the reproach to be fastened on me that I sneaked out of the army secretly. So, please let me know as soon as you can if there will be any conveyance going to-morrow to Königsberg?"

A storm of indignation arose. They all left their seats, some seizing his hand, some forming a circle round him, as if to prevent his departure by physical force.

"Stay at least a little longer, lest the fête we are organizing in your honor should fall through," exhorted Karl Engelbert, the young host, as soon as he could make his voice heard above the hubbub.

Baumgart turned to him with a quick gesture of inquiry.

"In *my* honor?" he exclaimed. "Are you mad?"

"There's no getting out of it now," was the

answer. "It was all settled the day you turned up here. I despatched Johann Radtke at once with a list of all our brothers-in-arms in the country round who are at home. Then, you know, we have representatives of six or seven regiments living about here. . . . Especially did I impress on him that he was to go to Schranden, where Merckel lives. Merckel," he added, "went over to the reservists too; for if he hadn't, he couldn't have made sure of his lieutenancy. So there was more sense in his taking the step."

Baumgart winced at the mention of this name, but quickly recovering himself, convulsively gripped the arms of the battered easy-chair, and with head bowed, listened in silence to what his well-meaning friends had to say about the gala-day arranged in his honor. He gave up protesting further, because he saw open resistance was useless. But the uneasy glances he cast about him seemed to indicate that he was meditating immediate flight.

His friends, however, did not observe his restlessness. After the excitement of war which had stirred their blood out of its normal channel, they found it irksome to subside into the ordinary routine of private life, and hailed with delight any excuse for varying its monotony with a few hours' roistering and dissipation. They were now engaged in eagerly discussing the result of their messenger's mission, whose return from Schranden, a few miles away, they had been expecting hourly all the morning.

"I wonder," said Peter Negenthin, the youth with the black sling, "how the Schrandeners are getting on with that fine landlord of theirs?"

Lieutenant Baumgart started and listened with all his ears.

"They set his house on fire long ago," remarked another. "For five years he's been roosting among the blackened ruins like an owl."

"Why didn't he build his castle up again?" asked a third.

"Why? Because the peasants and farmers down in the village would have thrashed any one at the cart-wheel who dared to work for him. Once he tried getting laborers over from his foreign estates, thinking that as they couldn't understand German it would be all right; . . . but there was a free fight one day down at the inn, and heigh presto!—the Poles were hounded back to where they came from. Since then he hasn't made any more attempts to cultivate his land."

"How does he live then?"

"Who cares how he lives! Let him starve."

In the midst of laughter, mingled with growls of hate which this humane remark had called forth from these doughty sons of the soil, the anxiously awaited ambassador entered the room. He was a

The Cats' Bridge

stoutly built short man, whose straight fair hair, as yellow and bright as new thatch, hung over his round face, which was the color of a lobster from exposure to the heat of the sun. Steaming with perspiration, and breathless from his hurried ride, he seized the stone jug of monstrous girth that stood in the middle of the table, before speaking a word, and held it to his lips with both hands, where it remained so long that it had at last to be torn away from his mouth by force, much to the amusement of the company. After a fusilade of banter and jokes had been discharged at him from all sides, he blurted forth his news. The idea of the fête had, it seemed, been caught at with enthusiasm. Every one in the neighborhood was willing to lend his countenance to festivities in honor of those who had done such splendid service in the cause of German Unity. The only difference of opinion was as to where they were to come off. The Schrandeners, with Lieutenant Merckel at their head, declared that no spot on earth could be a more appropriate scene for their celebration than their own village.

"Then you see, lads," exclaimed the messenger, "the Schrandeners have private reasons for being particularly gay just now. They are dancing in front of their houses, and scarcely know whether they are standing on their head or their heels. I'll tell you why. Perhaps you know that little hymn that they've for the last seven years been singing in church?

> 'Our gracious Baron and Lord
> Of Schrandeners' souls abhorr'd,
> For the shame he's brought on our head,
> O God, let the plague strike him dead.'

"Well, in a fashion their prayer has been answered. The betrayer of their country, who never tired of cursing and damning them up hill and down dale, and heaped on them every foul epithet he could lay tongue to, may now lie and rot in a ditch for all they care. They have sworn not to bury him."

Then arose excited shouts and eager questioning.

"Is he dead, the dog?"

"Has the devil taken him to himself at last? Ha! ha! Bravo!"

Suddenly, above the din of voices, a grinding, crunching noise was heard. Baumgart's arm had clasped the back of his chair with such vehemence that the long-suffering worm-eaten wood had collapsed. He sat rigid and motionless, staring at the speaker with wide, strained eyes, unconscious of the injury he had inflicted on the ancestral piece of furniture. Then garrulous Johann Radtke proceeded:

"Yes, happily enough, they were the cause of his death at last. They have never ceased to harass

and torment him, and it was while they were trying to demolish the Cats' Bridge that he had a
stroke of apoplexy from rage, and fell down foaming at the mouth."

"Lieutenant, have you ever heard of the Cats'
Bridge?"

Still he neither moved nor uttered a word; only
set his teeth on his under lip till it bled. As if
turned to stone, he sat gazing fixedly up into the
speaker's face.

"It was by the Cats' Bridge that the French
made the famous, or rather I should say infamous,
sortie which surprised the Prussians, and it was
the Baron who showed them the secret path which
leads to it. You have heard of the Schranden inva-
sion, of course. It's recorded in every calendar?"

The lieutenant nodded mechanically like a
doomed man, who, swooning, resigns himself to
inevitable fate.

"The stroke took him before their very eyes,"
Radtke went on. "His precious sweetheart, the
village carpenter's daughter, the baggage who
lived with him, you know, threw herself on his
body, for the Lord only knows what liberties they
might not have taken with it when their blood
was up."

"And now they refuse to bury him, you say?"
interrupted the good-natured Karl Engelbert,
shaking his head meditatively. "Is such a scan-

dalous outrage as that allowed to pass unpunished in a Christian country?"

Johann laughed scoffingly.

"The Schrandeners are like a flock of sheep. If one declines to pollute his hands with bearing such carrion to the grave, all the rest decline also. And who can blame them?"

"But," some one suggested, "suppose it came to the ear of the law?"

"The law! Ha, ha! Old Merckel is their magistrate, and he says, as far as he is concerned, they might have flayed—"

He broke off abruptly, for with a smothered cry of pain, and a gesture half threatening, half self-defensive, the young lieutenant had started to his feet. He was whiter than the whitewashed wall behind him, and a thin thread of crimson trickled from his blanched lips over his chin.

"Stop, for God's sake!" he stammered in a strange, muffled, almost inaudible, voice, and those who caught his words shrank away in horror.

"He was my father!"

The Cats' Bridge

CHAPTER III

THE moon had risen and flooded the tranquil
heath with its soft bluish radiance. Down in the
marshes the alder-bushes were tipped with crowns
of light, and the white, slender trunks of the
birches which flanked the highway in interminable
rows shone and shimmered, till the road seemed to
stretch away and lose itself between hedges of burnished silver. Silence reigned everywhere. The
last note of the birds' evening song had long since
died away. Peace, the peace of well-being, peculiar
to late summer, pervaded the wide-stretching level
fields. Even the grasshopper in the ditch, and a
field-mouse scurrying in alarm through the tall
blades of corn, hardly broke the stillness.

A traveler with staff and knapsack came along
the road, gazing absently before him, evidently oblivious of the magic of the moonlit landscape. It
was the young lieutenant, on his way home to bury
the father whose memory was held in such univer-
sal detestation. His host had put his best equipage
at his disposal, but his comrade had firmly refused
to accept the offer, and he had been obliged to
content himself with accompanying his guest part

of the way on foot. At parting he had solemnly affirmed that the compact of eternal friendship that they had entered into as brothers-in-arms after their first baptism of fire would hold good now and always, "the sins of the fathers" notwithstanding. Whenever he was in need of help and sympathy in the future, he might rely on the good-will of him and his neighbors.

This was meant well, but brought no comfort to the young man's sore heart. The allusion to "the sins of the fathers" stung him to the quick. It sounded very much like an insult, yet an insult that he was powerless to resent openly, as there was no shuffling off the incubus of shame which, as his father's heir, now weighed on his innocent shoulders.

Thus fiercely brooding he walked on, and pictures of the past involuntarily rose before his mental vision. He had never loved his father—the harsh, tyrannical man who flogged the peasants, whose laughter was more terrible than his oaths, to whom he, his only son, had been not much more than the pet dog that one minute was allowed to bite his heels when he was in a good humor, only to be hurled across the room the next with a savage kick. As long as he could remember, the small muscular figure, the sallow face with its high cheek-bones, coal-black goat's beard, and little keen gray eyes, had been the terror of his childhood. His mother he had never known. She had succumbed, a few years after his birth, to a long and tedious illness. It was rumored at the time, in the village, that her lord's ungovernable passions had been the death of her—that his love was as terrible as his hate.

Her picture had hung at the end of a long line of ghostly portraits in the dimly-lighted picture-gallery with its vaulted roof, where one's footsteps echoed uncannily between the stone walls, and where it was possible to shiver with cold on the hottest summer day. . . . The picture of a gentle, tired-looking woman with thin bloodless lips, and half-closed lids that seemed to droop from sheer weariness and lack of spirit.

Many a time, unseen, the boy had stood by the hour before this picture, and waited—waited for the heavy lids to lift, that one warm ray of maternal love might at last be shed into his lonely young life. He would fold his hands in prayer, and lift a tear-stained face in eager anticipation, while his heart beat for fear; but the picture never came to life. Tired and slumberous as ever, as if already half-closed in their last long sleep, the heavily shadowed, star-like eyes continued to look down on him with a strange, cold, metallic gleam, till he could bear it no longer, and would rush from the spot half distracted with disappointment.

Not far from his mother's picture hung another still more remarkable—the portrait of an exquisitely beautiful woman with blue-black hair. The artist had represented her in the act of mounting a horse. A red velvet cloak, embroidered with gold and bordered with fur, hung over her left shoulder, and in her right hand, which was covered with a long, wrinkled, gauntleted glove, she tenaciously grasped her riding-whip. It was easy to imagine her bringing it down with a will on the back of a too enterprising admirer. The whole figure was instinct with indomitable spirit and energy. Life glowed in the dark eyes that flashed imperiously from the canvas, as if demanding the homage of all who came within their radius. This was his grandmother in her youth—the old lady whose shrill scolding tongue, and witch-like appendages in the shape of gold-headed canes, liqueur-glasses, and snuff-boxes, were indissolubly associated with the boy's earliest memories. She had been the evil star of his house. Before her marriage, one of the most admired beauties of the Polish court in Saxony, she had instilled into his father with the milk from her breast love for the country of the Pole, so that he, a nobleman of German name and lineage, living on German soil, grew up to hate the land of his birth, and to set all his affections on the moribund chimera of Polish nationality. Though he had married a German lady, he had not hesitated to give his son

The Cats' Bridge

a Polish name, and to bear it at a time when the spirit of hypersensitive patriotism was rampant in the land seemed a worse misfortune by far than being afflicted by some hereditary disease.

But what was the innocent name of Boleslav compared with the indelible disgrace that his father, through his insane infatuation for the Poles, had since brought on him and his race?

And now he was dead, this father, and of the dead one should speak no evil. Yet even as he repeated this truism to himself, the consciousness of the stain with which he was branded, which no power on earth could remove, overwhelmed him with acutest anguish.

Passionately he threw up his arms toward the soft, blue, star-spangled heavens, as if he fain would demand that the soul of his father should be instantly brought to judgment, no matter in what remote planet it might be hiding.

Then came a reaction. His vehemence was succeeded by a gentler mood. He flung himself on the dewy grass by the roadside, and buried his face in his hands. He felt he should like to cry. But his lids remained dry and burning. The thought of his immediate future was almost more than he could bear. He reflected that in a few hours he should find a forsaken wilderness, a scene of desolation, where once bathed in all the rosy radiance of his boyish vision he had beheld a scene of sylvan peace and beauty.

For though he had been a lonely, motherless boy, it would have been wicked and ungrateful to maintain that even *his* childhood had not had its share of sunshine, and boasted its hours of unalloyed delight. Had he not been allowed to roam where he listed, through field and forest, untrammeled by conventions about meals and bed-time, as free to do as he pleased as any Robin Hood or gipsy in Arcadia? When the soft May zephyrs breathed on the shaking grasses, and the yellow butterfly danced from flower to flower, he had lain on his back between the tall blades and meadow-sweet, looking up into the blue sky, his day-dreams undisturbed. He might have stayed there from morning till night; so long as he was not hungry he did stay, and it mattered to no one.

If he took it into his head to wander off with the shepherd to the distant moorlands, to partake of black bread from his wallet, and quench his thirst at the babbling streams, who was there to prevent it? He was his own master. Round the Castle, which commanded an extensive view of the country, flowed the sparkling, merry river, in great serpentine curves, between its wooded banks and green terraces. By the river-side there was always something of interest going on. There the grooms watered the horses, the tanner washed his

The Cats' Bridge

skins, and the boys winked from behind their fish-
ing-rods at the servant-girls paddling bare-legged
in and out of the water. But greatest delight of
all—when the sun went down behind the alders,
the stately wild deer would venture cautiously out
of the neighboring thicket, climb down the steep
incline, through bush and brier, and thirstily lap
up the moisture with parched tongue. Often it
was necessary to lie in ambush more than half an
hour without moving so much as a hair to witness
this enchanting spectacle, otherwise it would have
vanished like a mirage. And what in the world
could be more glorious than when the moon rose
and cast a silver network on the ripples; when the
alders looked like white-veiled princesses, and the
lively wenches sang over their griddle snatches of
plaintive song, to plunge into the depths of the
wood, and with a canopy of foliage overhead, and
moonbeams dancing round you, dream the night
away, and wake to greet the dawn? He let his
hands fall from his face; and stared round him
with vacant, wild eyes. The fields lay white and
still in the moonlight.

Only the tree under which he rested cast dark,
jagged bars of shadow over the peaceful landscape.
A pitiful sound like the scream of a child in distress arose in the distance. It came from a young
hare that had lost itself in the furrows, and, frightened and hungry, was crying for its mother, little

suspecting that every yell was but a fresh signal to its murderers. He was thrilled with compassion for the sufferings of dumb creation, as he rose and pursued his way. . . . Reminiscence still kept pace with his footsteps.

Now it was his school-days that came vividly back to him—the time when the old Pastor Götz had undertaken his education, and the white parsonage among the nut-bushes became his second home. No more vagabond roamings now, for the gray-bearded, fiery-tempered old parson was a stern disciplinarian, and kept his pupils in good order. There were ten or twelve of them—boys and girls together—children of the well-to-do farmer class. He had, of course, never associated with the children of the peasantry, who were allowed to run wild and grow up like young cattle. This was not to be wondered at, considering that the village schoolmaster, an ex-valet of his father's, useless through drink, spent in the various taverns of the neighborhood most of the time that should have been engaged in teaching the children.

Felix Merckel, son of the village innkeeper, was the one of his comrades he remembered best—a strapping, unruly lad, who, at the age of ten, wore top-boots and carried a gun, and whose tendency to bully kept the whole school in subjection. Even Boleslav himself, though two years younger, and of a retiring nature that had little in common with the elder boy's somewhat bumptious temperament, was much influenced by him. Yet his position as the squire's son was never lost sight of, and Felix joined with his other schoolfellows in paying him a sort of sly homage in deference to it. Felix was his mentor in all boyish accomplishments. He taught him to swim, to row, to snare birds, to make fireworks, to shoot rabbits, and even to plunder the poor peasants' garden during church time on Sunday evenings. And though the fruit in his own garden, which he was at liberty to pick whenever he liked, was a thousand times sweeter and more luscious than the hard, sour stuff he clambered after at the risk of breaking his neck, he could not withstand the allurements of those secret raids. Afterward he was often seized with remorse on account of them, and was so heartily ashamed of himself that he would pay back in the morning a hundredfold what he had stolen over night. Such acts of reparation, nevertheless, were only received with scowls or smiles of malice, for the unfortunate peasants were compelled by benighted feudal laws to plow and delve on his father's estates, and were sorely oppressed; therefore it was only natural that the boy should reap to the full the harvest of bitter hate sown by the father.

Of his other companions, especially of the girls, he had nothing but the haziest recollection. There was, of course, *one* exception. Her bright image had floated before him, through all the pain and heartache that had gradually darkened his whole existence, pain which even the fascinations of war could not alleviate. It was her image, that like a loadstar had led him into the thickest of the fight and had not faded from him as he lay wounded, and, as he believed, dying.

Intense longing for her had become identified with that vague yearning after happiness which still sometimes possessed him, just as if his chances of happiness had not by his father's misdeeds been irretrievably ruined.

How this love had sprung up in his breast and grown apace, becoming stronger every day, till at last the whole world seemed filled with its reflection, he hardly knew himself.

As a child, the pastor's small daughter had always been distant in her manner. The fresh, neat, fairy-like little creature never could be coaxed by any of them into jumping a ditch, even if the bottom was dry, and was very particular at hide-and-seek not to allow her frocks to be caught hold of lest "the gathers should go." Now and then, when they were alone together, Helene would show off with pride the glories of her doll's house, and point out that the tiny towels had hemmed edges and a monogram. They would be getting quite confidential till, in an outburst of boyish spirits, he was sure to do something rough or clumsy, which brought down on his head a gentle rebuke, and he was reminded of the limitations of their friendship. Hurt and ashamed, he would afterward try to keep out of her way, but a smile of forgiveness never failed to bring him to her feet, for there was a kind of sovereignty in her little person that was not to be resisted.

Felix resented her power. He called her affected and a molly-coddle, and teased her as only he could tease. She, on her part, had an aggravating trick of turning up her nose and appearing to look down on him, though he was a good head taller, which goaded him, into tormenting her the more, and ended in her running to her father, and with streaming eyes begging that Felix might be punished.

At twelve years old, Boleslav left his birthplace. Some relations on his mother's side, belonging to the old Prussian official nobility, proposed to continue his education. His father had every reason to congratulate himself at getting rid of him. The life he had led since his wife died was scarcely of a character to bear the scrutiny of innocent, questioning, childish eyes. The Baron was in the habit of bringing back to the castle from his visits to the capital curious company, chiefly women, and many a half-opened bud, indigenous to the soil, had fallen a victim to his unbridled lust. Not that he carried on his intrigues openly and unashamed. It was simply that in his private life he refused to recognize the restraint of any moral law, and, after all, what he did was only, for the most part, what his fathers had done before him. Such amours were a part of the traditions of his house and were not likely to excite surprise or comment, unless it were from the boy, who was aware of these doings.

There were many other transactions besides these going on at the castle that were not meant for his eyes. When the great Napoleon's call to arms roused that miserable catspaw of European ambitions, the lacerated country of Poland, from its death-throes, mysterious movements were set on foot in every quarter where the peculiar hiss of Polish speech was heard, and even extended so far as the unadulterated German regions of East Prussia.

Foreigners with slim, supple figures, and sharply cut features used to arrive at Schranden Castle, driving through the village at express speed in small carriages, and leave again in the middle of the night. The post brought innumerable sealed packages bearing the Russian postmark; and for weeks together the Baron's study was locked against all intruders. He himself became taciturn and preoccupied, going about like a man in a dream, actually permitting the stripes and wheals on the backs of his serfs to heal and fade away.

The Cats' Bridge

It was at this time that Boleslav migrated to his relations in Königsberg. Afterward, years passed calmly away, years in which he grew in stature and developed in mind under the watchful care of the widow of a former chancellor, who stood in the place of a mother to him. All the leading families in the town opened their houses to him, and by degrees the old familiar scenes and faces of his home became little more than shadowy memories. His father's rare and hurried visits only demonstrated how estranged he had become from his son, and how little love was lost between them.

Then came that terrible winter in which the war fury was let loose, devastating the old Prussian provinces, and the victorious march of Napoleonic cohorts resounded between the Vistula and the Memel. Scores of provincial fugitives sought refuge from the invaders within the walls of Königsberg. Every house, from cellar to garret, was crammed with human beings, and in the streets smoldered the bivouac-fires of the soldiers who were camping out in the open air.

In the midst of war's alarms, to the accompaniment of beating of drums and bugle-blasts, it was vouchsafed to Boleslav to dream for the first time "love's young dream."

He had lately turned sixteen, and his upper lip was already shaded with a penciled line of down. He knew Horace's odes to Chloe and Lydia by heart, and the passion which Schiller, who had recently died, had cherished for his Laura was no longer a mystery to him. One January evening on his way home from school, as he crossed the castle square where Russian and Prussian orderlies were galloping hither and thither, he caught a glimpse of a pair of blue eyes which seemed turned on him with an expression of friendly inquiry. He blushed, but when he ventured to look round the eyes had vanished. The same thing happened again the next evening. Not till it happened a third time could he summon sufficient courage to watch more carefully and discover that the eyes belonged to a fair young face, which could boast, besides a straight little nose, delicately curved lips, which naïvely smiled at him. The face reminded him of an old altar-piece in the cathedral representing the Virgin Mary standing in a garden of stiff white lilies and short-stalked crimson roses. Of something else it reminded him too, and it puzzled him to think what. He was racking his brains to remember, when a rosy glow tinged the girl's fair cheeks, and the charming lips opened.

"Boleslav!" they lisped. "Is it you?"

Now, of course, he knew.

"Helene! Helene! *You!*" he exclaimed joyously.

Had she not bashfully evaded him, he would have embraced her then and there in the middle of

42

the crowded square, regardless of spectators in
the shape of giggling servant-maids and ribald
soldiers. They withdrew into a more secluded
street, and she told him that on the advance of the
enemy her father had sent her for the sake of
safety to board with an old aunt, who had set up an
institution for the daughters of poor clergymen.
Here she was very happy, and was making the
most of her time, studying French and music, for
she hoped that in the future she might render her
father assistance with his school, for it was not
likely she would ever marry.

All this she related in a quiet, old-fashioned
way, which excited his respectful admiration, casting smiling sidelong glances at him as she talked.
Of his father she could not tell him much; the last
time she had met him he had looked very fierce.
It was some time since she had had any news from
home, because the French were quartered there;
but Felix Merckel was in Königsberg, and she saw
him now and then. He was apprenticed to a corn
merchant, and thought himself quite the fine gentleman. He wasn't likely to come to any good,
though, for he smoked cigars and wore loud neck-
ties. She ended by giving him leave to call on her
at her aunt's on Friday—Friday being the day for
visitors at the institution.

Then she tripped lightly away, swaying her
slender limbs from side to side, and as he watched

her, he felt as if the Virgin in the altar-piece had graciously condescended to appear to him in the flesh, and was now returning to her lilies and crimson roses.

On Friday he pulled the bell of the institution and was admitted. He did not find her, it is true, among lilies and roses, but there were some fuchsia and geranium plants in the room, whose faded, dusty leaves made a pretty background to the girlish figure. The glow of the winter sunset came through the diamond-pane windows, and spread a rosy veil over her face. Perhaps, too, the pleasure of meeting an old friend made her blush a little. The aunt, a toothless, antique spinster, with patches and a powdered topknot, exhausted herself with courtesying and compliments, and after regaling the distinguished visitor with chocolate, in a bowl of superb old English china, vanished as noiselessly as if the earth had swallowed her up. That was the first of a succession of blissful, beatific Fridays.

Troops went forth to battle and returned, but he did not even notice them. The thunder of cannons at Eylau reverberated through the town, but he was deaf, and heard nothing. It often seemed to him, as he looked up at the sky, that he must be lying far down in the depths of the blue sea, and that the world in which he had lived before was somewhere a long way off on the other side of the

The Cats' Bridge

azure empyrean. But that he still in reality belonged to that world, he was forcibly reminded one Sunday afternoon, when the door of his attic-chamber, where he was dreaming over his books, was boisterously flung open, and his heaven invaded.

"Hurrah! my boy!" cried the intruder, with outstretched arms. "I've been looking for you everywhere for a year past, and it's been as difficult as searching for a needle in a bottle of hay. Even now I mightn't have tracked you out if that pious little Helene had not given me a hint of your whereabouts."

It was the harum-scarum Felix, and the gaudy necktie of which the beloved had spoken, flapped over either shoulder in aggressive fly-away ends.

Boleslav returned the greeting more heartily than a few weeks ago he would have thought possible; since his meeting with Helene, the old home and the old life had come back to him very distinctly, and his heart felt drawn to this once inseparable friend of his boyhood.

Felix did not stand on ceremony, but threw himself on the sofa, and as he stretched his legs on the leather cushions looked round him in amazed admiration. The room seemed to him the embodiment of luxury and magnificence.

"You are domiciled here like a prince in the 'Arabian Nights,'" he exclaimed; "that's what comes of being born a scion of nobility, I suppose. I wish I was. Such as we have to rough it, and—"

He paused in order to shoot through his front teeth a stream of dark-brown saliva, a habit he had learned from the sailors on the quays. After this, he frequently visited Boleslav's sequestered retreat, devoured the dainties his aunt sent up to him, borrowed money and books, and initiated him in the mysteries of life at the water's edge. In short, he conducted himself as do most "men of the world" between fifteen and nineteen years of age, who are apt to gain an ascendency over deeper and more thoughtful natures than their own.

Boleslav sometimes thought of making him his confidant in his love affair, but never, when it came to the point, could find the right words in which to express himself. So his secret remained, as he thought, buried in his heart of hearts. But one day Felix astounded him by saying:

"Don't think I am blind! I discovered some time ago that you are head over heels in love with a certain little prude. She's pretty enough, but a bit too holy for me."

The blood mounted swiftly and angrily to Boleslav's brow, and he demanded with dignity that henceforth no disrespectful word be spoken of the fair Helene in his presence. And Felix, though he made a contemptuous grimace, was careful not to offend again by any jibing allusion to his love.

The Cats' Bridge

Later he announced his intention of enlisting in the English navy as a midshipman, that he might be "revenged on the tyrant of his downtrodden Fatherland," as he expressed it, and Boleslav looked up to him in consequence with a profounder reverence than ever.

Then a day came when this friend passed him in the street without bestowing on him a shake of the hand, or even a nod. Only a scornful shrug of the shoulders indicated that he had seen him at all. Utterly disconcerted, he gazed after the rapidly disappearing figure that seemed anxious to get out of his way as quickly as possible.

What could be the meaning of this extraordinary behavior? The same evening, with tears pouring down his face, he wrote asking for an explanation. Before there was time for an answer, a messenger brought him a parcel of books and a note that ran:

"To the Nobly-Born Baron Boleslav von Schranden.

"Having become apprised of events that have recently taken place in Schranden, I consider that it would be beneath my dignity, and contrary to all my patriotic principles, to continue our intercourse. The books you have lent me are therefore returned. The money will follow in due course as soon as I have earned the same. Meanwhile the messenger will hand you five silver Groschen. In humble submission, your Lordship's obedient servant,

"FELIX MERCKEL."

The Cats' Bridge

Boleslav felt as if some one had struck him a
blow from behind. He was so bitterly humiliated
that for a whole day he daren't look any human
being in the face. At last he resolved to tell Helene
of his trouble, in the hope that she might be able
to give him tidings that would at least end his
fearful suspense. She had forbidden him to speak
to her in the street, because she considered such
meetings out of doors unnecessary and improper,
as he was allowed to call at the institution. Yet,
in spite of her veto, he waylaid her and showed her
Felix's letter. As usual, she smiled sweetly and
consolingly, but could throw little light on the matter. The last time she had heard from her father,
the letter had been full of nothing but the unfortunate engagement which had taken place in the
wood near Schranden, when the Prussian soldiers
had been completely routed. That had been in all
the newspapers. There was only one means of
learning the whole truth. Helene could walk
along by the river's bank, where the clerks from
the great warehouses lounged away their spare
time, and make inquiries of Felix. This she consented to do, though reluctantly; and he, in a
fever of anxiety, waited for her return on one of
the bridges.

"He does think too much of himself!" she said,
as she came back slowly from her errand, the
color deepening in her cheeks. "And so they all do,

these merchants' clerks. It's not likely that I should allow any of them to make love to me!"

She smiled, and hid her burning face in the blue silk reticule she always carried.

"But you needn't mind him, dear Boleslav. Since he has determined to go as a midshipman, he has got love for the Fatherland on the brain."

"How have I interfered with his love for the Fatherland?" asked Boleslav. "Don't I abominate that bloodhound Bonaparte as much as he does?"

Helene was silent, and gathered the folds of her cloak closer about her slender limbs, to keep out the bitter winter wind. Then she continued:

"You may rely on me. I will never bear a grudge against you for it."

"For what? Good God, tell me at once!"

And then at last the mystery was cleared up.

"You mustn't take it too much to heart, dearest Boleslav. At home in the village they all say that your father showed the French the path by the Cats' Bridge in the middle of the night, so that they might surprise the Prussians; and that gipsy-looking Regina, the carpenter's daughter—you remember the little curly-headed thing who was at school with you and me—she confessed it, because it was she who really led the way. And now the people call your father the betrayer of his country, and refuse to work for him any more, and have burned down his house."

The Cats' Bridge

Ah! so that was it. Now he knew all. In that hour his life's budding joys and hopes were withered like the blossoms of a tree struck by lightning in May. How intolerable were these memories of darkest hours of silent torture—hours in which he was oppressed with a sense of crime, and when shame literally consumed him!

It was some time before the news of the betrayal was openly spoken about in Königsberg. Months passed before the first signs that it had become known manifested themselves, and during these months his whole character underwent a complete change.

His glance became shifty and uneasy, his color often forsook him. Shy and awkward, he withdrew more and more from society, and frequented none of his old haunts. He would start and tremble at every word unexpectedly addressed to him. Then came days when the masters at the school began to look askance at him, and the pupils to shun him—days in which his aunt kept her room to escape his morning greeting, and the family sat in conclave behind closed doors, while the servants began to set his orders at defiance, and from time to time spat on the ground as they passed his door.

So he watched it creeping on, nearer and nearer, the cold, clammy monster, that, snake-like, was to bind his limbs and freeze the blood in his veins. He watched its wriggling progress, heard the gloating hiss of its approach, and, defenseless, paralyzed, he stared it stonily in the face, lacking the courage to cry out, or even to moan.

He had lost Helene too. Not through any fault of hers. She had still allowed him to go on pulling the institution bell on Fridays as if nothing had happened, and had been friendly as ever, and had even tried to distract his thoughts from the painful subject on which they incessantly brooded, with mild little jokes. But was it because he was himself so altered that he could only see the rest of the world through a distorting mist of shame, or had she really, since that day of the revelation, adopted a tone of pitying compassion toward him? Anyhow, he became more and more embarrassed in her presence, and dared not meet her eye.

One day, instead of Helene, the old schoolmistress received him alone. She courtesied and grinned as usual, and assured him, a hundred times at least, that she was his humblest servant; but what she proceeded to unfold seemed to Boleslav the last straw. Her dear nephew, the *Herr Pastor,* she stuttered, thought it best that the intimacy between his daughter and the young nobleman should terminate, and in order that there should be no further temptation to continue it, had decided to remove her instantly from the town of Königsberg. A note sealed with blue sealing-wax contained Helene's farewell:

The Cats' Bridge

"DEAR, DEAR BOLESLAV—My father commands me to give up my friendship with you. I must obey him. Good-by. I shall always be fond of you—always. I swear it. Your   HELENE."

Six hastily scribbled lines! Were these to be his food and drink through a life of longing and renunciation? Yet had he any right to expect more? Had she not promised to be true, and to hold to him, though every one else had cast him off? From that time forward she became for him transfigured and a saint. Her face became more than ever identified in his imagination with that of the Madonna he had seen in the Cathedral, and whenever he pictured her he beheld her adorned with an aureole, and surrounded by lilies and roses.

Had it not been for his extreme youth, energy and self-reliance might possibly have helped him over the abyss of enervating grief; but a habit of childlike respect, a latent instinct of veneration, put the idea of asking his father to explain what had happened, much less of calling him to account for it, out of the question. It was his unexpected appearance on the scene that at last roused in him a spirit of revolt.

He was now seventeen, and would have been ready to pass into the university, even if the school authorities had not repeatedly hinted that his withdrawal would be in every way desirable. Even his

The Cats' Bridge

kindly aunt, who had carefully avoided referring to the rumor through which she herself suffered keenly, had, as mercifully as she knew how, spoken to him about the advisability of his going somewhere else to finish his studies.

Under other circumstances, his pride, his zeal for fair play, and his own honor would have rebelled against this unjust dismissal. But now in his unspeakable bitterness he cherished only one wish, and that was to hide away somewhere with his disgrace, and be seen by no human eye.

And in this mood he stood one day face to face with his father.

The baron had come to town, to call in the aid of the law in dealing with his rebellious peasants, but had found every door shut in his face. His fury knew no bounds; he appeared to have lost all control over himself, and his demeanor was one of desperate defiance.

At the sight of the short stubborn figure, the bull-neck and the gray fiery eyes rolling in their red sockets, Boleslav was seized with the old boyish terror. He had to pull himself together with a tremendous effort before he could bring the fatal question over his lips.

"Father, is it true what people are saying, that—"

Suspicion blazed up in the small gray eyes.

"Eh?—what are people saying?" he interrupted.

The Cats' Bridge

"That it was through you that the French found out the path by the Cats' Bridge."

"And what if it was through me, you Hottentot? What if I did avenge the wrongs of the down-trodden Pole on this pack of cowardly Russian thieves—these hulking, stupid, lazy serfs, who would only get their deserts if the great Napoleon extirpated them altogether from off the face of the earth? Don't gape at me like that, clown! What I did was done as a sacred duty. Heavily chained, scourged human beings cried out imploringly to me, 'Save us, save us!' I could not save them, it is true; that work was reserved for a greater than I—but I could at least *help*, help him, who like an avenging angel swept over Europe and laid it waste—help him to annihilate a handful of ruffians I saw providentially delivered into my hand."

As he held forth thus, his short figure seemed to grow. His eyes flashed fire. The demon of fanaticism that so strongly resembles inspiration, its angelic sister, enveloped him in its red-hot, glowing mantle.

Boleslav shrank away, trembling. He felt keenly how completely every tie between him and this man was now severed.

"Let them whisper, and nudge each other as I pass," he continued, "and make faces; what the devil do I care? They dared not do it so long as the Corsican lion held them in his claws. And after all, who is to prove it against me? If it hadn't been for that fool Regina, who let her father hunt her down in the Bockshorn, every one would naturally have supposed that General Latour, with his inventive brain, had found out the way over the river and through the wood of his own accord. As it is, the wretches are all at my throat. . . . The peasants are no longer to be brought to heel with the knout. They've always been so fond of me, you see. If what the papers say is true, and the king is willing to let the mutiny continue, they'll kill me, as sure as fate. You will have good cause to congratulate yourself on your succession, my boy!"

Those were the last words his father had ever spoken to him, for the conversation, which had taken place in his own study, was interrupted at this point by the entrance of his aunt.

The aristocratic old lady recoiled from the touch of the Baron's red muscular hand as from that of some poisonous reptile. But mastering her repugnance, she asked for a few minutes' private talk with him.

What decision they came to over his future he was never to know, for even before the short interview had elapsed his former life already lay behind him like a nightmare, and he stood in the street and reflected through which of the city gates he should wander out into the wide world. Finally, the goal of his travels proved to be a small property in a remote corner of Lithuania, where he found rest in hard work, and an opportunity of fitting himself for the duties of a landed proprietor.

Years went by. For him they meant unremitting labor for his daily bread—a struggle for existence full of hardships, which, however, could be engaged in without shame, or any wounding of his self-esteem. For now he no longer bore the abhorred name of his fathers. If at the same time he only could have cast off, like a soiled garment, the host of bitter recollections with which it was associated, he would have been happier. But consciousness of the infamy that clung to the discarded name remained ever present. Love for his country, which hitherto had only slumbered in his heart, now bounded into full life. The passion of patriotism grew and grew, till it became a tormenting demon which scourged him with scorpions, drove the blood from his face, the sleep from his eyes, and heaped the guilt of Prussia's misfortunes on his shoulders.

Only once during this time did news of his home reach him. That was when he read in a Königsberg news-sheet that Schranden Castle, which had enjoyed such an unenviable notoriety in the winter of 1807, had been burned down with all its outlying buildings. Then he had folded his hands,

The Cats' Bridge

and a sound had escaped his lips like a prayer of thanksgiving.

Expiation! expiation! must be the watchword of his soul.

But as yet nothing could be expiated. Still the unhappy Fatherland lay crushed beneath the heel of the dictator. Then came the downfall of the great army on the snow-covered plains of Eastern Europe, and the rising of Prussia quickly followed.

Now the hour had come. His hour! He would die—give his life for the Fatherland, and expiate his father's sin with his own blood.

In the volunteer Baumgart, who entered Königsberg on the 5th of March, 1813, no one recognized the youthful Baron von Schranden, who, just five years before, had fled from the town unable to face the dishonor brought upon his name; and there were many now hailing him with shouts and cheers of welcome, who then would have driven him out with stones and brickbats.

He attached himself to a cluster of intrepid sons of the soil, from whose mouths the dialect of his lost home fell familiarly and musically on his ear. He became their friend and their leader, till suddenly a well-known face cropped up in the camp, the sight of which immediately drove Lieutenant Baumgart out of it.

Felix Merckel, he knew too well, would not have hesitated to betray him to his comrades, and to inform them who it was that led them to battle.

What followed was like a ghastly confused phantasmagoria, in which bloodshed, salvos, and death-rattles played their part. Why had he not died? How had he lived through it? These were the questions he asked himself on first regaining consciousness and opening his eyes on the world, after lying for months between life and death. For him, it seemed, no French sabre had been sharpened, no French bullet fired.

The one complete atonement his conscience told him it was in his power to make had been denied him. Was a heavier one awaiting him now, as he drew near the dusky woodlands of his birthplace in the dim gray dawn of day?

The Cats' Bridge

CHAPTER IV

IT was eight o'clock in the morning, and already the rays of the sun had strengthened, as Boleslav left the wild tangle of the forest behind him, and beheld the native homestead stretched out at his feet.

He had not set eyes on it for ten years. His first fierce impulse now was to shake his fist at the village which lay there so hypocritically idyllic in the calm of early morning, with its white toy cottages set in bowers of green bushes, its curls of blue-gray smoke, and opalescent slate church spire rising peacefully against the sky.

Beyond were the magnificent groups of old trees with dark, almost black foliage and yellowish trunks belonging to the Castle park, which sloped away on the eastern side of the hill. But the Castle itself, that had crowned the hill with its shining battlemented twin-towers, and had queened the landscape far and wide—where was it? Had the earth opened and swallowed the imposing structure whole? For a moment he was startled and shocked at its total disappearance. Then he remembered. How stupid it was to have forgotten! They had burnt it down, razed it to the ground.

Many and many a time he had thought of that deed of violence, which had laid waste the inheritance of his fathers, with a sort of grim satisfaction. But now, when he saw with his bodily eyes the scene of the conflagration, he felt sullen resentment rise in his heart.

"Incendiaries! Accursed incendiaries!" he cried, and once more shook his fist at the homesteads of his enemies. *His* enemies? Yes, in the flash of a moment it seemed clearly demonstrated that his father's enemies must be his enemies. Had he not inherited them, together with these woods and fertile valleys, with yonder smoked, blackened heap of ruins (he now noticed it for the first time) that reared itself like the mighty hand of a giant calling down the wrath of Heaven—together with that awful crime, which no one on earth hated more than he did, from which no one had suffered as he had suffered. . . . And though, instead of filial love, he had cherished nothing but a sensation of paralyzing fear toward his father, though for years he had deliberately cut himself adrift from ties of kindred, and the performance of duties that custom and civilization impose on those who are destined to hand down an ancient name and inherit vast estates—in spite of it all, the fact remained that it was his father's blood

The Cats' Bridge

flowing in his veins, and he felt it at this moment coursing through them tumultuously, and rising in hot anger at the wrong that had been done his race.

A wild gleam shone in his eyes as he fumbled with his left hand for the leather case strung over his shoulder, from which obtruded the burnished knobs of a pair of cavalry pistols.

"Won't bury him!" he murmured through his clenched teeth, clasping the pistols close. "Won't bury him, indeed! We shall see!" And with a bitter, mirthless laugh, he walked resolutely down into the village.

The one long straggling street lay before him, deserted and basking in the brilliant sunshine. The cart-ruts in the rich clay soil shone as if they had been glazed; bottle-glass and rags from old besoms filled the interstices to prevent the accumulation of stones. On either side of the road stood the thatched cottages of the peasants, shaded by limes and chestnuts, some of whose leaves were even now beginning to look autumnally sere and yellow. These peasants had formerly been under the jurisdiction of the Castle, and only since the new rural laws came into force had been relieved of their service and joined the freemen.

Here and there he saw a new fence painted in glaring colors, as if the owner wished to mark off his recently acquired possession from the rest of the inhabited globe. In other respects the new *régime* had left everything much the same. Sunflowers and herbs bloomed in the front gardens as they had always done; damp mattresses hung out of the windows to air just as of old. Only the number of taverns had increased. Boleslav counted three, whereas once the Black Eagle had reigned supreme and met all the requirements of the place.

Nearer the church were the white houses of the free artisans, burghers as they were called, who paid ground-rent to the Castle, and therefore enjoyed the privilege of cultivating their own vegetable plots as they pleased. There were a couple of blacksmiths with the sign of a horseshoe over the entrance of their forges, two or three cobblers, a wheelwright, a basketmaker, and a—

He paused and let his eyes rest on a dilapidated tumble-down hovel, the most wretched in the whole row. A dirty green shield hung over the door, bearing the almost obliterated inscription:

HANS HACKELBERG
CARPENTER AND PARISH UNDERTAKER

A coffin, also painted green, supported by pillars, loomed down on the neglected garden, and gave to those who couldn't read the necessary information. At the sight of it an incident long forgotten occurred to Boleslav with extraordinary distinctness. He saw again a little untidy girl with great, dark, tearful eyes and a tangled cloud of black, curly hair flying about her face and shoulders in wild dishevelment. She had clung to this garden gate with one hand, while with the other she held the corner of her blue print pinafore convulsively pressed against her bosom. A pack of village hobbledehoys were pelting her with sticks and stones. He was not much taller than she was, but at his approach the little crowd made way for him, shy and awestruck. For he was the "young lord," who had only to lift his finger, they thought, to bring down blessings or curses on their heads.

"What is going on here?" he had asked, whereupon the persecuted child had humbly advanced, and opened her pinafore just wide enough for him to get a glimpse inside.

"Beasts! They wanted to take it away from me!" she had exclaimed, lifting her wet eyes to his, blazing with indignation.

A poor unfledged sparrow, which somehow or other had fallen out of the nest, reposed in the pinafore.

"Give it to me," he had demanded, for he loved young birds; and obediently she had held out her pinafore for him to snatch it away. As beseemed a lordling, he had not said thank you, or troubled himself further about the giver.

And that was *she*—the girl who, it was said, had

The Cats' Bridge

shown the French the path by the Cats' Bridge, and had lived with his father as his mistress to the last.

Why had he defended her then? Why had he prevented the pack hunting her down? One blow on the forehead from a stone might then and there have cut short her mischievous career!

He walked on. Now and then a dull, dirty face peered at him curiously through the small, dark window-panes, or a cur barked. But he passed unmolested through the village. It was unlikely enough that any one would recognize him. The parsonage came in view with its shady veranda, trim flower-beds, and nut trees. It looked as quiet and peaceful as on that morning long ago, when, with a sigh of relief at escaping from the pastor's stern rule, he had seen it for the last time from the post-chaise, and Helene had waved him farewell with her little cambric handkerchief. With lowering brow he now took a short cut that he might avoid passing it. It seemed as if Helene must still be standing on the lawn waving her handkerchief. But what if she had been there? It would have been impossible for him to go to her. A path on his left led down to the river, which divided the Castle domain from the villagers' territory. As he turned into it he became aware of the frightful ravages the fire had made. Instead of the long line of barns and stables which had been ranged

The Cats' Bridge

on this side of the river stood a row of ruins, falling walls and scorched beams, grown over with celandine and valerian. Beyond could be seen, through gaps in the walls, the courtyard, now a weedy, grass-grown rubbish heap, and on the summit of the hill, behind a lattice formed of the leafless branches of dead elms, a black ruined mass of fantastically jagged brickwork—all that remained of the once proud Castle.

His arms fell heavily to his sides. A sound escaped him like a sob, a sob for vengeance.

He dragged his way laboriously along the banks of the river to the drawbridge, which was the main mode of access to the island; for, since his grandfather's time, the whole of the Castle grounds had been, by means of an aqueduct, practically converted into an island. The drawbridge, at least, was still visible. It looked like a remnant of antiquity as it hung with its gray, projecting timbers on its black, clumsy buttresses, at the foot of which the ripples broke with a gurgling sound. The rusty chains were tightened, and between *terra firma* and the floating edge of the bridge was a space of about three feet, which could be jumped with ease. Some one had evidently tried to draw it up, and failed in the effort.

Boleslav sprang over and passed through the stone gateway, whose nail-studded doors, half-burnt, were thrown back on their hinges. Suddenly he heard a sharp clicking sound at his feet resembling the snap of a bowstring. He stopped, and saw, to his horror, the iron semicircle of a fox-trap half-buried in the rubbish, and carefully covered with birch-broom. The long pointed teeth of the iron jaws had closed on each other in a tenacious grip. By a miracle he had escaped an accident which might have laid him up for many weeks.

Feeling the ground with his stick, he pursued his way more cautiously through the refuse and litter, among which he came across occasionally a disused wagon or the rotten barrel of a brandy cask held together by iron hoops. He went on, up the hill to the Castle. The path was overgrown with brambles as tall as himself, and again he came on traps, their wide open maws greedily eager to seize him by the leg. The whole place seemed strewn with them—the only signs of civilization he had as yet encountered.

The Castle lay before him, with yawning window-frames and sundered walls, a complete ruin. Piles of fallen tiles and plaster, between which rank grass and weeds had sprung up, formed a mound round its foundations. The vestibule, with its drooping rafters, had become a perfect bower of creepers and evergreens, whose luxuriant growth seemed almost impenetrable. A white tablet hung among the leaves, on which, in his father's

The Cats' Bridge

handwriting, were the words: "*Caution to tres-passers.*"

He shuddered at this, the first trace he had seen for six years of the man to whom he owed his existence, and whom he had now come to bury.

In a few moments he would be standing prob-ably beside his corpse.

But how was he to find it? What resting-place could his father have found here while yet alive?

No door or unbroken window, no signs of a hu-man habitation, were visible amid all this fearful wreckage. He turned, and walked slowly the length of the Castle's frontage, past the towers which flanked the gabled roof; here over the blackened stonework the ivy had begun to grow afresh, enshrouding it in a peaceful melancholy. From this point his eye caught a vista of the park, with its giant timber and wealth of undergrowth. And then he saw a few yards off, on the grass plot where once had stood the statue of the goddess Diana, of which nothing now was left but the shat-tered fragments and pedestal, a woman. . . . She was a slender, strongly built woman, with long plaits of dark curling hair hanging down her back. Her primitive costume consisted of a red petticoat and a chemise. She was digging energetically with a heavy spade in the dark rich soil, and was apparently too engrossed to notice his approach. She set her naked foot at regular intervals, as if beating time on the hard edge of the spade, and with the slightest possible pressure drove it deep into the earth. As she dug she sang a song on two notes, a high and a low, which welled out of her full breast like the sound of a sweet-toned bell. The chemise, a coarse and roughly made garment, had slipped off her shoulders, laying bare the strong, magnificently molded neck. When he addressed her, she drew herself erect with a sudden movement of surprise and alarm, and stood before him half naked.

She turned on him a pair of lustrous, large dark eyes. "What do you want here?" she asked, grasping the spade tighter, as if intending to use it as a weapon of defense. Then lifting her other arm she calmly raised the chemise over her shapely bosom.

"What do you want?" she repeated.

Still he did not answer. "So this is she," he was thinking, "the traitress, the courtezan, who—" Should he point his pistol at her, and drive her instantly from the island, so that the ground he trod on might at least be clean?

Meanwhile his bearing seemed to have convinced her of the peacefulness of his intentions.

"This place is prohibited to strangers," she went on. "Go away again at once. You are lucky not to have been caught in a wolf's trap."

She stood, drawn to her full height, and waved

The Cats' Bridge

him off. Then gradually she became confused under his searching glance, and regarded him nervously out of the corners of her eyes. Tossing back the black tangle of hair from her sunburnt cheeks, she began to fidget with her inadequate garment, seeming conscious for the first time of her half-nude condition.

"Show me his corpse!" he cried imperatively.

She started and stared at him for a moment with astonished, questioning eyes, then threw herself weeping at his feet.

"Oh, master!" she murmured, in a voice stifled with emotion.

He felt her fingers seeking his hand, and pushed her violently from him.

"Show me his corpse!" he commanded again, "and then you may go."

She rose slowly, kicked the spade away with her foot, and led the way down to the park. As they neared some bushes she turned round and said timidly: "There's a trap here." He stepped quickly to one side, otherwise he would have walked straight into the snare. She held back the brambles of the thicket through which they were making their way, to prevent the thorns scratching his face. They came to a clearing in the wood where stood a small one-storied cottage with a tall chimney, surrounded by broken hot-house frames and lime heaps. It was the gardener's house, in

which as a boy he had often played with flower-
pots, seeds, and bulbs; the one solitary building
the ravages of the fire had left untouched, because
the incendiary had been unable to find his way to it.

Again his guide warned him. "Take care! That
is dangerous," she said, pointing to a heap of earth
like a mole-hill. "Whoever steps on it is a dead
man," she added, half to herself. He knelt down,
and with his hands dug out the bomb that lay concealed in the soft earth, and hurled it far away
with all his might, so that it exploded with a loud
report against the trunk of a tree. She cast a shy,
half-scandalized glance at him over her shoulder,
for to her what he had done was an act of dese-
cration.

Then she opened the door, and he found himself in a dark passage. The cottage had only two
rooms. The one on the left of the front door had
been the gardener's dwelling-room, the other his
workshop.

From the former, the door of which stood ajar,
issued the odor of a corpse.

He went in. A body velled in white lay on a
low bier in the middle of the close, gloomy little
room.

"Leave me," he said, without looking round, and
he threw back the cloth.

His father's rigid features, covered with bristles,
stared up at him. The eyes had sunk far back in

his head; the brows were contracted. In the hollows of his cheeks bushy black hair had sprouted, while the beard had turned partially gray. The short, thick nose had shrunk, and close to the firmly-shut lips that had not parted in death lay a deep line, denoting intense suffering, and, at the same time, defiant scorn; as Boleslav looked down on it, the line seemed to deepen still more, and at last to quiver and play round the mouth that was still forever.

He dropped on his knees, and with folded hands prayed a paternoster. His tears fell fast, and rained heavily on the waxen face of the dead man.

"Your guilt is my guilt," he whispered hoarsely. "If I don't defend your memory, who else will? No one in all the world."

Then he covered up the body again with the white cloth, for flies were swarming round it. As he turned away, he observed the girl's dark head pressed against the foot of the bier. Her symmetrical neck and shoulders shone out in relief from the shadowy background.

"What are you doing here?" he demanded roughly. She crouched down, shivering, and raised her left shoulder, as if to ward off a threatened blow. Her eyes flashed a warm ray through the masses of her curly hair.

"No one has ever driven me away from him before," she murmured.

The Cats' Bridge

"But *I* drive you away," he answered with decision.

She rose and quietly vanished. He tore open a window, for he felt half suffocated, and then took a survey of the apartment. It was small and wretched enough, and was filled up without any attempt at arrangement with the most inappropriate and heterogeneous assortment of furniture, most of it evidently rescued in haste from the fire; a gold-legged table harmonized ill with rickety kitchen chairs; a peasant's canopied bed stood near gorgeous brackets of inlaid marble, and a cracked Venetian mirror hung beside a bullfinch's simple wicker cage. But nothing looked more out of its element than the life-size portrait of the beautiful Pole, his grandmother, and the original cause of all the evil that had befallen him. Her haughty, arrogant eye still pierced the distance triumphantly; the small gloved hand still grasped the flexible riding-whip. "Kneel, slave," the full proud lips seemed to say. Only the diamond pin which used to glitter in her bosom like a star was gone, for just there the color had warped, and the gray canvas beneath was exposed to view. The once elegant and artistically carved frame representing a garland of gilded roses and cupids had suffered too, being chipped and cracked in various places, where patches of coarse orange paint had been daubed on to repair the damage.

72

The Cats' Bridge

"Probably he took every care to save that first," thought Boleslav, and had not the presence of his father's corpse restrained him, he would have pulled it down from the wall, and trampled it under foot.

A case containing arms stood in a corner. The newest and most costly of shooting weapons were ranged there, including every variety of pistol, sword, and spear. Above it was unrolled a plan of the Castle island, showing the spots where ingeniously contrived man-traps, mines, and spring-guns awaited the trespasser—roughly calculated, there were over a hundred of them.

Boleslav shuddered. Surely this unhappy man had been punished enough for his misdeeds in the life he had been compelled to lead during his last few years on earth! Caged up like a hunted wild beast, his murderous contrivances were a perpetual source of menace to himself, for to have forgotten for a moment the position of one of his death-traps must have instantly proved fatal.

When Boleslav went out at the door he stumbled over Regina, who was cowering on the threshold. She started to her feet with a low cry of pain, like the whine of a trodden-on dog. He felt a momentary thrill of compassion for her, but it vanished before he had spoken the kind words that involuntarily rose to his lips.

"Why were you lying there?" he asked harshly.

The Cats' Bridge

"It's my place," she answered, always regarding him with the same humble, luminous glance.

"Indeed? It's a dog's place as a rule."

"It's mine too."

"Your name is Regina Hackelberg?"

"Yes, your lordship."

"It was you who led the French over the Cats' Bridge?"

"Yes, your lordship."

"Why did you do it?"

"Because I was told to do it."

"Who told you?"

She cast down her eyes.

"Why don't you answer?"

"Because I was forbidden to tell."

"Who forbade you; my— *He?*"

"Yes; the noble master."

"So that's what you call him, eh?"

"Yes, your lordship."

"Call me 'master,' and not 'your lordship.' "

"Very well."

"I shall expect you to tell me everything," he went on. "Do you hear?"

"The noble master did not wish me to speak about it—not to any one."

"Did he say not to *any one?*"

"Yes."

He bit his lip. Why should he inquire further into the matter, when it was all as clear as day-

74

The Cats' Bridge

light? This creature had been used as a tool because she was stupid, and bad enough to let herself be so used.

"How old were you at the time the French came?"

Again she cast down her eyes.

"Fifteen, master."

Once more he felt softened toward her, but almost immediately dark suspicion stifled his pity.

"You were paid for your work?" he asked between his clenched teeth.

"Yes," she responded calmly.

He was overwhelmed with disgust.

"How much was it? Your bribe?"

"I don't know."

"What! You mean to say you did not stipulate for a certain sum beforehand?"

She seemed unable to comprehend.

"My father took it all away from me," she answered. "He said it was the wages of sin. It was a whole big handful of gold. I know that."

He looked at her in amazement.

The fine head, with its wealth of wild hair clustering on her neck, was humbly bent. She appeared not to have the slightest perception of the scorn she had aroused in him; or was she so used to it that she took his contempt as a matter of course?

"What were you doing at the Castle when the French were quartered there?"

The Cats' Bridge

A dark flush suffused her face, neck, and bosom. He had struck some chord of memory that awakened in her a spark of shame.

"I was helping with the sewing," she stammered.

"Why did you come to the Castle?"

"My father told me I must. He said I was to go up and ask the noble master if there was any sewing for me to do. I was to earn my bread somehow, he said."

"Oh, indeed!" There was a pause, then he continued: "Go and put on a jacket, Regina."

She passed her hand over her bosom and drew her linen garment tighter round her chest, till the string cut into the swelling flesh.

"Well, why don't you go?"

"I haven't got a jacket."

"What! Didn't he clothe you?"

"They tore my jacket off my back yesterday."

"Who?"

A gleam of burning hate flashed from her eyes.

"Who? Why, they—the people down there, of course," and she spat in the direction of the village.

A feeling of mingled surprise and satisfaction arose within him, for here was a being who could share his hatred; some one whom fate was to associate with him in the coming struggle with the villagers below.

"So the people down there are your foes?" he said.

The Cats' Bridge

She laughed jeeringly.

"I should just think they were. They throw stones at me whenever they get the chance—stones as big as this." She joined the hollows of her hands together to show the size.

"For how long have they thrown stones at you?"

"It must be six years," she said after a moment's calculation.

"And how often have they hit you?"

"Oh, lots of times. Look here!" and she let the chemise slip down again, to display a scar extending from her shoulder to the root of her bosom, which marked the warm olive skin with a thin line of scarlet.

"But now I always take the tub with me."

"The tub?"

"Yes; the wash-tub. I hold it over my head and neck when they come after me."

What a wretched existence was hers—worse than a dog's!

"Why have you gone on staying here when they treat you thus?" he asked. "There are other places in the world."

She gazed at him in astonishment, as if she did not grasp his meaning.

"But I belong here," she said.

"You might at least have left the island, and betaken yourself somewhere where your life would not always be in danger."

The Cats' Bridge

She gave a short laugh.

"Was I to leave *him* to starve?" she asked; and then, growing suddenly red, she added, correcting herself shyly, "I mean the noble master."

He nodded to reassure her, for she looked as if she expected to be chastised on the spot for her slip of speech, poor miserable creature!

"I don't go down there oftener than I can help. Generally I go over the Cats' Bridge by night to Bockeldorf, three miles away. There, at Bockeldorf, I could get flour and meat, and everything else that *he* wanted, if I paid double the price for it, and be back by the morning. But sometimes it's impossible to get there—in a snowstorm, for instance, or a flood. So when the weather was very bad I was obliged to go down to the village, and had to pay still more money there, and even then perhaps get nothing but blows. So"—she laughed a wild, almost cunning laugh—"I just took what came handy."

"That means—you thieved?"

She gaily nodded assent, as if the achievement was deserving of special praise.

She was so depraved, then, this strange, savage girl, that she was quite incapable of distinguishing the difference between right and wrong!

"And what were you doing in the village yesterday?" he questioned anew.

"Yesterday? Well, you see, *he* must be buried.

The Cats' Bridge

It's time, quite time. And I thought to myself, however much I cry, that won't get him under the earth."

"So you cried, did you?" he asked contemptuously.

"Yes," she replied. "Was it wrong?"

"Well, never mind: go on."

"And so I took the tub and went down to the pastor's. But the pastor said I mustn't contaminate his house by coming near it, so on I went to landlord Merckel, who is mayor as you know, master. And there the soldiers saw me—"

"What soldiers?"

"The soldiers who have just come from the war." She paused again.

"Go on!" he commanded.

"And the soldiers cried out 'Down with her—strike her down!' and then the chase began, and my father joined in and called out 'Down with her!' too, but he was only drunk, as he nearly always is. . . . The stones flew about, and the women and children caught hold of me and held me fast, that they might strike me; but I had the tub and held it with both hands high over their heads, hacking with it right and left like this." She illustrated her story by holding up her rounded muscular arms in the air, and bringing them down again like a pair of clubs.

The tall, magnificent figure before him re-

minded him of some antique statue in bronze.
Strange, that in spite of all the degradation and
vileness amid which she had been reared, it should
have blossomed into such fulness of triumphant
splendor. There was something classic, too, in the
mere unaffected freedom with which she exposed
its charms. But of course in reality she was nothing but a shameless hussy, long since lost to all
sense of decency.

"Perhaps you have got a shawl, if not a jacket,"
he suggested, turning his back.

"Yes, I have a shawl, a woolen one."

"Then put it on at once."

She disappeared silently through the door before
which they had been standing, and after a few
moments returned in a brilliant red tippet which
she had crossed over her breast and tied in a knot
behind. Now that she had awakened to the fact
that her half-clothed condition shocked him, she
began to be ashamed of even her naked arms,
which she had no means of concealing. She kept
them folded behind her back, and crept into the
darkest corner of the passage.

"Did they refuse to bury the noble master?" he
demanded.

"No—no—one said anything," she answered,
"because I never asked."

"Why not?"

"Because I couldn't for the stones that were

The Cats' Bridge

hurled at me. And then I thought it was no good. Nobody would ever come and fetch him. I might as well shovel him in myself, as best I could."

"*You* proposed to do it! Without help?"

"If I could carry him from the Cats' Bridge into the house without help, I ought to be able to bury him too."

"Where—in the churchyard?"

"The churchyard? Ha! ha! That would have been a pretty piece of business. I should never have got him through the village and been alive afterward to tell the tale. It was in the garden, over by the castle. I was in the middle of digging the grave when you arrived."

Now he felt strongly inclined to praise her. Such canine fidelity, unquestioning, unhesitating, touched him deeply. Did not the girl who had faced death readily a thousand times for her master's sake deserve some sort of reward? Yes. He would repay her in coin; good hard cash would doubtless be more acceptable than anything else, poor thing! And, directly he had laid his father in his last resting-place, he would dismiss her from his service. Till then she might stay where she was.

But, at all costs, his father's bones must lie with those of his ancestors. His first duty, his bounden duty as a son, was to procure for him a decent burial, such as was granted to every Christian

81

human being. No matter what difficulties might stand in the way, he determined to accomplish the sacred task, even if he were driven to resort to extreme measures, and call in the aid of the law. He knew at least one magistrate in Prussia, a relative of his mother's, who would take his side, and enforce justice with an armed contingent if the worst came to the worst.

He was just in the act of walking off in the direction of the village, when it occurred to him that it was impossible to take a hundred steps on his own property without being snared into a hundred death-traps. Without the woman he detested to guide him, he was as helpless as a child.

"Lead me to the drawbridge," he said; "and while I am gone clear away all the traps."

"Yes."

But she remained motionless, as if rooted to the spot.

"What are you waiting for?"

"I beg the master's pardon, but he has been traveling all night, and I thought——"

"What did you think?"

"That he must be very tired, and hungry perhaps; and——"

She was right. He could hardly stand from sheer exhaustion. But the idea of taking even a crust from her hands filled him with loathing. Rather would he be fed by his enemies.

The Cats' Bridge

CHAPTER V

MEANWHILE in the Black Eagle a group of Schrandeners, burghers and burghers' sons, were enjoying their morning pint together. The Schrandeners, who had always thought the ideal of a happy life was to spend as much time as possible in the tavern, were now at liberty to indulge their taste from morning to night. What work they did must have been accomplished very early in the day, judging by the hour at which they began their recreation.

Young Merckel presided at their carousals. He had grown up into a fine, broad-shouldered young fellow, with a cavalry mustache aggressively curled up at the ends, which suited his cast of countenance, and a manner that even in bouts of clownish dissipation retained a certain swaggering good nature. At the conclusion of the war, instead of getting his discharge, he had come home on leave, to consider at his ease whether or not it would be advisable to attach himself to a standing army. His profession was not likely to interfere with his decision one way or the other, as practically he had none.

The Cats' Bridge

Till his twenty-fourth year he had been employed in "seeing life" in different parts of the world at his father's expense, and had hailed with joy the outbreak of war as a legitimate outlet for his energy, which otherwise might have been turned into unworthy channels.

Like Baumgart he had entered the army as a volunteer riflemen; like him had passed into the militia and had been promoted to the rank of lieutenant, but unlike him, he wore as a recognition of his bravery the iron cross dangling on his proudly swelling breast. For the time being, he had no intention of leaving his birthplace again, where he was perfectly content to be regarded in the light of a hero and a lion.

He drank, blustered, and helped to fan the flame of hate against the traitor, hate which since the return of the victorious soldiers had blazed up more fiercely than ever. At his instigation the Schrandeners had gone forth to destroy the Cats' Bridge in order to cut the baron off on his island. That he would be struck dead before their very eyes none in their boldest dreams had dared to hope, and without having achieved their mission they had hurried back to the village to proclaim the glad tidings.

It was a foregone conclusion that the man who had betrayed his country would be refused Christian burial. This would put the crown on their work of vengeance. They gloried in reflecting on it. The mayor was on their side; the parson appeared to shut his eyes to what was going on; and there was no reason to be afraid of the interference of higher authority.

That a champion of the dead would arise at the eleventh hour was the last thing any one expected. As for the son—God alone knew what had become of the son—had he not totally disappeared, probably to die of shame in a distant land? . . .

"There's some one coming, wearing a reservist cap," said Felix Merckel, looking out through a crack in the blinds on to the market-place, which lay glaring and dusty in the heat of the midday sun.

The sounds of revelry subsided, in expectation of the advent of a stranger. Felix Merckel stretched out his legs and began to toy indifferently with his medal.

The door swung back. The newcomer brought a momentary stream of sunlight into the cool, darkened room. Without a word of greeting he walked to the buffet, behind which a barmaid sat knitting a stocking, and inquired if he could speak a few words with the mayor. The mayor was not at home; he had just gone out into the fields, the barmaid told him.

Master Merckel was fond of leaving the inn in charge of his son, for he found the beer disappeared twice as fast from the barrels when he was not present. Felix adopted a method of stimulating customers to drink, which would not have been becoming in the host. He couched his invitations in military slang and in figures of speech learned in the camp; to resist them would, the Schrandeners held, be casting a slight on their lieutenant, so it followed that Felix was the means of adding treasure to his father's exchequer.

He was piqued at the stranger in the reservist cap not vouchsafing him a salute, although he must have seen the officer's badge on his coat, and determined to ignore him.

"Can I wait here till the mayor comes back?" the stranger asked.

"Of course. This is the tap-room," the barmaid replied.

He took a seat in the farthest corner from the topers, with his back turned to them, put down his knapsack, and bowed his head in his hands.

Herr Felix regarded such conduct as a kind of challenge to himself. Like the true son of his father, he was indignant at a stranger coming in and ordering nothing to drink.

"Ask the gentleman, Amalie, what he will take," he called out, bursting with a sense of his own importance. Apparently the stranger didn't hear, for he took no notice. The barmaid stood behind his chair and stammered something about the excellent quality of Schrandener beer.

"Thank you; I will drink nothing," he replied, without looking up.

Herr Felix twisted the ends of his mustache with vigor. It was clear that a rebuke must be administered to the stranger for his churlish behavior. He therefore rose to his feet, and swinging his tankard, began in a somewhat blatant tone to address his boon companions.

"Dear comrades and fellow-burghers and every one present, Prussia's glorious battles have been fought. Our beloved Fatherland has risen from the dust in new and unsuspected splendor. Most of us have bled on the field of glory, and felt the enemy's bullets pierce our breast. Whoever is a true Prussian patriot will now drink with me his country's health and honor!"

With high-pitched hurrahs, the mugs with one accord were lifted to the revelers' mouths, but before they could drink, an incisive "Halt!" from the lieutenant stopped them.

"I see there is some one here," he cried, "who seems inclined to shirk this sacred duty;" and he rose and walked with clanking spurs across the room to the stranger's table.

"Sir," he asked aggressively, "do I understand you don't wish to drink to Prussia's fame and glory?"

The Cats' Bridge

"I wish to be left in peace," answered the stranger, not turning round.

"What, sir? You who wear the honorable symbol of a defender of your country in your cap, decline—"

A sudden movement on the part of the stranger, who grasped his pistols, made him break off. The next moment he saw firearms gleam in his hand, saw him spring up, and stood aghast, staring into a pale, overcast face that he knew well, but from which two such angry eyes had never blazed at him before.

He understood the situation at once; he stood face to face with a man desperately resolved to go to any extremity if necessary.

"Look at me, Felix Merckel," said the stranger, who was stranger no longer, "and learn that I wish to have nothing to say to you. But understand that if you or any of your friends come too near, they will rue it. The first who approaches an inch I will shoot down like a dog."

Felix Merckel quickly regained his composure.

"Ah! the Master Baron!" he exclaimed, with a profound bow. "Now I am not surprised that Prussia's—"

The click of the double trigger of the cavalry pistol made him stop short again.

"I warn you once more, Felix Merckel. I am an officer as well as yourself."

The Cats' Bridge

And the reiterated warning had its effect.

"Certainly, it is not my concern," Felix said, and with another low bow, went back to his place; this time the clatter of his spurs was scarcely audible.

The Schrandeners put their heads together and whispered, and then old Merckel entered the room. His round, sleek, clean-shaven face beamed with prosperity and self-satisfaction. As beseemed the village patriarch, he passed by the common drinking-table with a dignified gait. A heavy silver watch-chain hung on his greasy satin waistcoat, suspended from a gold keeper in the form of a Moor's head, to which was also attached an amber heart.

"The gentleman wished to speak to me?" he asked, with a profound obeisance, which, however, he seemed to repent, when his little gray lynx eyes remarked that the stranger had no glass before him. To be obsequious to a non-drinker was a waste of time.

The Schrandeners kept their ears open. Felix had jumped up as if to seize this favorite opportunity of going for his whilom friend with his fists.

"I say, father, it's the young Baron," he exclaimed, with a discordant laugh.

Old Merckel withdrew a few steps. His benevolent smile died on his lips; his fleshy fingers fumbled nervously with the Moor's-head keeper.

The Cats' Bridge

"Can I speak to you alone?"

"Oh! Herr Baron—of course—is the Herr Baron going to stay?"

He flung wide a side door, which opened into the little best parlor reserved for gentry. A sofa, covered with slippery oilcloth, and a few velvet, bulky armchairs, were ready for the reception of distinguished customers. Over a cabinet containing tobacco hung a placard with the inscription: "Only wine drunk here."

Before the host closed the door behind Boleslav, he made a reassuring sign to his fellow-burghers as if to allay their anxiety. Then from under his drooping lids he took a rapid survey of the newly-returned young aristocrat's person, which seemed to fill him with satisfaction, for again his smug, slimy smile played about his fat lips.

"How the young Herr Baron has grown, to be sure!" he began. "Wonderful!"

Boleslav fixed his eyes on him silently.

"And he has come home to find the old Herr Baron no longer alive. A pity he was not in time to close the eyes of the sainted dead—"

He broke off, and caught violently at his amber heart, for Boleslav's piercing, threatening gaze began to make him feel uneasy. What if this were a desperado, who would think nothing of taking him by the throat?

"At any rate I have come in time," Boleslav

burst forth at last, "to repair the shameful scandal that has been perpetrated here in refusing my father the last honor due to his position."

"Shameful scandal?"

"I advise you, my good man, not to put on that air of saint-like innocence. I can read you through and through. Something has come to my ears concerning you, for which you deserve to be thrashed on the spot."

"Herr Baron!" and he showed signs of taking flight through the door.

"Stay where you are!" commanded Boleslav, barring the way.

Thank God that in confronting this scum he felt the old inherited instinct of conscious power come back to him. "Is this the gratitude you show my house, to whose favors you owe everything?"

This was true enough. The present landlord of the Black Eagle had once hung about the castle in search of a situation, and had finally, as its ubiquitous steward, amassed a considerable fortune, although he now chose to adopt an attitude of injured virtue, and rubbed his hands self-righteously.

"Dear Herr Baron," he said, a paternal kindliness suffusing his broad countenance, "I willingly pardon the insults you have just heaped on me, and will give you the best advice, as if nothing had happened. Now, you will surely understand how friendly are my intentions."

"I decline your friendship," thundered Boleslav. "As mayor of the village of Schranden, you will answer my questions. Beyond that, I have no dealings with you."

"The Schrandeners are really terrible people. I always have said so. I said so many times to my dear wife. You knew her. Why, of course, she often took the little heir in her arms, little thinking that—"

"Keep to the point, if you please," Boleslav interrupted.

" 'Marianne,' I used to say, 'these Schrandeners, when once they get an idea into their heads, nothing will move them.' Once they took it into their heads not to drink my brandy! Good, pure, beautiful Wacholder brandy! In the same way they've now got it into their heads not to bury the old noble lord, and—well, upon my word, no god and no devil will force them to do it. It's no good *your* trying either, Herr Baron. I'll tell you why. The hearse belongs to the corporation, and they won't let you have it. Horses, too, they wouldn't let out. . . . As for bearers—dear God! Go round the village and see if you can find one, and if you can, see if he is not well flogged for it quarter of an hour afterward. Oh! these Schrandeners! And then there is the Herr Pastor—who really in the end has the most voice in the matter. Go to the Herr Pastor, and hear what *he* says. Putting ceremonials and paternosters out of the question, you won't even get the coffin made."

"We shall see," said Boleslav, gnashing his teeth. He felt his spirit of resistance rise, the more clearly he saw the web that hatred and malice were weaving around him.

"You *shall see*," exclaimed old Merckel in badly concealed triumph, "if you wish it!"

He opened the door of the tap-room, from whence proceeded a low hum of many voices. Half the village seemed to have collected there during Boleslav's interview with the mayor.

"Hackelberg! come here!" he called, and then hurriedly banged the door to again, for he saw hands laid on it that threatened to tear it off its hinges.

"If he has got over his debauch of yesterday, he will certainly come and himself give you his views on the subject." For a moment the little lynx eyes sparkled with malignant joy. Then resuming his benevolent patriarchal smile, he went on, twisting the amber heart.

"You have repudiated my friendship, young man. You have insulted me, and shown no respect for my gray hairs—I don't resent it. You wouldn't have done it if you had known how I, at the risk of my life—for if the Schrandeners had

got wind of it they would have done me to death—
how I saved many a time the noble baron, of
blessed memory, from starvation.

"Ask Fräulein Regina—your deceased father's
best beloved. She is a pearl, Herr Baron; you
ought to hold her in high esteem, and take her
away with you on your travels. Often in the darkness of the night have I stuck a loaf and a sausage
in her apron, and sometimes a pound of coffee,
while I have made my own breakfast off rye bread
for fear of the embargo."

"Weren't you paid for your trouble?"

"Well; yes, yes. When one risks one's life one
expects to be paid. There is still a little bill due,
however, left standing from last winter; if the
Herr Baron will have the goodness to—"

"Write out your account, and the money shall
be sent you."

"There's no hurry, Herr Baron. I have confidence; I can trust you. What I wish to say
is, take the advice of an old and experienced
man, and go home now without more ado; dig a
grave behind the Castle, and lay his deceased lordship in it—do it at night, mind, on the quiet, quite
on the quiet—Fräulein Regina will assist you—
then make the turf perfectly smooth, so that no
one will know where you've laid him, and before
the dawn of another day ride away again with
Fräulein Regina on your saddle to where—"

The Cats' Bridge

He paused suddenly, for Boleslav's hand was on the butt end of his pistols. How the devilish mockery beneath this suave old hypocrite's counsel was goading him into drastic measures! While he listened to it, a new thought had flashed across his brain with vivid distinctness. The funeral would after all only be the first step in the work that it was incumbent on him to complete. Never would he slink away under cover of night like a criminal, and abandon what remained of the inheritance of his ancestors to utter ruin. No! he would stay and endure all things, set at defiance all these malicious hyenas, the worst of whom stood before him, now grinning, with greedily gleaming eyes, only awaiting his opportunity to pounce on the masterless, unowned possessions.

Endure! Endure!

Renunciation for the sins of the fathers must ever be his lot. And did not the foul act that had laid waste his property deserve retributive justice? He would be a deserter and renegade, indeed, were he now to turn his back on his native place, and on the beloved, who, though she seemed lost to him eternally, might still be cherishing timid hopes of meeting him once more. No! for the future his flag should wave over the ruins of Schranden Castle, with the single word "Revenge" blazoned on it in fiery characters. And who but a cowardly cur would leave his flag in the lurch?

The Cats' Bridge

He stepped nearer the mayor, and with a threatening glance that seemed to penetrate him through and through, almost roared in his ear:

"Who set fire to the Castle?"

Herr Merckel winced as if his conscience pricked him. Every Schrandener did the same when any question arose as to who it was had perpetrated the crime. Every Schrandener except one, and he was the criminal himself.

Herr Merckel was gathering up his strength for a glib answer when the suppressed murmur in the tap-room gave place to a sound which had a louder and more riotous note in it.

The landlord made a movement in the direction of the door, to bolt it on coming events, but before he could take the precaution it was stormed and burst open. A troop of wild-looking creatures led the assault, at the head of whom was a man of puny stature, in rags and tatters, with straight, black hair hanging in oiled ringlets to his shoulders, a gray, stubby beard, and a pair of glassy, besotted eyes that rolled under red, lashless lids. He beat the air with his fists and cried:

"Where is the fellow—the brute? Let me catch the brute and I'll strangle him!"

Then he beheld Boleslav's tall, resolute form, and swallowed his words with a gurgling hiss. Behind him was a phalanx of angry, heated, inquisitive faces all turned on Boleslav as on a recently captured beast of prey.

"Every man's hand is against me!" he thought, and his blood rose.

"Are you the carpenter Hackelberg?" he asked, holding the drunkard in thrall with his searching glance.

He was associated with one of the dark memories of his childhood. Once his pitiable howls had frightened him out of his quiet, boyish slumbers, and on looking from his window he had seen him being whipped round the courtyard for poaching. Now he stood shaking his fists, grunting and spluttering with rage.

"You supply the village with coffins, I understand?"

The carpenter shook his head, stared vacantly in front of him, and then answered in a sepulchral voice:

"I am at work on only two coffins—one for myself, and one for my poor erring daughter."

The Schrandeners laughed in their sleeve. This formula was so familiar. When any one died in the village the carpenter had to be fetched by force, locked up with a bottle of brandy and the necessary boards, and not let out till the coffin was finished. Taken all in all, this Hackelberg was a dangerous fellow, and no one knew it better than the Schrandeners, who never let him out of their sight for long. He was watched and shadowed, and many an arm was ready to strike him down when the right moment should offer itself.

Nevertheless they courted his society in the tavern, made him drunk, and humored him. Sometimes they hung on his lips, at others stopped his mouth. Either they put him under lock and key or allowed him to bully them. It was as if they had endowed their own bad conscience with flesh and blood, and allowed it to run wild among them in the shape of this unkempt, half-crazed sot.

"Who else makes coffins in the village besides you?" Boleslav asked again.

The Schrandeners burst into jeering laughter. They knew how difficult he would find it to get any direct answer to his question.

"My poor, wretched child," he growled, fastening his glassy eyes on Herr Merckel's amber heart, which appeared to possess a fascination for him. Then suddenly rousing himself once more from the half-stupor into which he had collapsed, he threatened Boleslav with his fists, and cried out excitedly:

"What do you want from me? A coffin? Is that what you want? For whom do you want it? For the scamp, the dog, who betrayed his country —who seduced my child? Do you think I'd make a coffin for *him?* Look at me. Did you ever see such a spectacle?" He wrenched open his shirt,

The Cats' Bridge

and exposed to view his shaggy breast. "I'm a beauty—mere offal, that dogs would turn up their noses at. And whose fault is that, my dear young nobleman? Why, the Herr Baron's, your deceased father's. He it was who reduced me to this, and made me an unhappy, forsaken, childless old man, such as you see." He wiped his eyes with the ragged sleeve of his corduroy jacket, while the Schrandeners applauded, and backed him up in his maudlin oration. "My child, my only child, was torn from my bosom. He robbed me of my child—"

"I believe you yourself sent her to the castle," Boleslav interposed, without, however, making the least impression.

"He degraded my child, but what's worse, young sir—what most lacerates my father's heart—for though I'm a blackguard, I'm a patriot; for in Prussia even blackguards love their country—if there *are* any blackguard Prussians—but my child —ah! do you know what he did with my child?— forced her with the lash to go out in the dark night and— But since then do you think I'd own her? No—she is my child no longer. I've cursed her—cast her off! I said to her, 'You are my own flesh and blood no longer.' That's what I said, and—"

"But you took the wage of her sin all the same," Boleslav was on the point of interrupting, but

The Cats' Bridge

recollected in time that in saying so he would be admitting his father's guilt to this pack of wolves.

" 'And you are free,' I said. 'You may go where you like, and whoever you meet may kill you outright for all I care. Go to your noble master,' I said, 'and ask him to protect you.' I said—"

At this juncture the shouts of the other Schrandeners became so much louder that they drowned the carpenter's speech. They closed round him, and he was lost in the crowd; only his rasping laugh was still audible.

"What did I prophesy, Herr Baron?" asked old Merckel, with his unctuous smile.

Boleslav leaned against the end of the sofa, and regarded the crew of Schrandeners pressing ever nearer with clenched teeth and unflinching eye.

"If one strikes me," he thought to himself, "the rest will tear me to pieces."

He felt how imperative it was to remain calm.

"Come, you people," he said, making a passage through their ranks with his hands, "let me pass."

And whether it was his commanding air of cool determination, or the cross which shone in his military cap, that awed the tumultuous throng, not one of them attempted to impede his progress. He passed into the thick of the mob, expecting every moment to be struck a fatal blow from behind;

but nothing of the sort happened—unchallenged he found himself in the open air. Felix Merckel had kept in the background.

The whole mob, now including women and children, surged after him down the road.

As he reached the parsonage garden, whose white walls blazed in the rays of the midday sun, he was aware of an aching sensation at his heart, that rose in a lump to his throat. His last hope rested in the hands of the old pastor. Would he too spurn him from his threshold? But at this moment that was not his only anxiety. How could he help feeling anxious as to what *her* reception of him would be, she in whose power it was to exalt him from the mire of shame and misery into a world of peace and purity. If she saw him in his present condition, dirty and disheveled, with this escort of hooting ruffians behind him, would she not recoil in horror?

And she did.

A terrified hand threw back the glass door of the veranda. It was she—it must be she! For a moment he saw the glimmer of a white, slender figure; saw her raise an arm, as if to wave off the approach of him and the mob: and then, before Boleslav could give one questioning, imploring look at the beloved features, she vanished with a faint cry of alarm.

There was a mist before his eyes. Half stunned,

he went up the steps of the veranda, closed the door behind them, and awaited the next turn in the course of events.

The Schrandeners blockaded the veranda, and some flattened their noses against the glass in order to see better what passed within. A pane fell out; one of them had pushed his neighbor through it, whereupon the revered voice of the old pastor was heard raised in remonstrance. He appeared on the veranda flourishing a thick, notched walking-stick. His white hair blew about his lofty temples. The nostrils of his hawk-like nose dilated furiously as if they snorted battle. Beneath the snow-white shaggy projecting brows his eyes glowed like fiery torches. Such was the venerable Pastor Götz, who, in March of the year 1813, had gone from house to house, holding the big cross from the altar in his hand, followed by a drummer, and had beaten up recruits for the holy war. And had he not been left fainting by the roadside on the march to Königsberg, in all probability he would have accompanied his soldier-parishioners into the field of action.

The Schrandeners stood in no little dread of his discipline, and no sooner did they catch sight of his formidable stick than they retreated quickly from the windows, and tried to regain the garden gate.

"You craven sheep!" he shouted from the glass

door. "Come to God's house on Sunday and I'll give you a dressing."

Then turning on Boleslav, he measured him from head to foot with a scowling glance. His eye rested on the military cap he held in his hand.

"You were in the campaign?" he asked.

"Yes."

"If it were not for the cross I see on the brim of your cap, I should ask was it for or against Prussia?"

Boleslav, whose thoughts had followed the fleeting vision of light he had seen on the veranda, at first did not understand him; then he met the insinuation with signs of passionate resentment. But the old pastor was not the man to be easily intimidated, and while they both glowered at each other, he cried:

"Boleslav von Schranden, am I, or am I not, justified in cherishing such a suspicion?"

Then Boleslav's eyes fell before the condemnation in those of the minister, who opened the door of his study, where between the book-shelves hung pipe-racks and firearms, and said:

"Out of respect for the cap I will not refuse you entrance here. But make what you have to say as brief as possible. In this house no Schranden is a welcome guest."

He put his stick in a corner, and drawing his

flowered dressing-gown close about his loins, paced up and down the room.

Boleslav cast about for words. He felt like a criminal in the presence of this man, whose speech was like molten brass. Of a truth it was no easy matter, this taking the guilt of another on to one's own guiltless shoulders.

"Herr Pastor," he began, stammering, "can't you forget for a moment that I bear the name of Schranden?"

The old man laughed bitterly. "That's asking a little too much," he murmured; "a little too much."

"Regard me simply in the light of a son who wishes to bury his father, and who is prevented from fulfilling that most sacred duty by the wickedness and malice of that scum."

For an answer the old parson contracted his shaggy brows without speaking.

"I appeal to you as a priest of the Christian Church. Will you suffer such a scandal in your parish?"

"Such a thing can not happen in my parish," the old man declared. "Wherever it is my duty to lead souls to God, every one must be granted a decent burial."

"And yet they dare—"

"Stop! Whose burial is in question!"

"My father's."

The Cats' Bridge

"The Baron Eberhard von Schranden?"

"Yes."

"That man has been dead for seven years."

"Herr Pastor!"

"For seven years he lived ostracized from the society of his fellow-creatures. Seven years he practically rotted in the earth. Therefore, don't trouble me about him further."

"Herr Pastor, I was once your pupil. From your lips I first learned the name of God. I always thought you a brave, upright man. I retract that opinion now; for what you have just been saying are lying, cowardly quibbles."

The old man drew himself up. His beard worked; his nostrils expanded. With lurid eyes he came nearer to Boleslav.

"My son," he said, "do I look like a man who would countenance a lie?"

Boleslav maintained his defiant attitude. But, much as he struggled against it, he felt the old, long-forgotten sentiment of respect for the schoolmaster awaking in him once more.

"My son," went on the old man, "a word from me, and the rabble that waits for you on the other side of that hedge would slay you; but, as I said before, for the sake of the cap you wear, I will be merciful. If you like, I can prove that what I said just now is no lie."

He went to a cupboard, where stood a long line

of ragged folios, containing church and parish documents, took out a volume, and, opening it, pointed to a page dated 1807.

"Here, my son, read this."

And Boleslav read:

"On March 5th, died Hans Eberhard von Schranden. *Ex memoria hominum exstinguatur.*"

Beneath were three crosses.

"That is a forgery!" exclaimed Boleslav.

"Yes, my son," the old man answered solemnly, "that is a palpable, shameless forgery; a stain on my office; and if you choose to report it to the magistrates, I shall be suspended and end my days in prison. Do exactly as you think fit. My fate lies in your hands."

A shudder of mingled horror and reverence passed through Boleslav. He had himself experienced too often the hot glow and reckless delight of making sacrifices for the love of his country, not to understand what impulse had driven the old clergyman to this insane confession.

"With those crosses," he continued, "I buried the man seven years ago—the man who, in spite of his cruelty and ungovernable passions, had till then been my friend. From that day, whoever dared to breathe so much as his name in my house was sent out of it. Then came that night of arson, when these walls were illumined by the reflection of the burning Castle. I jumped out of my bed, and, throwing myself on my knees, prayed God to forgive the incendiaries, for it began to burn at all four corners at once, a sure proof that the fire was not an accident. Now, I thought, not only the deed, but the scene of it, will be erased from men's minds. I didn't concern myself in the least about the spectre that was doomed to haunt the ruins of Castle Schranden. And now you come, my son, and tell me that that spectre was no spectre, but a living creature, who only a few days ago gave up the ghost, and now waits interment. Well, I forbid it Christian burial, on the strength of this register. I never bury any one twice. Report me, and—and I shall be tried for my offense. But you know I am prepared. Do as you like. Bury the corpse with all the honors you consider due to it; have a procession grander and more imposing than an emperor's, but kindly leave me out."

He settled himself in his green-cushioned armchair, supported his face with his wrinkled, muscular hands, and stared vacantly at the open register. There was nothing to hope from this iron-willed man of God. It would be madness to keep up any illusion on the subject, and that other illusion, that the loved one might still be won on earth after long waiting and renunciation, must be abandoned too. All the shy dreams and hopes that he had yet dared to cherish in his embittered heart now seemed finally wrecked.

The Cats' Bridge

"So this is the divine grace, the forgiveness of sins, you preach!" he cried, tears of wrath filling his eyes.

The old man rose slowly and let his hand fall heavily on Boleslav's shoulder.

"Because of your cap, my son, I will reason with you, although the sight of you is hateful to me. Listen! It is a year and a half now since there came here from Russia a rabble of ragged French beggars, starving and frost-bitten. The Schrandeners would have felled them to the earth with their scythes and pitchforks, and perhaps would have had right on their side, for they were mere carrion-serfs in the pay of Napoleon. But I opened the church door to them that they might take refuge in the shelter of God's altar. I kindled a fire for them on the flagstones, and had a hot supper cooked for them and gave them straw to lie on. I told the Schrandeners that, though they were enemies, they were human beings like themselves, bearing the cross of human suffering as the Saviour once bore it on his shoulders. I told them to go home and pray that God might spare them as they had spared those miserable Frenchmen. So you see I *can* be pitiful and show mercy— To return to the subject of the funeral. I have never refused any sinner his lawful resting-place. If I could have my will, even suicides should not be excluded from the churchyard. That those who have been unhappy in their lifetime should be comfortable in death has always been my principle. And if the body of a man who had murdered his mother was brought here from the scaffold, I would go to his grave side in full canonicals and pray the King of kings 'to forgive him, for he knew not what he did.' Yes, I'll extend mercy to all, only not to your father. For he who sins against his country outrages every law, human and divine; he disgraces the mother who bore him and the children he propagates. Such a one is a social outcast. He is like the leper who brings death and corruption with him wherever he goes, or a mad dog who spurts poison from his jaw on every living thing that comes in his way. And do you realize the extent of your father's guilt, the mischief it has worked? It is not so much the lives of those two or three hundred Pomeranian youths whose bones lie buried there on the common that are to be reckoned against him. They would probably have met death somewhere, later. The grass grows high on their graves; even their parents have long since become reconciled to their loss. No, it is not on their account that I bear the grudge. But— come here, my son—"

He clutched Boleslav's hand and led him to the window.

"Look out—what do you see on the other side

of the garden hedge? A gang of turbulent wild animals thirsting for the blood of their prey, and yet too craven-hearted to spring on it, even when they have it within their reach. And look at me, my son. I am here, appointed by God as His minister to preach the gospel of love, and I preach hate. Words sweet as honey should flow from my lips, and instead, scorpions spring out of my mouth directly I open it, for I too am become a wild animal. And this is what your father's crime has made us. There is no goodness left in Schranden; the venom of your father's hate ferments in us, is inoculated into our children and children's children. So will it ever be till the Lord not only wipes the scene of infamy, but your accursed name with it, from off the face of His blessed earth. Amen!"

He stood with raised hands like some anathematizing prophet of the Old Testament, and foam rested in the corners of his mouth.

Boleslav, half-dazed and horror-stricken, turned in silence to the door. The old man did not call him back. As he crossed the hall he started violently, for he was sure he heard the rustle of a woman's dress behind a half-opened door. But not for the world would he meet her now. Not in this dark hour, when he was completely overpowered by a sense of having had the remnants of all that was good and noble in him shattered and laid in the dust.

The Cats' Bridge

"If *they* are become wild beasts, I can become one too," he thought, as he thrust his hand in the breast-pocket that held his pistols, and walked toward the Schrandeners. The old pastor was right. Though they danced, whooped, and jostled around him with the lust of murder gleaming in their savage eyes, they dared not lay a finger on him.

.   .   .   .

When he reached the drawbridge, behind the palings of which a girl's figure crouched, awaiting his return, he was full of a desperate resolve. His father should be carried to his last resting-place by an armed force.

"Are you ready to earn another large sum of money?" he asked the girl, who flushed and stood up quickly at his approach.

She looked at him for a moment in reflective surprise, and then, as his meaning dawned on her, she shook her head violently.

"Why not?" he demanded.

She began to tremble. "What's the good of money to me?" she asked, in subdued, bitter tones. "They would only take it away from me."

"Who?"

"People—those people. Please, oh please, give me no money."

"Her mind is clearly unhinged," thought Boleslav.

The Cats' Bridge

"Besides, there is money enough," she continued in a whisper, glancing round her timidly, "in the cellar—great boxes full—where the wine is. I used to take what I wanted from there—for him, I mean—the noble master. For myself I never want any, unless it's to buy a new jacket with."

"Will you earn a new jacket?"

"There's no need to earn it. Next time I go to Bockeldorf—for the master must have food—I can get one."

So, unreasoning as a beast of burden, she performed her duties, and expected no return except her food!

"Will you, then, without earning anything, go a long way for me this very night?"

"Oh, yes, master, if you wish it."

The Cats' Bridge

CHAPTER VI

THE next day the village of Schranden received an unexpected visitation that proved no small shock to its inhabitants. At about five o'clock in the afternoon two coaches appeared in the village street, each of which contained half a dozen occupants, young fellows in military uniforms, with their muskets slung over their shoulders from wide leather belts.

In the first coach there was also a female occupant, who, the moment the horses' heads turned in the direction of the space opposite the church, alighted with a wild leap, and scudded away toward the castle.

Every Schrandener recognized in her the deceased Baron's sweetheart, but all were too much taken aback to think of following her.

The coaches halted before the Black Eagle, the windows of which were eagerly opened, and before the strangers had moved from their seats, an enthusiastic welcome was extended to them.

"The Heide boys—hurrah!" shouted Felix Merckel, who had many a time fought side by

The Cats' Bridge

side with these comrades of the Sellinthin squadron, and he stretched a foaming jug out of the window.

His father threw open the door of the little room reserved for "gentry," where only wine was drunk, in the hopes that some at least of these wealthy yeomen would patronize it. But, without answering the warm greetings, they proceeded in gloomy silence to unharness the horses, and to take out of their vehicles all manner of tools, such as hatchets, files, and spades.

The Schrandeners were astounded.

"Good gracious! have you lost your tongues?" Felix Merckel called from the window. "And why haven't you brought your paragon, Lieutenant Baumgart, with you?"

Still no answer.

The Schrandeners began to think these strangers must be playing off a joke on them, and burst into extravagant laughter.

Then Karl Engelbert, who evidently had the command of the expedition, came under the window from which Felix's broad-shouldered form obtruded itself, and, greeting him with a half-military salute, said:

"With your permission, Lieutenant, we have come here not to take part in any festivities or anything of that sort. We are a funeral party."

"But here in Schranden no one is going to be

buried," cried Felix Merckel, still laughing, but his face appreciably lengthened.

"Indeed, Lieutenant! Nevertheless, we have been invited to a funeral."

"Who has invited you?"

"Our former officer, Lieutenant Baumgart."

"Nonsense! There no Lieutenant Baumgart here. I thought you were going to bring him with you."

"Pardon, Lieutenant, he is here already."

"Where is the fellow hiding, then?"

"Probably you know him better under another name—Baron von Schranden."

The stone jug in Felix's hand fell and crashed to pieces at Engelbert's feet. The beer splashed his legs up to the knee.

A tumult arose inside the inn. As if in preparation for battle, windows were speedily closed, and Johann Radtke, driven by thirst to ascend the steps to the main entrance, found the door banged in his face.

"Hunted from the threshold like tramps!" grumbled the dark-haired Peter Negenthin, and clenched his fist in his sling.

"Do you wish to perjure yourself?" asked Engelbert in a low voice, coming close to him. "If so, then go back. What is required of us we must do. Whoever forgets the church at Dannigkow is a cur!"

The Cats' Bridge

"And if we are dry we must wet our whistles with holy water, I suppose," added Radtke with a sigh.

Engelbert shouldered his musket and gave the orders to move on. The procession filed off in the direction of the Castle, a handful of natives, out of respect for the muskets, bringing up the rear.

Boleslav stood on the bridge to receive his friends.

He rushed toward them in delight, and could hardly articulate, for emotion, the words of gratitude that rose to his lips.

Engelbert held out his hand in silence. Boleslav was going to embrace him, but he drew back. In his excitement Boleslav did not notice the rebuff.

"I knew you'd come," he stammered forth at last—"knew that I had friends who would not leave me undefended to the tender mercies of this pack of wolves."

No one made any response. They stood drawn up in an unbroken line, their eyes looking beyond rather than at him, in embarrassment. Engelbert was the first to break the silence.

"You have summoned us, and we have come—but our time is short; tell us what you want us to do."

For a moment Boleslav wondered at being addressed in this curt, somewhat surly fashion, by the

116

comrade who, of all others, had been his favorite. But it was only for a moment. Why should he doubt them? Had they not come? And then, incoherently enough, he related how his father's disgrace had descended on him, and what he had resolved to do, with their help.

All the time a pair of shining eyes watched him from the other side of a rubbish heap, and a woman's figure that sat cowering there trembled like an aspen.

"They are here—they are in the village!" she had called out to him in timid excitement, as she had flown into the yard like a Mænad. At first he had not recognized her in a light cotton skirt, a bed-jacket buttoned over her panting bosom, and a handkerchief of many colors on her head, tied under the chin, according to a fashion of the peasant girls in the neighborhood.

"They gave me these things to put on," she had added apologetically, on observing his puzzled looks.

And then in pleasure at the news that his friends had arrived, he had forgotten her, till, while waiting for them on the bridge, he had caught sight of her hovering about the ruins. The headdress had fallen on her neck, and the wild black tresses escaped, and waved in confusion about her sunburnt face. She seemed to be smiling absently to herself.

He was ashamed to think his friends had seen

this woman, and decided to pay her off and dismiss her on the spot, so that they should not encounter her again.

"What are you doing here?" he demanded.

She started.

"Nothing," she replied, guiltily lowering her eyes.

"Why did you smile?"

"Ah, master," she murmured, "I was so glad."

"Why?"

"Because I had got safely back here again."

What strange fascination had this spot of earth for the abandoned creature who had suffered on it nothing but shame and degradation and endless misery? He remembered to have heard of domestic cats who, when the house to which they belong is deserted by its inhabitants, prefer to starve beneath its moldering roof rather than take up their abode elsewhere. And if this cat-like propensity were incurable in her—what then? After all, perhaps it would be cruel at this moment to pass sentence of banishment upon her. She might as well stay till to-morrow morning, so long as she kept out of his way.

"Go," he had commanded, "and don't come near me and my visitors again."

And she had hung her head humbly, and vanished behind the rubbish heap, and there she cowered now, in terror of being discovered.

The Cats' Bridge

When Boleslav had finished his story, Engelbert exchanged significant glances with his friends, then said:

"We have brought the requisite tools with us. If you can supply us with the wood, we will knock you up a coffin in a very short time."

"Naturally it won't be a very grand one," remarked Peter Negenthin with a stony smile.

Engelbert looked at him reprovingly. A subdued growl passed from mouth to mouth through the little party, which Boleslav, in his almost light-hearted confidence in his friends' good-will, did not hear.

"Do you remember," he exclaimed, "that coffin we made for the young Count Dohna in the dark? We took two hours over it, though we couldn't see an inch before our noses."

But his reminiscences met with no response.

"One of you hold the horses," said Engelbert, "and the rest of us will go and look for wood. All must be ready before nightfall."

Boleslav bethought him of the wine in the cellar, which the fire had spared, where also was the frugal larder, containing bread and salt meat, but not enough with which to entertain his friends.

"I have next to nothing to offer you to eat," he said, "but I wish you would at least refresh yourselves with a bottle of wine before setting to work."

The Cats' Bridge

The friends were silent, and their faces clouded.
"Never mind refreshment," said Engelbert,
trying hard to assume a facetious tone. "Wine
makes a man lazy, and we haven't a minute
to spare."

He stooped to test some scorched rafters that
lay about among the stable ruins.

"This will do," he said, "but we won't saw off
the blackened part; that will serve us instead of
paint."

And he walked on farther with Boleslav to look
for more rafters. Something white rose suddenly
out of the earth in front of them, and disappeared
in a twinkling behind a neighboring wall.

Boleslav instinctively balled his fists, for he had
recognized Regina.

"I ought to apologize," he said, "for not being
able to send you a better messenger. I had no one
else to send."

Engelbert was about to speak, but seemed to
think better of it."

"You were obliged to supply her with clothes, I
understand?"

"Yes," answered Engelbert, his natural loquacity
getting the upper hand. "I found her lying on the
doorstep with scarcely a rag to her back. She was
dead beat. I got up in the night to see what the
dogs were barking at."

"What? Was it in the night?"

The Cats' Bridge

"Two o'clock in the morning. Here is a sound rafter. We can use that. . . . She walked the twenty miles in seven hours. I should never have thought it possible; she lay like an otter that has been shot down—so straight and fair—and gasped for breath. Your sheet of paper she clung to with both hands. She tried to stand up, but fell backward. Then I fetched her brandy, rubbed her temples, and gave her—"

One of his companions who was following behind now came up, and gave him such a look of astonishment and reproach that he broke off in the middle of a sentence.

For the next few hours an industrious sawing and hammering proceeded from the Castle island, which sounds fell disagreeably on the ears of the fierce and much perturbed Schrandeners on the opposite bank of the river. It seemed to portend that their nicely laid plans were to be frustrated at the last moment.

Old Hackelberg appeared in the street with his gun, which, as a rule, lay buried in a dung-heap, because he was afraid that it might be taken away from him, as had once happened when he amused himself by shooting bats in the market-place, declaring that they followed him in swarms wherever he went. With this famous gun he used in old days to go out poaching every night, but since his once unerring hand had become weak and tremulous from drink, he had been obliged to give up the trade. Only when he had drunk even more than usual did the old sporting instinct rise strongly within him, and he would rush to the shed, unearth his gun, and bring down a swallow in full flight through the air.

Now he was on the war-path, and with the babbling rhetoric peculiar to him, shouted:

"Schrandeners, duty calls! Arm yourselves against the traitors. I am an unhappy father, robbed of my child. I'll shoot him dead, the brute."

"But he *is* dead," some one interposed.

"Is he? Well, it doesn't matter—the other must be shot—all must be shot down."

Meanwhile Felix Merckel was tramping about the parlor of the Black Eagle like a bull of Bashan. He remembered enough about the Heide youths to know that when once irritated or attacked they would go to any length. The inevitable result of offering them opposition would be such bloodshed as the rioters outside had no conception of.

And then—what then? Would not he as ringleader be the first object on which the wrath of the outraged law would expend itself?

On the other hand, did the swindler who had dared under a false name to obtain a lieutenancy and abuse the confidence of his comrades, thereby

The Cats' Bridge

incurring the contempt and abhorrence of every
honorable brother-in-arms—did he deserve to be
allowed to score such a triumph?

While his son was debating thus, Merckel,
senior, was also troubled with anxiety from another
cause. It struck him as a pity that such a quantity
of noble enthusiasm should be seething about aim-
lessly in the open air, and determined to put an
end to the nuisance.

He stepped out on the porch, and addressed the
rabble in his suavest, most paternal tones.

"I, as your local functionary, can not bear to see
you, my children, turning our public square into a
bear-garden. Go under cover, and then you may
make as much noise as you please."

Of course, "under cover" could only mean the
parlor of the Black Eagle; and, five minutes later,
the consumption of inspiriting stimulants left
nothing to be desired.

Felix had bowed his curly head between his
hands, and stared gloomily into his glass.

Surely no Prussian patriot who had ever worn
a sword ought silently to look on at what was
coming to pass this night? Rather die! Rather!—
He jumped up, and began to speak eloquently to
the crowd.

His speech was not without effect. One after
the other stole out and returned with some sort
of weapon, a flint gun, a bent sabre, or a scythe.

The Cats' Bridge

"Calm, and patriotic, my children!" exclaimed old Merckel, grinning, and counting the empty tankards with his argus eye.

Night had come. The two flaring tallow candles in the bar illumined the overcrowded, oppressively hot room, and were reflected in the polished blades of the scythes. Then two or three boys, who had been stationed as spies on the drawbridge, burst in, shouting at the top of their voices:

"They're coming! They're coming!"

There arose a howl of fury. Every one pressed to the door. Felix Merckel hurried into his bedroom to take his sabre out of its scabbard, but he did not come back. Probably the sight of the weapon he had so often wielded in honorable warfare brought him to his senses.

His father continued to exhort the rioters to calmness and caution, especially those who had not yet paid for their drinks.

"Forward!" spluttered old Hackelberg, "avenge my poor child. Mow them down!"

Outside, in the market-place, the whole population of the village was assembled. Even babies in swaddling-clothes had been snatched out of their cradles, and their squalling mingled with the babel of many tongues. The moon came out from behind some clouds, and shed a pale twilight on the scene. The church tower rose dark and forbidding against the sky, and the parsonage, too, remained silent and dark. The old veteran had kept his word. He heard and saw nothing of what was passing. A dark-red fiery glow appeared behind the cottages that lined the road to the river. Above the low roofs rose columns of thick black smoke. Like the reflection from a conflagration the purple vapor encroached on the pale dusk of the summer night.

With one accord the rabble took the path to the churchyard, which, a few yards from the last straggling houses, lay close to the street. There by the gate they would best be able to bar the way to the invaders. Those who had been in the war fell into rank and stood ready for action. As far as they were concerned, it would be a case of soldiers pitted against soldiers.

"Where is Merckel?" one of them exclaimed in astonishment, expecting to hear the lieutenant's word of command. "Where is Merckel?" was echoed in consternation from all sides.

But the feeling that he must be coming, and had only gone to arm himself, allayed any momentary suspicion of his having shirked the business at the last. The lurid glow drew nearer and nearer. Soon the eye could distinguish something black and square, framed as it were in flames.

"The coffin—the coffin!" the crowd exclaimed, and involuntarily shuddered. Then, suddenly— who began it no one knew—it was as if it had flashed across every brain at the same instant, in a booming chorus the mob set up the weird song:

"Our noble Baron and Lord
Of Schrandeners' souls abhorred;
For the shame he has brought on our head,
O God, let the plague strike him dead."

And the coffin advanced. Already the light from the torches shone on the faces of the singing mob, and women and children retreated screaming.

The crowd opened wide enough for the procession to pass on, and closed again behind it. Six men carried the coffin on their shoulders and swung flaming pine branches in their disengaged hands, which scared the throng and made it draw to one side. Six others followed with loaded muskets. At their head Boleslav, with his pistols cocked in his hand, his military cap on the back of his head, piercing his antagonists with his burning gaze, cleared a road for his father's corpse. Deeper became the rent in the human vortex, thinner the space that divided the procession from the armed Schrandeners, who looked uneasily from side to side, conscious that they were leaderless.

When Boleslav stood face to face with them they were about to make a forward dash, but a short military "Halt!" such as they had often heard in the campaign, compelled them to take a step backward instead, for in spite of themselves, their limbs insisted on complying with the old habit of obedience. Boleslav, who had intended the order for the bearers, saw its effect on the armed line in front of him, and suddenly a new idea occurred to him.

"As you were!" he commanded again. No one moved a hair. His manner, his voice mastered them. "Which of you have been soldiers? Which of you has helped his king to make his country free?"

An indistinct, half-resentful murmur went through the ranks, but there was no answer.

"The king sent you home," he continued, "because he is now at peace with his enemies. Do you suppose that he would be pleased to hear you had taken it upon yourselves to break the peace once more in his realm? Bah! he wouldn't believe it of you! He might believe it of the Poles, but not of Prussians! So make room, my good people. Let us pass!"

The line wavered and began to break in places. For one moment the churchyard gate lay clear before Boleslav's eyes, but the next, fresh figures had moved up from behind and filled the breach.

Again the clamor arose, and mingling with it a loud, gurgling laugh of derision. In another instant something round, black, and polished was leveled at Boleslav's head, and behind it sparkled a pair of malignant eyes. He had only a second in which to realize what was going to happen, before a figure, supple as a panther's, shot past him and plunged into the midst of the Schrandeners' troops, which again showed signs of giving way. In the hiatus thus made, Boleslav saw two forms wrestling on the ground, one that of a woman, the other a man's. The woman overpowered her antagonist, and wrested from his hand the gleaming bore of a gun.

It was the carpenter Hackelberg and his daughter. She must, stealthily and unobserved, have followed the funeral procession, for since her disappearance on the other side of the stable ruins Boleslav had seen nothing of her. The crowd pushed forward, curious to find out who was struggling on the ground, and Boleslav, promptly taking advantage of the general confusion, passed the combatants and gained the churchyard gate, the coffin following close at his heels.

Behind was heard the report of the gun, which exploded in the hand-to-hand struggle.

"Guard the entrance!" he called to the six who followed the coffin, while the bearers made their way between the mounds and tombstones to the burial vault of the Barons von Schranden.

Karl Engelbert stationed himself as sentinel beneath the gateway, and saw, by aid of the last

The Cats' Bridge

flicker of the torches as they moved away, how the crowd closed round the wrestling father and daughter.

Three piercing shrieks escaped the girl's lips. Evidently the mob intended to wreak its thwarted fury on her. There seemed little doubt that she would perish at its hands, unless some one came quickly to her help.

"Leave her alone!" cried Engelbert, striking out right and left with his powerful fists. And then the figure, that had been so pitifully mauled and in such dire extremity till he interfered, emerged from the midst of her persecutors. She glided past him, dived into the dry ditch that skirted the churchyard wall, and then disappeared like a shadow, into the darkness. The Schrandeners began, with whoops and hoots, to pursue her.

"How about the burial?" cried he.

"The devil take the burial!" exclaimed another, and cast a shy glance at the men standing on guard by the churchyard gate—men who looked as if they were not to be trifled with. Certainly it was better sport to give chase to a defenseless creature than to risk one's skin in an encounter with them.

And the Schrandeners started off like bloodhounds. The carpenter Hackelberg tried to do likewise, but staggered instead into the ditch, where he lay full length and fell asleep.

CHAPTER VII

THE last of the stone slabs that covered the vault had crunched back in its place with a resounding crash. Hans Eberhard von Schranden lay with his ancestors. In the little chapel, the men who had acted as grave-diggers bared their heads and said a short prayer. The torches that had burned down to their sockets smoldered on the smooth surface of the flagstones, and cast a lurid glow as they flickered out over the stern faces of the worshipers.

Then without looking round at Boleslav they left the chapel. He stood in a remote corner with his hands before his face, brooding fiercely on the future that lay before him. The echoing footsteps roused him, and silently he followed his friends, letting the iron gate of the chapel that had been broken open when they came in, swing back in the lock.

The moon had again pierced the clouds, and illumined with a weird radiance the mounds and crosses that stood in regular rows, like columns drawn up for battle.

"Do you wish to bait me too?" Boleslav mur-

mured as he contemplated the graves for a moment
with a bitter smile. At the gate he overtook his
friends. They joined the men on guard, who now
had nothing to watch, for, with the exception of a
group of women and old men who stood gossiping
by the hedge, the street was empty. Hoots were
heard proceeding from the distant fields, where the
mob apparently were still in full pursuit.

"God have mercy on her, if they catch her!"
said Karl Engelbert with folded hands. Then two
of his comrades, one of whom was Peter Negenthin, came up to him and whispered earnestly in
his ear.

Boleslav was too lost in thought to notice their
strange and unnatural behavior toward himself,
and was not even aware, as they walked through
the village, that he was always left to walk alone,
though now and then he stepped confidentially to
the side of one or other of them. He had accomplished the first chapter of his work. His father
was laid to rest as befitted his rank, and yet it
seemed as if the real work was only just beginning.
He beheld all he had to do towering like a great
inaccessible mountain in front of him. The moldering ruins must be built up again; what was
now a waste overgrown by weeds must be restored
to a waving sea of golden corn; he must strive to
endow his neglected property with new wealth, and
his tarnished name with new honor: and then he

saw, as the goal of all this striving, the face of the beloved beckoning him onward. If he was too bowed down now with a consciousness of shame and disgrace to look into her pure, maidenly eyes, *then* he would be able to go to her and say, "Now, all is expiated. I am worthy to lay myself at your feet." Yes, he would struggle tooth and nail— work day and night—to attain this end.

At first it seemed almost madness to think of such a gigantic undertaking— But he had his friends to help him— After all, it would not be a single-handed struggle. Had not they to-day helped him to achieve the impossible? Would not they, true to their sacred oath, continue to stand by him in need with their advice and sympathy? And perhaps their noble example would in time break down the barrier that divided him from his fellow-creatures, and lead to his father's sin being at last consigned to the limbo of forgotten history.

Higher and higher rose his hopes as he meditated thus. They had left the village street behind them, and now reached the drawbridge, where the vehicles had been put up. The horses, each with its nose in a bundle of hay, waited patiently by the fence to which they were tethered. Immediately, without a moment's delay, the comrades set to work to harness them.

This frightened Boleslav out of his dream.

The Cats' Bridge

"What!" he exclaimed. "Off already, before I have thanked you?"

No one spoke.

"Won't you take a glass of wine now the job is finished? And I wanted to ask your advice about other matters."

Peter Negenthin strode up, and looking him straight in the face, drew his clenched first from the sling.

"We would rather die of thirst," he hissed through his set teeth, "than take a drink of water from your hand."

Boleslav staggered backward as if he had been hit between the eyes. He felt the earth reeling beneath his feet.

Then Karl Engelbert stepped forth from his sullen little band.

"It is much to be deplored, Baumgart—I call you so because you have been Baumgart to us till this minute—it is much to be deplored that you should thus be bluntly told of what our present feelings are toward you. Why did not you hold your tongue, Negenthin? But the words have been spoken and can not be recalled, so now you may as well know all. You summoned us, and we came. Some of us, it is true, were of opinion that we weren't obliged to obey your summons, considering you had deceived us about your name; but others said, whether it was Baumgart or not, we were bound by the oath taken in the church at Dannigkow, after our first battle—and none of us were desirous of breaking an oath. That is why we are here. You can imagine that we didn't come willingly. We are honest fellows, and to tell the truth, the work you gave us to do went against the grain. The long and short of it is, that when we go home, and people spit in our faces, we must put up with it, for they will have right on their side."

"Why didn't you say all this before?" Boleslav stammered forth. "Why, oh why have you let it come to my standing here before you—like a—like a— Ha! ha! ha! *If you spit in my face, I must put up with it!*"

"You need not reproach yourself on our account," Engelbert replied. "You have quite enough to bear without that. But now that we have discharged our duty—without grumbling, you must admit—I can only ask you, on behalf of myself and my comrades, to release us from our oath, as we release from yours. Of course we can not compel you against your wish, but all I can say is, that if you don't choose to do it, we must leave home and kindred, and wander forth into the world, lest people—"

"Stop!" cried Boleslav, feeling as if more would kill him. "Your desire is fulfilled. I now wish it as earnestly as you do. Of a truth I should deserve my disgrace, were I ever to ask another

The Cats' Bridge

favor of you— I will not even insult you by
saying 'Many thanks' for the service you have just
rendered me. May God reward you, and may He
forgive you for having put me in my present position; rather would I have thrown the corpse into
the river and myself after it; let us say no more.
Perhaps you will allow me to assist in putting the
horses in, as there is nothing else I can do for you?"

"I am sorry," Engelbert said, his voice quivering with emotion; "it pains us deeply. We are as
fond of you yourself as we have ever been—but,
you see—"

"I see all, dear Engelbert; no excuses are necessary."

"Well, then, we wish you farewell."

"Farewell!'

The horses were put in. All were in readiness
to start. Staring vacantly before him, Boleslav
leaned against the wall. Engelbert turned and
took a last look at him from the box-seat.

"And don't forget Regina!" he said. "That is
to say, if she escapes with her life. It is to her,
not to us, you are indebted."

"Very well," answered Boleslav, not taking in
the meaning of what had been said to him.

"Adieu!"

"Adieu, and *bon voyage!*"

The drivers cracked their whips; in another
moment the heavy wheels had thundered over the

loose flooring of the drawbridge. Like silver-girt phantoms the coaches disappeared in the misty moonlight.

He was alone—more alone than any outcast in God's wide world. What should he do?

He began wearily to drag his footsteps up the incline. The brambles that tangled the ground wound round his ankles. A firefly made a zigzag thread of flame in front of him. From the top of the hill the great, weird, dark masses of the Castle ruins looked down on him, as if threatening to fall on him and bury him beneath their débris. Through the yawning window-casements the moon shone, giving them the appearance of huge ghostly eyes. He roamed absently past the towers, a sudden exhaustion weighing like lead upon his limbs. If only he could fall asleep and never wake again.

He tried to remember what it was his friend had called out to him from the coach at parting. He racked and racked his brains, but his memory failed him.

The grass plot, where he had first found the half-wild girl, lay before him brightly illumined by the moon. The spot where she had begun to dig the grave stood out in uncanny blackness from the rest of the shining turf.

If only he had shoveled the corpse into it and gone on his way, perhaps somewhere at the other

The Cats' Bridge

end of the world some sort of happiness might still have been in store for him.

But now it was too late. Now all he could do was to endure—to complete the work of defiance begun to-day under such gloomy circumstances. Desolate and alone till the end. Never to feel again the clasp of a friendly hand, never to look with trust and affection into any human face, since the doughty comrades he had so firmly believed in had recoiled from him shuddering.

And had not the beloved shrunk from him too in horror? It seemed clear now for the first time why she had avoided him and hidden herself.

He was cut adrift from all the joys and sorrows that form a common bond between the hearts of men—cut adrift from love, hope, compassion, from everything but ignominy and hate.

With his face buried in his hands, he staggered over the lawn in the direction of the gardener's cottage, when his foot struck against something round and soft that lay across the path. It was the figure of a woman, lying with her head buried in the dry leaves and her limbs outstretched. Regina—positively it was Regina!

"What are you doing here? Get up."

There was not a sound or a movement. Where had he seen her last? Ah! to be sure; under the churchyard gateway, screening him from the gun that was pointed at his brain. That ghastly mo-

ment came back to him with all its terrors. For
his sake she had flung herself on the murderer;
for his sake risked her life. And how had he rewarded her? He had pushed carelessly past her;
consigned her to the mercy of the murderous,
bloodthirsty crew who were greedy to take her life,
without a shadow of a thought of how he might
save her troubling him for an instant. Even if she
were the most abandoned creature on the face of
the earth, she had not deserved such dastardly
treatment at his hands. Certainly she had not.

"Regina, wake up."

He bent over her and raised her, but her head
fell back lifeless among the bushes. There was
blood on his fingers from touching her. Her hair
was damp and matted.

Was she dead? No; it must not, could not be.
Sacrificed for him; that would mean adding original guilt to the sin he had inherited, and the idea
of owing so much to such a degraded creature was
in the last degree humiliating. She must at least
live till he had paid her. He tore open her chemise
with a rough, eager hand, and laid his ear on the
cool, rounded breast.

God be praised! Her heart was still beating.
And as he raised her once more, she slowly opened
her great eyes and looked round her vacantly. As
if shocked at being caught holding her thus, he let
her head slip out of his arms.

The Cats' Bridge

She moaned slightly as she sank back, for the swaying briers hurt her. Then regaining consciousness, she lifted herself on her elbow and gazed at him in dumb inquiry.

"Get up, Regina," he said.

The sound of his voice made her tremble. She tried to struggle on to her feet, but fell back helplessly.

"Let me lie where I am," she begged, with a timid, imploring glance.

"Stand up. I will help you."

"Must I go?" she asked, evading the proffered support. Grief and anxiety were depicted on her blood-stained, beautiful face.

"You would rather stay with me?"

"Ah, master, how can you ask?"

"But you'll have a bad time of it if you do."

"Oh, no. The noble master used to whip me every day. I am quite accustomed to it."

"But somewhere else they would treat you better."

"Somewhere else?" New consternation showed itself on her features.

"Good God! A woman like you, who is willing and hard-working, and has such strong limbs, is sure—"

She shook her head violently. "I shouldn't go far, master. If you hunt me away, I shall only lie down in a ditch and starve to death."

The Cats' Bridge

A softer look came into his eyes. No matter how bad, stupid, and corrupt she might be, she was the only human being in the wide world who clung to him. Why should he drive her from his threshold, when he himself was despised, ostracized, and a social outcast? Were they not both under the ban of the same misfortune?

The Cats' Bridge

CHAPTER VIII

THE next few days proved how little he was in
a position to live on his own estate without her
services. He was far more dependent on her than
she on him. Helpless as a shipwrecked mariner
on a desert island, he stole about the ancestral
grounds. Though the mines and wolf's-traps no
longer dogged his steps, finding his way among the
chaos of smoked and tumbling walls made him
giddy, and decay had altered everything so much
that the landmarks of his childish memories
afforded him no assistance. Even the park, where
once he had known every tree and bush, through
long years of neglect, had become such a wilderness that at every step he nearly lost himself in it.

When the first flush of his defiance and despair
had subsided, the question arose, "What was he to
do next?" It was a problem that pressed for solution, as the miserable rations of bread and meat in
the cellars were running out.

His pride prevented his seeking advice from
Regina; he had not spoken to her again. Apparently she understood the wisdom of making herself

scarce. But when he returned of a morning from the river, where he went for a bath, he found the red-flowered counterpane of the canopied bed neatly arranged, the floor swept, and strewn with sand and fragrant fir spikes, and saw awaiting him on the gold-legged table (the fourth leg of which was propped up with a brick) a steaming brown coffeepot, and dainty slices of black bread lying beside it.

His diffidence at taking food from her hands had soon been got over. At first he had still hesitated a little to break bread that she had brought him, but it looked so appetizing, and bathing in the cold autumn mornings so sharpened his hunger, that at last his scruples had gone to the wall.

At midday a soup made of bread and slices of roast meat stood ready for him, not to mention a bottle of good wine; and in the evening, by some clever stratagem, another meal of a different character was contrived out of the same unpromising materials. Thus she knew how to keep house with nothing but the scanty larder he had found in the cellar at her disposal.

He often saw her whisk past the window with pots and kettles, on her way to wash them in the river. When she came back she would cautiously peer with her lustrous eyes through the shrubs, to ascertain whether the coast was clear. If he happened to be at the door, or looking out of the window, she would immediately disappear in the wood.

She made the gardener's former workshop her domain. One morning after he had watched her go down to the river, he went in to look at it. He found a low, sloping room, with a roof composed of old greenhouse frames. The green, dusty, lead-bordered panes were much cracked, and in places let in the winds and rains of heaven. The ground was neither floored nor paved, but covered with a dark moist garden soil resembling peat. Attached to the walls were rude wooden shelves, once used by the gardener for his flower-pots. They now held all the house's scanty stock of crockery. Pots, plates, and dishes were arranged on them in perfect order, and had been polished till they shone. A blackened door off its hinges, evidently rescued from the fire, supported by two wooden boxes about two feet from the ground, was spread with straw and a haircloth of the kind that is thrown over the backs of horses to protect them from cold. This was her bed—"Many a dog has a better," he thought. The brick fireplace was in the opposite corner; a home-made contrivance of beams was meant to guide the belching smoke from the hearth into its proper channel, but only partially succeeded.

In this smoky hole, with its cold, damp floor, she was domiciled, and desired nothing better. Here her heart was centred as in a dearly cherished Paradise. Poor, wretched woman! and to be driven forth from it meant to her death and perdition.

And then one evening she disappeared. He had at last made up his mind to speak to her about the provisions, and went to call her. No answer came. The kitchen was empty. He sought her in the park, among the ruins, on the bridge, all over the island, but there was no sign of her. Her name rang clearly out through the night air as he called her, and had she been anywhere about she must have heard it. He became suspicious. Probably after the hard work of her lonely days, she took it out at night in the arms of a swain. She was, of course, well versed in the arts of vice, and would not scruple to yield herself to the embraces of some rustic gallant. Many of her persecutors below may have desired the body they stoned. How otherwise could her obstinate adherence to her present miserable mode of living, after his father's death, be explained, except by the existence of a new sin—a sin which, perhaps, had long been carried on hand-in-hand with the old. He was filled with loathing and disgust at the thought.

"If she can't behave herself, I'll pack her off early to-morrow morning;" and with this resolution he retired to rest. But he could not sleep for thinking of what the future would be without

The Cats' Bridge

her. To send her away would involve going himself the same day.

At about six o'clock he was awakened out of a doze by a stealthy opening of the outer door. He got up and dressed himself quickly, determined to call her to account without loss of time. He entered the kitchen and found her on the hearth with inflated cheeks, blowing the pine logs she had just set alight into a flame.

She turned on him slowly, her eyes big with astonishment, and said, "Good-morning, master."

He trembled in angry excitement. "Where have you been all night?" he thundered.

Her arms fell to her sides, and she shrank away terrified.

"Tell me at once."

"Oh," she stuttered, hanging her head, "I thought you wouldn't notice I had gone, and that I should be back before you were awake—"

"So if I don't *notice*, you amuse yourself by running about all night?"

She had retreated still farther from him.

"But—but—I was obliged to go," she said, stammering painfully. "There was scarcely anything at all left—and—and the master has eaten nothing but salt meat for so long."

The scales fell from his eyes.

"You went then to fetch food?"

"Of course. I have brought veal and fresh eggs

and butter—and sausage and lots of things. It's all in the cellar."

"Where did you get it?"

"Oh, I told you, master—in Bockeldorf. I know a grocer there who gets ready a supply of what we want beforehand, and when I knock at nights he lets me in at the back door. Not a living soul besides his wife knows. And he's not very dear. Merckel down in the village charges a thaler a pound for meat, and swears at me into the bargain."

"And you have walked six miles there and back to-night, and carried all those heavy parcels?"

Still frightened, she regarded him with surprise.

"I think you know, master, that I can do it, for I told you so before."

"But it's a physical impossibility. Don't lie to me, girl. From my experience during the campaign, I know how much fatigue a man can stand."

Now that she saw he was no longer angry she dared to draw herself to her full height. She exhibited her powerful arms proudly, and exclaimed with a pleased smile:

"I can stand more than any man, else I should be no good at all."

"For how long have you been going on these journeys, Regina?"

"For five years. Every week. Sometimes

The Cats' Bridge

oftener. In summer it's child's play. But in
autumn and winter, when the snow lies two feet
thick in the wood, or when the meadows are
flooded, it's no joke. But there's one thing to be
thankful for, the nights are long then, and at least
no one can see you. And I'd a hundred times
rather walk the six miles than go to that beast—
I beg pardon, I mean Master Merckel—who takes
a thaler for a pound of meat. Isn't that abomin-
able? And in the village—"

She paused suddenly, as if she feared being
scolded for talking too much.

"What were you going to say, Regina?" he asked
in a kindlier tone.

"Oh, nothing, but I should like to beg the master's pardon for having gone without leave. But
I thought he might perhaps like a change for
breakfast—a fresh egg—"

"Never mind, Regina," he said, turning away;
"you are a good girl."

He went down to the river to bathe. When he
came back he found his room tidied as usual, only
the coffee was not there.

"She is so tired out that she's fallen asleep," he
thought, and resigned himself to wait. At least,
she should not be reprimanded any more to-day.

But in consequence of his bath he was bitterly
cold, and found he could not forego the customary
warm beverage much longer. So, in order not to

wake her he went on tiptoe into the kitchen to see to the fire himself. But she was not asleep, though at the first glance it looked like it. She sat on the edge of her couch, motionless, with her hands before her face. Now and again a quiver passed through her frame, a symptom of the sleep of exhaustion. Yet on regarding her closer, he saw that glistening tear-drops were falling through her red, plump fingers, and her breast was shaking with gurgling sobs.

"What's the matter, Regina? Why are you crying?"

She did not answer, but her sobs became louder.

"Have I hurt your feelings, Regina? I shouldn't have scolded you if I had known where you had been."

She let her hands fall from her face, and looked at him with eyes swollen from weeping.

"Oh!" she said in a voice half choked by tears. "No one—ever—called me that before; and—it's not—true."

His mood changed and became harsh again. He was not conscious of having used any abusive epithet. It was too ridiculous of this creature, who was accustomed to being hounded about from pillar to post, to pretend to be thin-skinned and fastidious.

"What isn't true?" he demanded.

"What you said."

The Cats' Bridge

"What did I say? Good heavens!"

"That I—I was a good—" She broke again into convulsive sobs that stifled her voice.

He shook his head, perplexed at her distress. He had never looked very deeply into the most complex problems of the human soul, and did not know that even dishonor has its code of honor. Laughing, he laid his hand on her shoulder.

"Don't cry any more, Regina; I meant no harm. And now get my breakfast ready."

"May—I—bring it in?" she asked, still sobbing.

"Do you want me to come and fetch it?"

"I only thought I mightn't—" She moved to the hearth and began blowing the smoldering fire, using her tear-stained cheeks as bellows.

After that she was no longer shy of entering his room when he was there. Ever anxious to forestall his wishes, she seemed to read his countenance without a question passing her lips.

Boleslav had found, in the recesses of the cellar in which money and wine were stored, great masses of papers stuffed into chests, where chaos reigned supreme. They contained the whole of his father's correspondence, deeds, and documents of every description. His first search among them had brought to light nothing less important than his aunt's last will and testament, in which her Excellency bequeathed to Boleslav von Schranden, the only son of her favorite niece, the whole of her fortune, "to compensate him for the wrong," so ran the clause, "from which he will suffer to the end of his days."

Boleslav's pleasure at first was not great; it was only when he considered that here was a weapon put into his hands to use in the coming struggle that he began to appreciate the value of the gift. He scarcely gave a thought to the giver, who had always been kindness itself to him, so hardened had he become, so completely was his mind engrossed by contemplation of the grim work that it was his duty to carry on.

If only he could have seen a way clear before him, which he could have pursued instantly, without looking to the right or left, with the impetuous zeal characteristic of his nature! But for months the prospect must be one of paralyzing, hopeless inaction. The war which he had determined to wage against the Schrandeners must be conducted on an ambitious scale, if it were not to end in the pitiful failure that had soured and impoverished the last years of his father's life. It would need an army of workmen to inspire the serfs, who had so long run wild, with new respect. And where were these to be engaged, when there was not a soul in the neighborhood who would not have disdained to enter his service? But nearly everything is attainable with money, and doubtless many a swaggering patriot, who now spat at the mention

The Cats' Bridge

of his name, could be brought, cringing and servile, to heel, by the bribe of a triple wage. Only, for this his means were not sufficient. The cash that at the first glance had seemed such vast wealth proved, on nearer calculation, to be wholly inadequate to float his scheme. It was 4,500 thaler, left from outstanding debts, that the old Baron had hastily saved from the conflagration, when the whole world must have appeared to him to be melting into flame. For the sort of existence that, following his father's example, he was now leading with Regina, such a sum would last for years; but for the project he had in view it was a mere drop in the ocean.

Before the discovery of the will he had with a heavy heart entertained the idea of offering the fine old timber, which had been the pride of his ancestors, for sale, and to dispose of it below its value if the need arose. Now he had abandoned the plan as impracticable. Granted that he could find a market for it as easily as he hoped, it must be months before the actual cash came into his hands. Besides winter was at hand, one of those severe East Prussian winters, when work in the open air is out of the question. For this year at least neither building nor plowing was to be thought of. Why, then, make a sacrifice which with a little patience might be avoided altogether? If on the first of April he claimed his legacy, and was able with full pockets to enlist workers in his service, by May the building would be in full swing, and possibly the ground ready for the sowing of crops.

But till then—till then—! How would he be able to support the barren monotony of gray winter days spent in enforced and dreary idleness when his hands were burning to be at work? How endure the thought that his beloved was in the near neighborhood and he unable to ask her the fateful question on which his life and happiness hung? Would she wait? Would she forgive? Would she steel her heart against the atmosphere of hate and slander that surrounded her, and so keep her affection for him unchanged?

The Madonna in the cathedral came back to him. He wondered if she still resembled it. If only for one moment he might have gazed into her face! There was a white and red mist before his eyes; he saw lilies and roses, and a radiant virgin figure bending over them with a smile, but the features of the girl he had loved he could only dimly recall.

Veiled from his sight, perhaps she was destined to be the invisible guardian-angel who was to watch over his endeavors till his work was completed, when she would set the crown to it by revealing herself. He became gradually reconciled to the thought, and ceased to yearn for a meeting; and one word or sign to assure him that his hopes in her constancy were not ill-founded would have more than satisfied him.

More and more he buried himself in the chaos of papers, which seemed to increase instead of to diminish, in spite of his arduous sifting. The yellowed parchments stood in great piles against the wall of his sitting-room, reaching higher than the head of his beautiful grandmother, and yet in the vaults there still remained chests and boxes full, untouched. The whole archives of the family seemed to have been gathered together at a moment's notice, and hurled into a place of safety without the slightest regard to method or arrangement. Out of this confusion he wanted to find documents relating to the property, which were important, not to say indispensable. Among others were missing those that concerned agreements with the emancipated peasants relating to land boundaries. The rabble below were certain to have grabbed from the domain that had become ownerless more than their legal share. He saw how lawsuits would have to be fought over almost every inch of ground, and he must be able to back his claim with irrefragable documentary proof.

Nevertheless he felt an insuperable aversion to appealing to the courts. The picture of his father, as he had seen him the last time alive, stood out vividly in his memory; the ostracized baron, who had been bold enough to seek the aid of the law,

had then found every door closed in his face.
Truly Prussia at that time was not itself. The
walls of the State were tottering to their foundations, and the rats were having it all their own
way. But what guarantee was there that the son
of such a father would find the ear of justice less
deaf to his appeal? The law had shifts and re-
sources in plenty by which an unpopular person
could be rendered powerless to benefit by its help,
and he did not doubt that he would fall a victim
to such casuistry. His deserted and forlorn position so distorted his view of things that law and
order took the form of wild beasts lying on the
drawbridge in ambush for their prey. Even his
military duties had no interest for him now. Lieutenant Baumgart was on the list of killed. Why
trouble the authorities with the work of his resur-
rection? They would not thank him for it.

A text from the Bible came into his mind: "His
hand shall be against every man, and every man's
hand against him." The curse that accompanied
Hagar's son through life, he by dint of stubborn
defiance would turn into a blessing.

Weeks went by, but he hardly observed the flight
of time. He sat immersed day after day in his
papers, wandering forth of an evening to stumble
about the ruins, or to take a walk in the overgrown
park. There was only one place he carefully
avoided. That was the path which led to the Cats'

The Cats' Bridge

Bridge. When he chanced to find himself nearing it, his heart beat quicker, and he would hurry breathlessly by the shrubs that concealed it from view. Yet he was tormented by a grim desire to stand on the scene of the disaster, a desire which at length became almost irrepressible.

It was one evening toward the end of September when, for the first time since his return home, the moon was full. He roamed restlessly in the glades of the park, the dry leaves rustled at his feet, and the autumn wind shook the branches of the trees. The moonbeams shimmered on the grass like flocks of white sheep. Before him the shrubs rose in a dark, jagged line of wall. An impulse of sinister curiosity suddenly got the better of the superstitious repugnance that had hitherto held him back, and he plunged through the thicket that, with a sort of protecting aid, hid the path. The descent to the river was steep, almost perpendicular, and the mirror-like surface of the water was entirely concealed by alder-bushes. A faint rippling and splashing below fell mysteriously on his ear. From the top of the precipice a railed plank shot boldly out into mid-air. A rude scaffolding, planted firmly in the rock of the precipice, supported it with iron bars. On the opposite bank the trunk of a giant oak formed the support. In the middle there was a yawning gap of from ten to twelve feet. Like two arms longingly outstretched but never meeting, the planks branched forth on either side above the abysmal depths.

If they had never reached each other the crime would never have come to pass. But an easier job for a joiner could not be conceived. The plank on this side had two loose boards, which, by means of a wedge, could easily be pushed across; and the position of the hand-rail, by being unhinged, could also be reversed. Everything seemed to have been arranged expressly to facilitate the treacherous transaction. As a memorial of eternal shame, the dark, crude structure loomed out through the white mists of the brilliant night.

Beneath, the splashing from the invisible river grew more pronounced. It sounded as if its waters were still foaming with rage at the deed that so long ago had been enacted near at hand, and which death itself could not consign to oblivion.

Like a man in a dream, he stepped on to the plank, and looked down on the silver surface, which seemed to be emitting myriads of diamond sparks. Then he beheld the figure of a woman, who stood up to her knees in the water, with her skirts pinned round her waist. It was Regina, doing her washing, and wringing out the articles among the sandbanks and osiers.

His brows contracted. That he should encounter her *here* of all places! But in common justice he was obliged to admit it was not her fault.

The Cats' Bridge

Whenever she could she avoided him, and he had no reason to complain that he saw too much of her.

He leaned absently on the railing and watched her. She had no idea that he was anywhere in the neighborhood. She bent low over the water, the muscles in her neck and arms strained by her exertions, and shook the wet clothes with a will, sending up a spray of glistening drops. From time to time she chanted the song on two notes that he had heard her hum while digging the grave, breaking off abruptly when the water spurted into her nose and mouth.

What a hard worker she was! He had imagined her long ago gone to bed, and here she was instead, at this time of night, washing as if her life depended on it!

She started in alarm. His foot had disturbed some small pebbles, which fell splashing into the water close to where she stood. Her first thought was that some one was lying in wait for her among the shrubs, and, suspicious, she moved nearer the opposite bank. When at last it occurred to her to look up at the Cats' Bridge, she gave a startled cry.

"Don't be frightened, Regina," he called down to her. "I am not going to hurt you."

Whereupon she returned calmly to her washing.

"How do you get down there?" he asked.

She wiped her face with her naked arm. "I'm

a good climber," she said, looking up at him for a moment with blinking eyes.

"Doesn't the water freeze you? So late in the year, too!"

She made some response that he did not understand. He was curious to see how she would clamber up the steep declivity with her burden, so remained where he was and continued to watch her.

In a few minutes she packed up her washing and climbed on the bank. The moonlight cast a flashing halo round the masses of her hair, which to-day had been combed till it was almost smooth. She looked as if she wore a coronet. With one shy glance to ascertain that he was still standing there, she dived into the shrubs, and he saw her dart rapidly from branch to branch with the agility of a wildcat. At the top she let down her skirts, and would have flown with her basket, had he not called her back.

"Why do you do your washing at night?" he inquired, making an effort to look friendly disposed toward her.

"Because in the daytime they give me no peace."

"The villagers?"

"Yes, master."

"What do they do to you?"

"What they always do—throw things at me."

"Over the river?"

158

The Cats' Bridge

"Yes."

"The next time any one attacks you, come and fetch me."

She did not answer.

"Do you understand?"

She folded her hands, and looked at him beseechingly.

"What's the matter?" he asked.

"Please don't shoot at them," she stammered. "They like you to do that. He—the noble master, I mean—tried it once. Then they began to shoot too, from the other side, and there was firing here and firing there; the wonder was no one got shot. Don't you see, if they get into the habit of carrying guns about with them always, they are certain to hit me one day, for I'm obliged to go off the island sometimes?"

It was the longest and most sensible speech he had as yet heard from her lips. He had not suspected the existence of so much thoughtful wisdom behind that low brow, in its frame of wild hair.

"You are right, Regina," he replied. "For your sake I must forbear from provoking them."

He saw in the moonlight a dark flush suffuse her face.

"For my sake?" she said hesitatingly. "I don't quite understand what you mean."

"Oh, well, never mind," he answered evasively. "What I wanted to ask you, Regina, was—are you satisfied in my service? can I do anything to make you more comfortable?"

She stared at him in dumb amazement.

"You mustn't think, Regina," he went on, "that I am unfriendly. My mind is occupied with many things, and I prefer to be quite alone with my troubles. So if I don't speak to you often you will understand how it is."

Her eyes drooped. Her hands fumbled for the balustrade as if seeking a support, then the next moment she turned, and leaving her basket in the lurch, scampered off, as if driven by furies.

"Strange creature!" he muttered, as he looked after her. "I must be kinder to her. She deserves it." Then he leaned over the balustrade again, and gazing into the silver water fancied he saw growing there a garden of lilies and crimson roses.

The Cats' Bridge

CHAPTER IX

LIEUTENANT MERCKEL was far from being pleased at the course events had taken on the day of the funeral. He called the Schrandeners poltroons and old women, and declared they were unworthy ever to have worn the king's uniform.

When some one ventured to ask why he had not shown himself in it to the procession, and had left the mob leaderless at a critical moment, he replied that that was a different matter altogether: *he* was an officer, and as such bound only to draw his sword in the service of the king.

The Schrandeners, not accustomed to logical argument, accepted the explanation, and promised to retrieve their reputation the next time the opportunity offered itself. But this did not satisfy Felix Merckel.

"Father," he said, late one evening when the old landlord was counting the cash taken during the day, "I can't bear to think that scoundrelly cur holds the rank of Royal Prussian officer as I do. I am ashamed to have served with him. Our army doesn't want to be associated with people like him. It drags the cockade through the gutter, not to speak of the sword-knot. I know what I'll do; I'll call him out and shoot him."

He stretched his legs out on the settle, twisting his cavalry mustache with a bland smile. The old man let fall, in horrified dismay, a handful of silver that he was counting, and the coins rolled away into the cracks of the floor.

"My son," he said, "you really mustn't drink so much of that Wacholder brandy. It's good enough for customers, but you, Felix, shall have a bottle of light wine to-morrow, and perhaps some of them will follow your example, and so it won't cost me anything."

"Father, you are mistaken," Felix answered. "It's my outraged sense of honor that gives me no peace. I am a German lad, father, and a brave officer. I can't stand the stain on my calling any longer."

"Felix," said the old man, "go to bed, my son, and you'll get over it."

"Father," replied his son, "I am sorry to have to say it, but you have no conception of what honor is."

"I think," went on the old man, ignoring the taunt, "you haven't enough occupation. If you would only look after the bottles—of course the barmaid is there for the purpose—it would do you good. It would distract your thoughts. Or you might go out shooting sometimes."

The Cats' Bridge

"Where?"

"Lord bless my soul! there are the woods and forest of Schranden. Whether the hares devour each other, or you annex your share of them, is all the same."

"That won't do for me, father. I am an officer, and don't wish to be caught poaching."

"Good gracious, how you talk! Do you forget that I am magistrate here. I am not likely to sentence you to the gallows. But do as you like, my boy. Of course you *might* go oftener to the parsonage. The old pastor enjoys a game of chess; there's nothing to be gained by chess, I know, but some people seem to like it, and then there's— Helene."

"Ah, Helene!" said Felix, stroking his chin and looking flattered.

The old man examined the artificial fly in the centre of his amber heart.

"I have a strong notion that she would be a good match if the pastor consented, and she liked you."

"Why shouldn't she like me?" asked Felix.

"Well, there might be some one else who—"

Felix smiled sceptically.

"Or do you mean that she has already set her heart on you?"

Felix shrugged his shoulders.

"You see, Felix, my boy, that would be a great

piece of good fortune for us. People are constantly carping at the way in which they think I acquired my bit of money—without the smallest ground of course. If only the pastor gave you his daughter as wife, it would stop their mouths once for all. A man like Pastor Götz has great weight and influence. Well, then, as I said, it's worth while your hanging about there a little. Court her, and a fellow like you is sure—"

"Dear father, spare me your advice, if you please," interrupted his son. "Whether Helene becomes my wife or not is my own affair. I have not yet made up my mind. She has a pretty enough little phiz, but she is too thin. She might be fattened up with advantage. Then there's something old-maidish about her, something sharp and prudish that I don't quite fancy. For instance, if you put your arm round her waist she says, 'Ah, dear Lieutenant, how you frightened me!' and wriggles away. And if you squeeze her arm, by Jupiter, she screams out directly, "Oh, dear Lieutenant, don't do that, I've got such a delicate skin!' Of course that's all airs and affectation, and perhaps if a man caught hold of her firmly and didn't give in, she'd allow herself to be kissed at last; but as I say, I have not made up my mind, so don't build too much on it."

The old landlord, who with deft hand was rolling up his sovereigns in paper, looked proudly

The Cats' Bridge

across at this magnificent son of his. Then he became anxious again.

"And you won't think any more about the duel, eh? That's all nonsense. . . . You wouldn't go and risk your life so recklessly as that."

Felix threw back his chest. "In affairs of honor, father, please don't interfere, for you know nothing about them. Directly I can find a respectable second—"

"What is that?"

"Why, the man who'll take the challenge."

"Where—to Boleslav?"

"Of course."

"To the island?"

"To the island."

"But, Felix, what are you thinking about? No Christian dare set foot on the island. It swarms with wolf-traps, bombs, and other deadly instruments. Look at Hackelberg; he was caught in one, and limps to this day—but never mention it. It mustn't come out that Hackelberg was ever on the island. Do you see? . . . As I was saying, you wouldn't get any one to go on such a dangerous errand—or to come in contact with such a man as that. No, my boy, think no more about it. There's nothing to be gained by it."

"But I *will* challenge him all the same to meet me here," growled Felix.

The old man contemplated him with the greatest concern for a few moments, then rose, filled a liqueur-glass with peppermint brandy, and brought it over to him.

"Drink it up," he said, "it'll soothe you." Felix obeyed.

"Leave the matter in the hands of your good, honest old father. Trust him to find in the night some other means of satisfying your so-called sense of honor. Good-night, my boy."

"The good, honest old father" had not promised more than he was able to perform.

The next morning, when he met his son at the breakfast table, he asked in an accent of benevolent sympathy:

"Well, have you slept off all those silly notions?"

Felix grew angry. "I told you, father, that on that subject you were—"

"Totally ignorant! Very good, my boy. But I want to be clear on one point. Is it with the Baron von Schranden that you propose to fight a duel, or with Lieutenant Baumgart?"

Felix did not answer at once. A suspicion of what his father was darkly hinting dawned on him.

"Don't deal in subterfuges, father," he said. "I am an upright, simple soldier, and don't understand them."

"But, Felix, you needn't be so headstrong. I mean well. As the Baron von Schranden never was an officer, there is no reason why you should

The Cats' Bridge

concern yourself about him; and as Lieutenant Baumgart has proved a swindler, and assumed a false name, he is equally beneath your notice."

"That is true," said Felix, spreading honey on his bread and butter. "As a matter of fact, I oughtn't to do him the honor of challenging him."

Then a new idea seemed to occur to Felix. "If only," he added fiercely, "he could be stopped from entitling himself lieutenant. That's what offends my sense of honor more than anything."

His old father seemed prepared with an answer to this remark.

"Why should he go on calling himself lieutenant?" he asked, grinning and whistling under his breath. "Only because his superior officers are kept in ignorance of the deception he has practised. If they had an inkling of it, they'd be down on him fast enough."

Felix understood. "You mean we ought—" he began.

"Of course we ought."

But Felix's hypersensitive sense of honor again felt itself outraged. "Remember that I am an officer, father," he exclaimed indignantly. "Your proposal is in the highest degree insulting."

The host shrugged his shoulders. "Very well; if you don't wish it, leave it alone," he said.

Then the honorable young man saw a way of escape.

The Cats' Bridge

"If only it could be done without a signature," he meditated aloud.

"That difficulty is easily overcome," responded the old man. "I have a scheme in my head. Let *me* draw it up. All you've got to do will be to sign your name with the others at the foot. Then it will be only one of many."

On the afternoon of the same day, the parish crier, Hoffmann, invited all the country's defenders in the village to assemble at the Black Eagle. It was the merest matter of form, a tribute to the importance of the business to be discussed, for they were certain to have turned up there of their own accord sooner or later without an invitation. The tables were soon full (Schranden had sent a contingent of thirty warriors to the War of Liberty); and when Master Merckel saw glasses emptying to right and left of him, he stepped behind the bar, and exchanging glances with his son, rubbed his hands with satisfaction, and began the following harangue:

"Dear fellow-citizens, I desire to speak a few words to you. You are all brave soldiers, and have fought in many a bloody battle for your Fatherland in its dire extremity. You must have often been thirsty in those days, and have longed for even a few drops of dirty ditch-water. It's only to your credit, then, that after the heat and burden of the war, you turn into the Black Eagle occa-

168

sionally, for a good draft of beer. You have earned it honestly with the sweat of your brow. Your health, soldiers!"

He flourished the mug that he kept specially for occasions like the present, and then raised it to his mouth, holding it there till he had assured himself that no glass had been put down unemptied. Then making a sign to the barmaid, he wiped his lips energetically, and continued:

"I, as your Mayor and magistrate, could not accompany you to the seat of war, being obliged to remain and look after the wants of those who stayed at home." A murmur of approval came from the audience. "But I am a patriot like you; my warm heart beats true for the honor of the Fatherland, just as your hearts do, brave soldiers! Fill up, Amalie, you slow-coach! Master Weichert is nearly expiring for thirst." Master Weichert protested, but in vain; his glass was snatched out of his hand. "And my bosom swells with pride when I look at my son, a gallant, upright soldier, whom the confidence of his comrades and the favor of his king promoted to the rank of officer. I speak for you all, I know, when I call three cheers for the joy of the village, the dutiful son, the good comrade, the brave soldier, and honorable officer, Lieutenant Merckel—Hip, hip, hurrah!"

The Schrandeners joined enthusiastically in the

cheering, and Master Merckel observed with satisfaction that several glasses had again become empty. To give Amalie time to fill up, he made an effective little pause, in which, in speechless emotion, he fell on his son's breast: then he resumed the thread of his discourse:

"All the more painful is it, therefore, to see that the disgrace you, by your glorious deeds of arms, did your best to remove from our beloved and highly favored village, now rests on it again, through the presence here of the son of the man who wrought it such dire mischief. On the site of the fire he is now living with his father's mistress. I'll not enter into details, but you know, my children, what that implies."

There was a significant laugh, which changed gradually into a sullen muttering.

"Yes, and what's more, this immoral outlaw belongs to our glorious army. Under a false name he enlisted in its ranks, and raised himself to the position of officer. By lying, and cheating, and devilish craft, he succeeded in obtaining what you brave, honest fellows (with the exception of my son, of course) could not attain to. Will you tolerate this, you noble Schrandeners? Will you, I say, let a rascally cheat, the son of a traitor, continue to look down on you as his inferiors? Was it for this that his gracious Majesty made you free men?"

The moment was a favorable one for drink-

The Cats' Bridge

ing his gracious Majesty's health, and Amalie, in obedience to a signal, began the filling-up process anew. Master Merckel already felt he had cause to congratulate himself on the result of his stirring oration.

"No, brave Schrandeners," he went on, "such a scandal must not be tolerated! The army must be purged of this black spot; otherwise you will be ashamed, instead of proud, of calling yourselves Prussian soldiers."

"Kill him! kill him!" cried several voices at once.

"No, dear friends," he replied, with his unctuous smirk. "You mustn't always be talking of killing. I, as your Mayor, can not countenance that," shaking a warning fat forefinger at them; "but I can give you wiser counsel. The authorities, naturally, have no suspicion of who it is that has been masquerading as Lieutenant Baumgart; last spring no one had time to inquire into birth certificates and such-like details. But now there will be leisure to investigate the case of a Prussian officer passing under an assumed name. And the case presses for attention.

"Do you remember the story Johann Radtke related in this very room, the day he came over from Heide, when none of us had the slightest idea of what a savage kind of animal his celebrated hero, Lieutenant Baumgart, really was?"

The Cats' Bridge

He was interrupted by a laugh of pent-up hate and fury. It proceeded from his son Felix.

"He is said to have tramped home from France entirely alone, like a wandering journeyman. He had been wounded and taken prisoner, and all the rest of it. But, mark my words, that signifies more than you think. It means that he didn't get his discharge—that he sneaked out of the service like a thief in the night, in the same straightforward manner as he entered it. And do you know what that is in good plain Prussian? *Deserting!* It means he is a deserter."

A cry of jubilation arose, which Master Merckel greeted with profound approval, for, according to his ripe experience, shouting rendered the throat dry. He let the applause therefore exhaust itself, and then went on:

"It is our sacred duty, as genuine patriots and intrepid soldiers, to open the eyes of his Highness the Commander-in-Chief to this young man's true character. We owe it to our King, our Fatherland, above all, to ourselves. We'll get him cashiered out of our brave army, degraded, and ruined. What is done to him afterward, whether he is shot or cast into prison, is a matter of indifference to us. We are not responsible for him."

At the mere suggestion of such a vengeance the Schrandeners were beside themselves, and almost howled with rage.

The Cats' Bridge

Master Merckel drew a sheet of paper from his breast-pocket.

"I have drawn up a little statement, in which I have respectfully lodged a complaint to a general of high standing and noble birth. If you'll allow me, dear friends—"

He was in the act of unfolding the sheet when a still happier thought occurred to him.

"I could lay the document before you at once and ask you to sign it, but then it would be my composition, and not yours," he went on, beaming; "and I want every word well weighed and considered, and altered if needful. I therefore propose that a committee of five comrades be elected from among you, who shall withdraw with me and my son into the best parlor, where we can hold a quiet consultation over the wording of the address, while the rest of you remain here."

Then he gave the names of those he considered worthiest of filling this delicate office. They were five young men whom he knew to be lavish spendthrifts, and whom he expected to acquit themselves honorably in more senses than one. Half in envy, half in malice, his choice was agreed to.

The elected looked rather glum; they then knew what they had been let in for, but at the same time they were too flattered by the invitation to decline it.

Master Merckel, with the air of solemnity he al-

The Cats' Bridge

ways considered due to any occasion on which the best parlor was brought into requisition, flung open the door, over which was inscribed the alluring caution, fraught with so much significance: "*Only wine drunk here.*"

With a somewhat nervous air the chosen committee entered the sanctum of gentility, awkwardly twirling their caps in their hands. The last to go in was the son of the house. At the door, Master Merckel turned and called out in a loud impressive voice:

"Amalie, bring two bottles of Muscat for me and the Lieutenant!"

Muscat was a wine made at home, from rum, sugar, cinnamon, currant juice, and a judicious quantity of water, and was sold to the Schrandeners for a thaler the bottle. Master Merckel ordered two bottles, to demonstrate to his customers that he did not expect any of them to go shares in a bottle.

There was now a profound silence in the taproom. Its occupants gazed with serious excited faces at the closed door and then at each other.

Neither did any sound proceed from the reception room, where a dumb pitched battle was going on between the host and his guests. It was doubtful at one time who would come off victor. But a few minutes after the barmaid had hurried up from the cellar with the two freshly filled bottles,

The Cats' Bridge

Master Merckel tore open the door again, and shouted triumphantly:

"Amalie, five bottles more of Muscat!"

Tongues were loosened. The tension was over. As was generally the case, the customers had been mastered by the landlord. And soon the dull monotonous sound of reading aloud reached the ears of the listeners in the tap-room.

. . . .

Master Merckel, senior, when he retired to rest, felt that his day had not been wasted.

His son had abandoned his dangerous project: the fate of the last of the Schrandens had been sealed; and in the cash-box, beyond the usual takings, was a surplus of eight thalers and twenty-five silver groschen.

"Now I have killed three birds with one stone!" he mused, with a self-satisfied grin, and, folding his hands, fell into a gentle slumber.

The Cats' Bridge

CHAPTER X

WINTER had come. It had been preceded by a season of decay, inexpressibly cheerless and trying to the spirits. Boleslav, who had grown up in closest communion with Nature and her moods, could never have believed it possible that autumn's symbolic melancholy would affect him so profoundly and send such deathlike shivers through his limbs. The mere calculation of time dismayed and oppressed him.

His evenings began to be dismally long. Solitude swooped over his head like a flying vulture in ever-narrowing circles, till he began to fancy he felt the chill flap of the wild bird's wings across his face.

It was strange that he who all his life had been much alone from choice, should now, when almost every human being was his deadly foe, crave for the society of his fellow-creatures.

He buried himself deeper and deeper in the mass of papers and manuscripts, a dreary enough occupation, without much object unless it were to help the hours to drag a little less slowly. He tried to convince himself that the portion of the past he unearthed from these dust-heaps might be of service to him in the future. But in reality he had found what was absolutely necessary to his purpose without much trouble, and the rest might as well have perished in the flames.

Regina remained tongue-tied, and performed her household duties swiftly and noiselessly. She moved about his room without lifting her eyes to his face, and if he addressed a word to her, shrank away with a startled look. But her answers to his questions, though given in a hesitating and embarrassed manner, were always clear, comprehensive, and to the point. Sometimes days together went by without their exchanging a syllable. Yet it was on these days he observed her in secret all the more closely, watching her as she laid the table, following her with his eyes as she crossed the little plot of garden and disappeared into the bushes. He caught himself constantly wondering what was passing in her mind. What did she think about all day long? Was it possible that her whole existence revolved round him and his personal comforts—a man who was nothing to her, who had not even rewarded her labors so far with a brass farthing?

He felt ashamed when he thought of the innumerable self-sacrifices he accepted from her with such haughty indifference, and determined to be

more friendly and conversational toward her in the
future, so that she might feel the unpleasantness
of her position less acutely. But a certain unac-
countable shyness on his side seemed to hinder his
putting these good intentions into practise. He
no longer hated her. His aversion had yielded to
something like regard at sight of so much unsel-
fish loyalty and untiring industry; and the result
was that he felt more than ever a constraint in conversing with her. Something came between them,
a kind of mysterious veil that enveloped her and
rendered her unapproachable as a stranger. It
seemed almost as if the spirit of his father hov-
ered about her, preventing by its ghostly presence
any intercourse between them. Sometimes he wondered if it were her shame that invested her with
that strange fascination that vice is said to exercise
on inexperienced youth. Or was it the magnitude
of her misfortunes that gave her an unconscious
power and charm?

Often when she brought in his supper, or turned
back the counterpane from his bed, he would look
up from his work and endeavor to open a conversation, but his tongue would cleave to the roof
of his mouth. He could never think of anything to
talk to her about that was not beneath his dignity.
So, after all, only curt and harsh commands crossed
his lips.

He had remarked for a long time how much

more careful she had become about her personal appearance, which had wonderfully improved. She no longer went about ragged, unkempt, and with her neck exposed, but wore her jacket buttoned up modestly at her throat, with the ends neatly tucked under her waist-band. A woolen scarf was knotted round her neck by way of giving a finish to her costume, and her skirt was carefully brushed and kept in repair. Her hair did not hang about her as formerly, in untidy plaits and a hundred rough loose curls, but was combed and neatly dressed. Of a morning the top of her head sometimes presented a smooth polished surface, the effects of the shower-bath, by means of which she brought her unruly mane into subjection.

The weather grew bitterly cold, but she still shivered in her cotton gown, only throwing on her red cross-over when she went into the open air.

One evening as she was preparing for her regular weekly expedition for the purchase of provisions, and had come to him for orders, he said:

"Why have you brought no winter clothes back with you yet, Regina?"

She looked on the ground and replied:

"I should like to—only—"

"Only?"

The Cats' Bridge

"I wasn't sure whether I might."

"Of course you may. You mustn't freeze."

"There's a—" she began eagerly, then stopped and blushed.

"Well?"

"There's a jacket at the shop—a blue cloth one trimmed with beautiful fur. The shopman says—"

He smiled. "Thank God," he thought, "she is beginning to be human at last. A love of finery has awakened in her."

"What does the shopman say?" he asked.

"That it would fit me exactly. And I need something warm and comfortable for the long walks. But it's a real lady's jacket, and—"

"All the more reason why you should have it," he interrupted, laughing. "Don't come back without the jacket, now mind. Good-night, and a pleasant journey."

With a joyous exclamation she stooped to kiss his hand, but he evaded the caress.

When her footsteps had died away in the darkness, he took the lamp and went into the greenhouse, which was her private apartment.

The fire still smoldered on the hearth, but the room was icily cold and comfortless. A stray flake or two whirled through the holes in the roof, for outside a gentle dusting of snow had begun to fall.

The Cats' Bridge

"Why doesn't she doctor the laths?" he thought, and resolved that the next morning he would come and lay boards over the weak places. He climbed on one of the boxes and tested with a tap the glass roofing. Then he understood why Regina preferred to sleep half in the open air. The leaden framework of the panes had become rotten and brittle. At his mere touch the whole decrepit roof rattled and trembled in all its joints. Any attempt to mend it would bring it down altogether.

"It's a positive sin to allow her to be housed like this," he said to himself.

He went back to his room and drew from under his sheets as many of his feather mattresses as he could do without, and carried them, with one of his pillows, to her wretched resting-place. He carefully made up a bed, and then threw her horse-cloth over it, so that not a scrap of the bedding was visible.

"That will make her open her eyes," he thought, "when, worn out, she comes to throw herself on her pallet." And well satisfied with his evening's work, he returned to his papers.

The next morning, when he awoke, his walls shone with the dazzling reflection of the snow. In the night the world had arrayed itself in the garb of winter.

He dressed, and called Regina. There was no answer. She had not come back.

The Cats' Bridge

He waited two hours, and then went to prepare his own breakfast. Three snow-heaps had collected underneath the holes in the glass roof, and a fourth was accumulating on the hearth. A greenish twilight filled the room. He took the shovel and broom, and half mechanically swept the white mounds out at the door; then he fetched a sheet of strong cardboard that had served as a cover to the stacks of documents, cut it into strips, which he cautiously pushed through the holes so that they roofed in the bad places from the snow.

"That's the best I can do," he said as he shivered about the room, which he had now made nearly as as dark as night.

Then, sighing heavily, he went to the hearth, and lit the fire.

The day crept on, and still Regina did not return. In all probability the snowstorm would detain her at Bockeldorf till the next morning. He felt moved to distraction as he sat over his work. Now and then, to vary the dull monotony, he took a walk to the Cats' Bridge, over which she was bound to come. After he had bolted his cold dinner he did nothing but watch the clock, whose hands seemed hardly to move.

He missed Regina at every turn; for though she kept out of his way when at home, he knew he had only to whistle to bring her instantly to his elbow.

The Cats' Bridge

He put his papers aside, and to change the current of his thoughts began to draw. On the back of a coachbuilder's bill of fifty years ago he painted a long garden border of stiff rows of stately lilies and red roses. First he made a line of lilies, then one of roses, then lilies again, and so on until the whole resembled some gorgeous carpet. Then he threw himself on the creaking sofa, and dreamed of the Madonna who presided over that wall of flowers, and shed the blessed light of her countenance on all who had the courage to penetrate it.

Already it was dusk.

There was a sound of footsteps on the cobblestones before the door. He sprang to his feet and hurried out.

Regina came timidly over the threshold. She was laden with bundles and parcels, and covered from head to foot with snow; even the little curls on her forehead were powdered white. Her face glowed, but there was an expression of fear in her brilliant eyes as she lifted them to his.

"I ran as fast as I could," she panted, laying her right hand on her heart. "The shopman wouldn't let me start till daylight, because he thought—the jacket might—"

She broke off, looking guilty.

He smiled kindly. He was much too glad to know that she was back again to scold her.

The Cats' Bridge

"Go and cook me something hot as quickly as you can," he said. "You'll be glad of your supper too."

She gazed at him in mute amazement.

"Why don't you go?"

"I will—but, oh!" And then as if ashamed of what she was on the point of saying, she rushed past him into the kitchen.

"She almost claimed her flogging," he murmured, laughing, as he looked after her.

He was sitting at his desk where he generally worked, when she brought in the evening meal. The lamp with its green shade cast a subdued uncertain light over the apartment. He liked to watch her as she moved swiftly to and fro, in and out of the shadows. To-day her appearance almost frightened him. She looked resplendently, proudly beautiful. Not a trace of her former degradation was apparent. The once forlorn and half-tamed girl might have been taken for a duchess, so graceful and distinguished were all her movements; so pure and full of charm was the contour of her young erect figure. Was it the neat woolen dress, or the new jacket with its silver-gray fur—*kazabeika*, as they called it in Poland—that was responsible for the transformation? As she laid the table she smiled to herself a happy shame-faced little smile, and every now and then flashed a rapid stealthy glance across at him. It was evident she wanted to be admired, but dared not attract his attention.

When she came within the circle of light made by the lamp, in order to place it on the supper table, he turned his eyes quickly away to make her think he had noticed nothing. But all the same he could not resist letting fall a remark.

"How conceited we are of our new clothes!" he said banteringly.

A vivid blush spread over her face and neck.

"They are much too good for me," she whispered, still smiling, still glancing at him in half-ashamed coquetry. But she was not yet daughter of Eve enough to take a sidelong peep at herself in the glass.

On going to turn down his bed for the night, she was astonished to see how it had diminished in size, but gulped back an exclamation of surprise, lest he should be annoyed. Then wishing him good-night she left the room.

With a grin of inward satisfaction he thought of the great surprise that was in store for her, and soon became engrossed in his manuscripts again.

About an hour had elapsed, when he was startled by a rustling sound at the back of his chair. He turned round and found her standing beside him. Her face was very white, her lips trembling, her breath coming quick through dilated nostrils. The fur collarette was unfastened at the throat, and showed the coarse chemise underneath, the folds of which rose and fell with her billowing breast. In the excitement of the moment she had forgotten to arrange her clothing.

"How handsome she is!" he thought, filled with involuntary admiration of her strange beauty, and then he tried not to look at her.

"Now then, what's the matter?" he asked in his gentlest tones.

She made an effort to speak, but some moments passed before a sound escaped her lips.

"Oh, master!" she stammered forth at last, "was it you—did you do that with the beds?"

"Yes, of course. Who else should do it?"

"But—why—*why?*" and she lifted her swimming eyes in alarm and consternation.

Apparently his kindness frightened her. It was necessary to adopt a firmer tone in order to become master of his own emotions.

"Stupid girl," he said loftily, "do you think I wish you to die out there of cold?"

For a moment she stood like a statue, silent and motionless, and big sparkling drops rolled down her cheeks. And then suddenly she threw herself at his feet, clung to both his hands, and covered them with kisses and tears.

At first he was too unnerved and thrilled at the sight of her agitation to speak. He had never imagined that she would be so deeply moved. Then he collected himself, and withdrawing his hands commanded her to rise.

"Don't make a scene, Regina," he said. "Go to bed. I'm sure you must be tired out."

She would have wiped her eyes with her sleeve, as was her habit, only she remembered the new soft fur trimming in time, and so let her tears run on.

"Oh, master!" she sobbed. "I hardly know what's come over me. But were you really serious? I don't deserve all your kindness. First the beautiful jacket, and then when I expected a whipping for being gone the whole day—for you to— Oh—"

"Say no more. I won't listen to another word," he insisted. "You must have some sort of bed. Where used you to sleep before?"

She started and cast down her eyes.

"Before?" she murmured.

"Yes, in my father's time."

"Ah, then, I used to lie on the door-mat or—" she paused.

"Or where?"

She still remained silent, and trembled.

"Where?" he asked again.

Her eyes moved shyly in the direction of the canopied bed.

"You know; ah, you know, master," she murmured. And then overwhelmed with shame she covered her face with her hands.

Yes, he knew. How could he forget it for a moment.

"Begone!" he cried, his voice shaking with anger and disgust, and he motioned her to the door.

Without a word she crept out, her head still bowed in her hands.

The Cats' Bridge

CHAPTER XI

BOLESLAV was almost happy. He had hit on a new and brilliant idea, and the hopes of carrying it out brightened for a time the deadening monotony of his existence. He believed he could clear his father's memory.

How it had first occurred to him he hardly knew. He had found certain letters from Polish noblemen addressed to his father, which seemed to suggest that the deceased had felt himself bound by a hastily-made promise which at the time he had not meant seriously, and that a chain of tragic circumstances had compelled him against his will to be a party to the act of treachery. If this did not exonerate him from all guilt, it at least put the slandered man in a new light—the light of a martyr.

If by minute study of the documents he could trace the affair to its source, and make public a true history of the disaster, in which he would demonstrate that Eberhard von Schranden, far from having played the devilish rôle that rumor attributed to him, had only been a victim of circumstances, surely there would at least arise some who would hold out their hand in remorse to the sufferer's heir. The more he absorbed himself in this task of vindication the more he began to feel united with the dead man, and accustomed to the idea of sacrificing his own innocent reputation for his sake.

His brain was so much occupied with these schemes that he slept little at night, and in the daytime tore about the park like one possessed. The less hope he cherished in his secret heart that his plan would succeed, the more did he long for some human soul into whose ear he could pour his doubts and fears. But there was no one to speak to but the taciturn woman, who glided past him with eyes guiltily cast down.

One evening, when his solitude almost maddened him, he said to her:

"Regina, aren't you frozen in your kitchen?"

"I never let the fire out."

"But what do you do in the evening, when it's dark?"

"I sit by the fire and scw, till my fingers get quite stiff."

"Then you have a light?"

"I burn fir-cones."

He was silent; he gnawed his under lip, and hesitated as to what he should say next. Then he took courage.

"Regina, if you like you may bring your sewing into the sitting-room, after supper," he said.

She grew pale, and stammered out, "Yes, master."

He thought her wanting in gratitude.

"Of course, if you'd rather not—" he said, shrugging his shoulders.

"Oh, master—I should like to come."

"Very well, then, come—but you must make yourself look respectable. Why have you given up wearing your new clothes?" Since that evening she had taken to shivering about in the cotton jacket again.

"I thought it would hurt them."

"Hurt them! How?"

"I mean," she said incoherently, "that when you are angry with me—such as I are not fit—"

"Nonsense!" he interrupted quickly, feeling that if she went on he would be angry with her again.

After supper she appeared in some trepidation at the door. Snowy linen shimmered in her hand. She remained standing till he had impatiently invited her to sit down.

"You want people to stand on ceremony with you, as if you were some fine lady," he said.

She laughed in confusion.

"I am only nervous, because I am not quite sure —how to behave." And she turned to her work.

No more passed between them that evening, and it was more than a week before they broke into conversation again.

The Cats' Bridge

He sat brooding over his yellow papers, and she let her needle fly through the crackling calico. When the clock struck eleven, she gathered up her sewing, and whispering "Good-night," slipped out on tiptoe without waiting for an answer.

"What are you working at so industriously?" he asked her one evening, after he had watched her intently for some minutes.

She looked up and pushed a curl off her forehead with damp fingers.

"I am making shirts for you, master," was the answer.

"So you undertake that too?"

"Who else should do it?"

A short silence; then he questioned her further.

"Who taught you all you know, Regina? Your mother?"

She shook her head.

"My mother died very young. I can hardly remember her. People say my father beat her to death."

He thought of the thin pale face and tired eyelids in the picture-gallery, of which the last trace had perished in the great fire.

"Can you remember what your mother was like?" he demanded again.

"She had long black hair, and eyes like mine, at least, so I have heard people say; and I can remember her hair, for she often wrapped me in it

The Cats' Bridge

when I was undressed. I used to sit in it as if it were a cloak, and laugh; and when father—" She stopped in sudden alarm. "But you won't care to hear more?"

"Go on, tell me the rest," he exclaimed.

"And when father came home and wanted to beat me, because he was drunk, you know, she stood in front of me, and told me to get under her dress; and inside her dress it was like being in a cave, quite dark and still, and father's swearing sounded a long, long way off. And then she died. It was on a Sunday—yes, it was on a Sunday. For I was standing by the hedge and wondering whether she'd have a beautiful coffin—a green one, like the coffin on the trestle in the garden—when you went by on your way to church. At that time you were little, like me, and you had on a blue coat with silver buttons, and a little sword at your side; and you stopped and asked me why I was crying, and I couldn't answer, I was so frightened, and then you gave me an apple."

He had not the smallest recollection of the incident, but he remembered how he had taken the young sparrow away from her, and related the story. She had not forgotten it. Her eyes became illumined, as if lost in contemplation of some blissful sight.

"I wonder, now, that you gave it up so meekly," he said.

The Cats' Bridge

"How could I have done otherwise?" she answered.

"You might easily have refused," he said.

She bent over her work. "I was only so glad for you to have it," she said, in a low soft voice. "It's not often that a poor little village girl gets the chance of giving anything to a rich young nobleman."

He bit his lip. Truly he had taken more from her since than his pride and manliness should have permitted.

"And besides," she went on, "even if I hadn't wanted to give it to you, it was yours by right. You were the young baron."

How perfectly natural the argument sounded from her lips.

"Regina, tell me honestly," he said, "if you haven't entirely forgotten the days when you ran wild in the village."

"Oh, no, indeed I haven't," she replied, with an almost roguish smile. "For instance, I remember a great many things about the noble young baron."

He withdrew far back into the shadow of the lamp-shade. "What splendid stuff she has in her!" he thought, and devoured her with his eyes. And then he made her relate all her reminiscences of him at that time. He did not appear in a very amiable light. Once he had pushed her into a

194

duck-pond; another time sent her floating down the river in a flour-vat, till her cries of terror had brought people to the bank with life-saving apparatus; when she had on a new white frock, given her by the castle housekeeper, he had painted her hands and face with white chalk, and told her to stand motionless like one of the statues in the park. She had submitted meekly till the chalk got into her mouth and eyes and made them smart, and then she had burst out crying and run away.

She recalled all this with beaming eyes, as if his pranks had been a source of infinite happiness to her. Although when reminded of such and such an escapade he recollected it perfectly, he could not remember that it was Regina who had been the victim of his caprice. A sensation of shame rose within him. Instead of the dreamy, generous young cavalier he had been in the habit of picturing himself, he saw a cruel little village tyrant, who exercised his power over his small contemporaries with a relentlessness that was almost vicious.

"And did I make no amends for my wicked deeds?" he inquired, hoping to hear he had at least been capable of doing good sometimes.

"Oh, you used to give us things," she answered. "'Divide that,' you used to say, and scatter on the ground either apples and nuts, or broken tin soldiers, or a handful of counters. But, of course, the strongest and biggest got everything. Felix Merckel was the best at a scramble; the girls only had the leavings."

"And did you ever get anything from me, Regina?" he asked.

She flushed scarlet, and bowed lower over her work. "Yes, once!" she said softly.

"What was it?"

She was silent, and dared not lift her eyes.

"Good heavens! why do you look so ashamed about it?"

"Because—I—have it still."

"Oh, not really!" He smiled. A feeling of pleasure shot through him.

Without answering, she felt in the pocket of her dress, and laid before him on the table a little straw box plaited out of colored blades. It was hardly bigger than a baby's fist.

He held it in his hand, and examined it all over attentively. Something rattled inside.

"May I open it?"

"You needn't ask, master!"

It was a ring of glass beads—blue, white, and yellow, such as a little girl, following the first instincts of vanity, threads for herself. He took it out, and tried to force it on his little finger, but it was far too narrow, and he couldn't get it over his nail.

"Did I give you the ring too?" he asked.

The Cats' Bridge

"No, it belonged to my dear mother. It cut into her flesh once, and that's why I used to wear it day and night till the thread broke. Then she had been dead a long time, and as it was the only keepsake I had of her, I threaded the beads again, and have never parted with the ring, and I always have it on me."

"In my little box?"

She nodded, and her head drooped. "Why shouldn't I?" she said in a whisper, "it brings me luck."

He looked at her with a compassionate smile. "Luck? Brings *you* luck?"

"I'll tell you how," she exclaimed triumphantly. "Every bead you count—"

But at that moment he leaned back in his chair, and the ring slipped through his fingers on to the floor.

Regina started up and hurried round the table to pick it up, but could not find it.

"The earth seems to have swallowed it up," she said in alarm, and she dropped on to all fours close by Boleslav's side.

He saw the nape of her beautiful neck with its fringe of crisp, dark curls, gleaming near his knee. His heart began to beat, a cold shiver thrilled through his limbs. He stared down on her with a fixed smile.

"Here it is!" she exclaimed, and raised herself

The Cats' Bridge

into a kneeling position to hand him the treasured bauble.

He lifted his hand. He felt as if some occult power had lifted it for him, and that it weighed hundreds of pounds. Then with a timid, caressing touch he laid it on her cheek.

She drew back trembling. A great light swam in her eyes, that rested on him in dreamy inquiry. His arm sank heavily to his side.

"Thank you," he murmured hoarsely.

She went back to her place, and there was a profound stillness. It seemed to him that he had committed a crime, and that every moment of silence between them made it worse. He must force himself to speak.

"What was I asking you? Ah! to be sure. Who taught you to sew?"

She had unthreaded her needle, and was trying hard to pull the cotton through the eye again. But the small glittering shaft oscillated between her unsteady fingers like a reed shaken by the wind.

"I learned at the parsonage," she replied. "Helene had a class—" She paused, embarrassed, for at the sound of the beloved name, which he heard for the first time from her lips—such lips —he winced as if from the lash of a whip. She took his excitement for anger, and added apologetically, "I mean the Pastor's daughter."

The Cats' Bridge

"Never mind," he said, controlling himself with difficulty. "Go to bed now."

That night Boleslav fought a severe battle with himself. He felt as if his ideal of exalted purity had been polluted since his eyes had rested with favor on this abandoned woman. And he himself was polluted too by that involuntary caressing touch of her cheek.

It was absolutely necessary to regain his peace of mind and purity. He must come to some distinct understanding with Helene without delay, in order that he might be strengthened in his struggle against his treacherous senses and benumbing doubt.

So urgent did it seem that his resolutions should at once be put into force that he rose in the middle of the night, and by the glimmer of his night-light wrote to Helene assuring her of his undying love and eternal devotion, and imploring her to make some sign to show that she stood by him in trouble as she had once done in happiness, so that he might know for certain it was worth while his continuing to wage for her sake the fight against such enormous odds. With every line he wrote, his anxiety lessened, and when he lay down in his bed again, he felt that, through bracing his energies for the task, he had relieved himself of a load of care that had long heavily oppressed him.

"Can you undertake, Regina," he asked the next

evening, "to deliver this letter unseen to the young lady at the parsonage?"

She regarded him for a second with wide eyes, then looking down, she murmured, "Yes, master."

"But supposing they attack you down in the village?"

"Pah! What do I care for *them?*" she exclaimed, shrugging her shoulders contemptuously, as she always did when the villagers were in question.

Soon afterward he saw her glide by the window like a shadow and disappear in the gloaming.

Hours passed. She did not return. He began to reproach himself for having engaged her in his amatory mission when her life was at stake.

At last, toward midnight, he heard the front door latch click.

She appeared on the threshold with chattering teeth, blue with cold, the letter still grasped in her cramped fingers.

He made her sit down by the stove, and gave her Spanish wine to drink—and gradually she found her voice.

"I have been lying all this time in the snow under the parsonage hedge," she said, "but there was no possibility of getting at her. Just now she put the light out in her bedroom, so I came home. But don't be vexed. Perhaps I shall have better luck to-morrow."

The Cats' Bridge

He wouldn't hear of her repeating the adventure, but when she came to him the following evening equipped for her walk, he did not forbid her to go.

This time she came back with glowing cheeks, panting for breath. Two peasants on their way home from the Black Eagle had seen her and given chase.

"But to-morrow, to-morrow, I shall succeed."

She was right. More breathless than the evening before, but radiant with delight, she came into the room, and stood at the door, stretching out two empty hands in triumph.

"Thank God," he thought, "that I shan't have to send her a fourth time on a fool's errand."

In joyous excitement she told him all about it. Sultan, the big dog in the kennel, knew her; and as a hostage she had taken him a bone, then he had permitted her to stand at the back door and look through the keyhole. She had seen Helene standing at the great store-cupboard. "I knew that Helene—I mean the Pastor's young lady—went to the store-cupboard every night to put out coffee and oatmeal for the morning," she explained, "and sure enough I just timed her right, for there was her candle flickering in my face, and she standing within three steps of me—"

He gave a deep sigh. Happy creature! She had *seen* her!

The Cats' Bridge

"I opened the back door very softly, and called, 'Helene, Fräulein Helene!' And when she caught sight of me, she screamed and let the candle fell. 'Helene,' I said, 'I am not going to hurt you. Here is a letter from the noble young baron.'

"She trembled so she could hardly take the letter out of my hand. And then she shrieked in horror, 'Go! Go *at once!*' And almost before I could tell her about the letter-box on the draw-bridge, she had slammed the door and bolted it in my face. Ah, dear God!" she added with a melancholy little smile. "I am used to being treated in that way, but she might have been kinder because I brought a message from *you!*"

He leaned his head on his hands. Helene's conduct gave him food for meditation. Of course her reception of her fallen playmate was in every way excusable. No wonder that her chaste and maidenly soul revolted at the sight of this unfortunate girl!

Every day Regina now ran down to the draw-bridge to peep into the letter-box that was fastened to a pillar there, to see if there was an answer from Helene. But the letter-box remained empty; and Boleslav's brighter mood soon clouded again. He became more bitter and defiant than ever, and a prey to tormenting reflections. In his pride he would not allow that he had been spurned by the woman he loved; yet it was hardly any longer a matter for doubt that she wished in no way to be associated with him in his dishonor. He saw his great plans for the future fall in ruins in this abandonment of hope of winning the love of his youth.

Many days went by before he roused himself from his fresh depression—it was not till the feverish unrest of waiting had subsided that he slowly recovered his calmness and fortitude.

Then he threw himself with renewed energy into the search for proofs of his father's innocence. The evidence was contradictory and confused. Letters in which his father was referred to as the stanchest of Prussian patriots were counterbalanced by others in which he was addressed as the pioneer of Polish liberty. That might possibly have been a mere figure of flattering speech, designed to win over the vacillating nobleman, but to make it public would be once more putting the deceased's reputation in the pillory.

During these disheartening investigations of the truth, his only refreshment was the evening hours in which Regina's presence gave him something else to think about. So soon as she came and sat down opposite him he felt a curious satisfaction mingled with uneasiness. Sometimes, before she made her appearance, and he with bowed head listened to the sounds that came from her kitchen, he would be suddenly seized with anxiety, and feel as if he must jump up and call out, "Stay where you are! Don't come!" And yet, when she walked into the room he breathed more freely. "It is loneliness that attracts me to her," he often told himself. "She has a human face and a human voice."

As she sat over her work silently putting in stitch after stitch, he would pretend to be napping, and with closed eyes listen to the rise and fall of her breath. It was a full, slow, muffled sound, which fell on his ear like suppressed music. It resembled the ebbing and flowing of an ocean of restrained life and energy. After she had been sitting for a long time in a stooping attitude she would suddenly straighten herself, and stretch her arms with closed fingers over the sides of the chair, till the curve of her bosom stood out in powerful grandeur, and threatened to burst its bonds. It was as if from time to time she was obliged to become conscious of the fulness of life that pulsated and throbbed within her.

Then she resumed her old attitude and quietly sewed on.

It lasted all too short a time. These hours spent in her society had unconsciously become dear to him, and almost indispensable. The lamp seemed to give a brighter light since its rays fell on that pile of shining white linen; the hand of the clock accelerated its pace now he was not always looking

The Cats' Bridge

at it to hurry it onward. The wind that used to howl and whistle so dismally in the branches of the trees now murmured soft lullabies, and even the laths in the rotten roof cracked less ominously. He dreaded the evenings when she started on her journey to Bockeldorf at dusk, and more than once had meditated accompanying her.

But in their relations, that had become so friendly, there was one blot, and the knowledge of it pierced him at times like a poisonous arrow. Often, after he had been watching her in silence, he was tormented with a desire to penetrate into the secrets of her past, and to cross-examine her on the subject of her intercourse with the dead. For long he kept back the questions that burned on the tip of his tongue, feeling that little good could come of asking them; but at last he felt driven to speak.

"She is the only living witness of the catastrophe," he thought; "what's more, the only accomplice. She alone can give authentic information."

And one evening he broke the silence which had been so enjoyable to both, with a brusque demand that she should tell him all she knew.

She changed color, and dropped her hands in her lap.

"You'll only be angry with me again," she stammered.

The Cats' Bridge

"Do as I bid you."

She still hesitated. "It's—so long ago," she whispered piteously, "and I don't know how to tell things."

"But you can at least answer questions."

Then she resigned herself to fate.

"Who was it that first suggested to you the midnight sortie?"

"The noble master."

He clenched his teeth. "When and how?"

"The noble master ordered me to wait at table. The great candelabra, that was hardly ever lighted as a rule, was burning, and shone on the gold uniforms of the French officers, and it was all so dazzling I felt quite giddy when I carried the soup into the hall. They all laughed and pointed at me, and spoke in French, which I didn't understand."

"How many were there?"

"Five, and one with gray hair, who was the General, and had the most gold on his coat; and when I brought him the soup he caught hold of me round the waist, and I put the plate down on his finger and pinched it. Then they all laughed again, and the noble master said, 'Don't be so clumsy, Regina.' I felt so ashamed and vexed at his saying that that I said, quite loud, I didn't see why I should wait if I was only to be scolded for it. Then they laughed louder than ever, and the General began to speak German, like little children speak it. 'You are a plucky, pretty little girl,' he said; and the noble master told him I was a girl who might prove useful to him and them all—or something of the kind. And when I brought in the liqueur at the end of dinner, he drew me down to him and whispered in my ear. I was to go to him in the night."

He started up. "And you went?"

She cast down her eyes.

"Ah," she said imploringly, "why do you ask me? I wish you wouldn't. I had often done it before, and I saw no harm in it then."

He felt his blood boiling.

"How old were you at that time?"

"Fifteen."

"And so corrupt—so—" His voice died away in wrath.

She cast an unspeakably sad and reproachful glance at him.

"I knew you'd be angry," she said, "but I can't make myself out better than I am."

"Continue your story," he cried.

"And when I went to him at midnight he was still up, striding round the table, and he asked me if I should like to earn a great sum of money. 'Of course,' I said, 'I should like it very much,' for then I was very poor. Whereupon he asked me if I was afraid of the dark. I laughed, and said he ought to know best; and after a few more ques-

The Cats' Bridge

tions it came out what he wanted me to do. Could
I be trusted to show the French the way over the
Cats' Bridge and through the wood in an hour? I
began to cry, for the French had behaved dreadfully since they had been quartered in the castle,
running after and insulting all the servant-girls,
and I was afraid they might insult me too." '

"Oh, you were afraid of that, were you?" he
interposed with a contemptuous smile.

"Yes; and I told the noble master nothing would
induce me to do it. But then he became terribly
angry, and thumped me on the shoulders till I
sank on my knees, and he cried out that I was an
ungrateful hussy, and that he would have me sent
back to the village in disgrace, and would tell the
Master Pastor what sort of a wench I was, and he
would make me confess and do penance; and then
he took me by the throat, and when he had almost
throttled me, and I could scarcely draw a breath,
then, *then*——"

"Say no more," interposed Boleslav; and seizing the letters that were to establish his father's
innocence, he tore them to pieces.

The Cats' Bridge

CHAPTER XII

THE next morning he took one of the guns out of the case, and wandered into the snowy forest. He tramped about the whole day without meeting a single human creature. The deer and hares were left in peace, for he stared beyond them into vacancy. At dusk he turned his footsteps homeward, dispirited and worn out.

He saw Regina standing like a statue on the Cats' Bridge looking out for him. At first she looked as if she intended to run and meet him, but she changed her mind, and took the path to the house, smiling and murmuring to herself as she went.

But when she brought in his meal she was as silent as usual. He sat without looking at her till a sound like a short convulsive sob roused him from his reverie.

"What's the matter with you?" he asked.

Without answering, she ran out of the room. He made a movement as if he were about to follow her; then set his teeth and sat down again. A dull resentment devoured him. He could not forgive her for depriving him of the illusion on which

The Cats' Bridge

for weeks he had been building so many vague hopes.

Now there was nothing for it but to drink the cup of degradation to the dregs, no matter how bitter the bottom might taste.

In a little while Regina appeared again, in her outdoor things.

"You wish to go out to-night, then?" he asked harshly.

She kept her head half averted, so that he should not see she had red eyes.

"To-morrow is Christmas—the holy feast day; and the grocer says that on Christmas night he would rather not be disturbed."

Christmas! holy feast! How strange and like a fairy tale that sounded. Then there was still rejoicing and festivity going on in the world! People still joined hands and frolicked round glittering fir trees!

"You wish to get your Christmas presents, I suppose, Regina?" he inquired, smiling bitterly.

"Oh, no," she replied. "That has never been the custom here. Besides, now I should take no pleasure in such things."

"Why not?"

She hesitated, and then said in some embarrassment, "Let me go, master."

"I have a great deal to ask you yet, Regina."

"Please, not now, else—"

The Cats' Bridge

"Very well, go."

"Good-night, master."

"Good-night." Then he called her back. "Tell me first, what did that sob mean just now?"

A ray of half-ashamed happiness shone in the eyes that were swollen from weeping.

"Can't you guess?"

He shook his head.

"I had been so anxious about you. I thought perhaps you weren't coming back, and then when you did—" She turned and fled through the door. Her footsteps died away in the night. . . .

The following morning Boleslav was awakened by a great rushing and roaring that had for some time mingled with his dreams. A terrific storm was raging. The topmost branches of the poplars lashed each other in fury. Huge white clouds were swept along the ground, but the air was clear. Another fall of snow seemed improbable. To-day he could not rest in the desolate, cold little house, and went out to wrestle with the elements.

"She will have a bad time of it," he thought, as the north wind hurled in his face a shower of fine icicles that pricked like needles and almost took his breath away. In the wood it was more sheltered. There the tempest crashed and crunched in the tops of the trees, seeming to vent all its fury on them. He walked on, not knowing where he was going, and then found himself on the road to Bockeldorf.

"It looks as if I were running after her," he murmured, chiding himself; and he struck into the pathless thicket.

He thought how remarkable it was that this degraded being should creep so much into his thoughts. Of course it was because he had been thrown with her day after day, and depended upon her entirely for human society. Yet he was alarmed, for he realized now, perhaps more than he had ever done before, how he felt himself every day more drawn toward her, and how much there was in her that began to appear comprehensible, excusable, and even noble, that once had only seemed to testify to her innate coarseness, and repelled him from her in disgust.

But without a doubt contact with her was doing him no good. She was drawing him down into the slough of her own worthless existence.

Something must be done. Above all, it was necessary to stand in less familiar relations with her, to repress her, and lower her again to her old position of humble and despised servant-girl. The festival of Christmas was a good opportunity of paying her off with a loan, the handsomeness of which would discharge his obligations to her for all time. With a stroke of the pen he would provide for her future, and thereby purchase the

The Cats' Bridge

right to regard her as what she actually was—his humble dependent and menial. She should give him her company to-day for the last time. She had not yet finished her evidence, and as he had once broken the ice he might as well know everything. Of those two awful nights of guilt and shame, in which she had been a witness of bloodshed and arson, he would hear the worst.

"And then when she has confessed all," he said to himself, "she shall keep to her greenhouse, which is her proper place, even if she has to burn all the timber in the park to prevent herself from freezing."

It was not seemly that in this solitude he should associate so much with her, and he made up his mind to put an end to the intimacy once for all.

A hare crossed his path, and turned his thoughts into another channel. He aimed and hit it. The little animal rotated three times, and then lay motionless on its nose.

"She will be pleased," he thought, as he slung his booty over his shoulder. Ah! there he was, thinking of her again already.

The sky meanwhile had clouded. A sharp shower of prickly white flakes cut through the trees; a wild hiss now mingled with the roar of the wind that made him shiver involuntarily in every limb. By aid of his compass he found the way home. When he entered the open fields the snowstorm was in full swing. He could scarcely stand against it. The air was dark with the falling masses of snow. There was not a trace visible of the shrubs in the park only three hundred feet away.

"It's to be hoped she's got home," he thought as he struggled on.

Freshly-fallen snow lay thick on the Cats' Bridge; there were no footprints in it, but they might easily have been obliterated.

With a sinking heart, he ran to the house and called her by name, but got no answer. The hearth was unswept, the fire out, the beds unmade as he had left them.

She had been overtaken by the storm that she feared more than she feared the Schrandeners. A torturing uneasiness took possession of him. He rushed from one room to the other, lighted the fire and extinguished it again, tried to eat, and then threw down his knife and fork impatiently. It struck him as ludicrous that he should be so anxious. Had she not for six winters gone backward and forward in wind and rain and snow, and never yet met with an accident? Why should anything happen to her to-day? To kill time he sat down to his desk, and with numb fingers made out a check. The sum amounted to three figures. Regina ought to be satisfied.

Darkness set in. The hand of the clock pointed

The Cats' Bridge

to three, and yet it was already like night. He could contain himself indoors no longer. He would at least go as far as the Cats' Bridge and see if there was any sign of her. To prevent the wind pitching him over, he was obliged to hold on with all his might to the balustrade. The rickety woodwork shook in all its joints. On the ice beneath him danced a maze of spiral patterns; lily-stems grew upward and sank again in heaps of white dust, which in their turn were whirled away to make room for other fantastic forms. The Madonna's garden rose for a moment and then vanished; for a figure drew nearer and nearer out of the twilight, casting its shadow before it.

"Regina, thank God!"

He was on the point of rushing to meet her, when he was overcome with a sensation of shame that paralyzed his limbs and drove the blood to his heart.

On this very spot where he now waited for her, she had yesterday waited for him; looking out into the dusk because she had not been able to rest for anxiety about him, just as to-day he could not rest for anxiety about her.

For a moment he felt a strong inclination to dive behind the bushes, so that she should not see him; but the next he was ashamed of being ashamed, and stepped forward to meet her on the Cats' Bridge.

"You have had a bad time of it, Regina," he

called out; and tried to relieve her of the sack she carried on her back.

But she quickly dodged him, holding out her elbows in protest. She was muffled to the eyes in shawls, and could not speak. They walked to the door in silence. On the threshold she turned and tore the wraps from her face.

"I have a favor to ask," she said breathlessly.

"Well, what is it?"

"Would you mind staying out another half-hour, or going into the kitchen, so that I can warm the room and tidy up a little?"

"But you must rest first."

"Not now, master, if you don't mind."

And she went in, letting her parcels fall to the floor in the darkness.

"She may bustle about in there for a few minutes if she likes," he thought; and turned to look for a temporary shelter among the ruins.

Warm air ascended from the cellars. He struck a light, and went down the slippery steps. He felt curiously light-hearted almost, as if Christmas had brought him joy.

The rows of wine-bottles with their red and green labels peeped at him festively from their places.

"She shall not forget it's Christmas," he said, smiling; and drew from the farthest niche, where the treasure of treasures was stored, two or three

The Cats' Bridge

bottles covered with dust and cobwebs. In these reposed a nectar which had not seen the light since an eighteenth-century sun had shone on it.

His latest resolution occurred to him. Of course, he had not meant to put it into force till to-morrow —not on Christmas evening, when people consort together, who at other times are not congenial to each other. On Christmas evening no one ought to be lonely and sorrowful.

Obedient to Regina's wishes, he patrolled the ruins for half an hour beneath a roof of sparkling icicles. Then he put the bottles under his arm, and staggered out into the stormy night.

As he approached his dwelling, he saw with amazement that the shutters were closed, a thing that had never happened before. His first thought was that the storm had penetrated the chinks, but on nearer view he learned they were still weather-proof. Not till he stood in the vestibule did he find a happy solution to the problem. Regina met him beaming, and half-ashamed, and threw the parlor door wide open. Astounded at what he saw, he remained rooted to the spot. He was greeted by a festive shimmer of candles and a fragrant odor of firs. In the centre of the dining-table, covered with its pure white cloth, stood a Christmas tree, adorned with wax tapers and gilded apples. The whole apartment was brilliantly illuminated.

The Cats' Bridge

Never in his life before had a Christmas tree been lighted for *him*. Only from the thresholds of strangers had he sometimes looked on with dim eyes at strangers' happiness. And where was Regina? She had retreated behind him, and stood in the remotest corner of the vestibule, watching him with shy yet proud delight.

He took hold of her hand and led her into the room.

"Who put it into your head, child?" he asked.

"The grocer's wife was trimming her Christmas tree when I got there at three o'clock, and I thought it so pretty I said to myself, *he* shall have his tree too, and shall know that there is at least one person to think of him. I asked her to show me how to gild apples, and gilded a supply while I was there, and bought the lights and got a sack to put the tree in, so that you shouldn't see it."

"And who gave you the tree?"

"I cut it down myself at the edge of the forest not far from here."

"In the middle of this storm?"

She laughed contemptuously. "A little wind wouldn't hinder me." And then with a sudden outburst of joyous ecstasy, she exclaimed: "Oh, just look, how beautifully it burns! How pious it looks. Hasn't it really a sort of pious face, as if an angel had brought it?"

The Cats' Bridge

He assented, laughing, and expressed his thanks in a few words of forced condescension, for he was afraid of being too gracious.

But she was more than satisfied. "Why should you thank me?" she asked reproachfully. "It's all bought with your money. I have none. I'm only a poor girl. Else, ah, else—" She threw up her hands and clasped them above her head.

The check came into his mind. "This is to show you," he said, handing it to her, "that I have thought of your Christmas too."

She looked at him in bewilderment. "Am I to read it?" she asked, respectfully taking the piece of paper between two of her fingers. After studying it carefully, she still looked perplexed.

"Don't you understand what it is?" he asked.

"Oh yes—I understand— But to begin with, you can't be in earnest. And even if you are— what good is it to me?"

"It will provide for your future."

"My future is provided for—I have all I want. Good food—and I am dressed like a lady. What can I possibly want besides?"

"But we may not go on living always together like this."

She gave a cry of dismay. "Are you thinking of sending me away, master?" she asked with tightly clasped hands.

"Not now. But suppose I were to die?"

The Cats' Bridge

She shook her head meditatively. "I should die too," she said.

"Or I might have to go to the war again?"

"Then I should go with you as a vivandière."

Her persistence annoyed him. "Do as you like," he said, "only take what I give you."

A bright idea seemed to occur to her.

"All right, master," she exclaimed, "I'll take it, only next Christmas I shall buy you something with it that will be worth having." And happy at the thought, she scampered away.

The candles on the Christmas tree had burnt out. It stood now dark and neglected in the corner by the stove, only occasionally casting a glimmer from its golden fruit on the table where master and servant sat opposite each other.

Regina had been accorded permission to take her supper with him this evening, and had been too overcome to swallow a mouthful. She was almost stunned with this great and unexpected pleasure.

Now the dishes were cleared away, and only bottles and glasses stood between them. She drank, thoughtlessly, of the old fire-kindling wine in long immoderate drafts. Her face began to glow. The pupils of her brilliant eyes seemed to melt beneath their drooping lids. She rocked to and fro on her chair. A wild abandon had relaxed her in every limb.

The Cats' Bridge

"Are you tired, Regina?"

She shook her head impatiently. For once her constraint in his presence had disappeared. There was something even approaching audacity in the brilliancy of her glance as she turned it on him from time to time. She was intoxicated with happiness. He too felt the wine flame up in him; and his eyes were riveted on her figure, which swayed before him with the graceful motions of a Mænad.

All the time the tempest raged outside. It whistled in the chimney and hurled a rattling fusilade against the window shutters. There was a grinding and crunching among the rafters of the roof, which sounded as if the moldy wood were collapsing.

"I am afraid something will be blown down," he said, as he listened.

"Maybe," she answered with a dreamy smile, huddling herself together. And then she began to babble in a fragmentary but quite unrestrained fashion. "Perhaps it isn't good for me," she said, "that you are so kind to me. All my life I have never got anything but blows and abuse—first from my father, then from *him,* not to mention other people. But if you spoil me, I shall get proud—and pride is a great vice, I have heard the pastor say—I shall begin to think I'm a princess who needn't earn her bread."

She burst into a peal of wild laughter, and let

The Cats' Bridge

her arms fall to her sides. Then in a low tone, as if conversing with herself, she went on:

"Sometimes I do wonder if I am only a servant. I often feel really as if I were some enchanted princess, and you, master, the knight who is to deliver me. Will you be the knight?"

She blinked at him over her wine-glass. He nodded in friendly acquiescence. Let her revel in her strange fancies. It was Christmas.

"There have been cases," she continued, "in which princesses have been turned into quite common sluts. They have had stones thrown at them, and been spat at, and men have called after them, 'Strike her down, the dirty slut!' And all the time they were princesses in disguise."

"Do you believe in fairy tales, then?" he asked, wonderingly.

She laughed to herself. "Not exactly. But when one passes so many hours alone, and has to take long solitary walks as I have, one must think. And when the rain beats down, and the wind blows— Hark at it now, what a to-do it's making— Think of me tramping along in this —and I have often been out when it's as bad, but I've never lost my way. And sometimes, when I come into the wood, I have asked myself, 'Which would you rather be? A queen sitting on a golden throne, or the Catholics' Holy Virgin, who had our dear Lord and Saviour for her little boy; or

222

would you rather be the devil's grandmother, and bury all the Schrandeners in a manure-heap; or a noble lady and—'" She paused.

"And?" he queried.

She drew herself up, and laughed in embarrassment.

"I can't tell you that—it is too silly. But I had only to choose which I'd be. And as I march along through the night shadows, I often imagine I am one or other, till all of a sudden I find myself in Bockeldorf, just as if I'd flown there—often I think I am flying. Ah! things do happen in real life, after all, very much the same as in the fairy tales. Don't you think so, master?"

He contemplated her with curiosity and wonder, as if he had never seen her before. And truly it was the first time he had looked into her secret soul. Now, when her tongue was loosened by wine, much was revealed in her that before he had either not observed or not understood.

"Blissful creature!" he murmured.

"Am I?" he replied, boldly planting her elbows on the table, and regarding him with an expression of joyous inquiry. "You mean, because I'm sitting here with you drinking wine and being treated as if I were human? Oh! it's exactly like being in heaven— Do you think I shall ever go to heaven? —I don't. I am far too wicked!— And I think, too, I should be afraid to go there. It must be much livelier in hell— I should be more at home there. The Pastor often said I was like a little devil and I never fretted about it. Why should I? It seemed quite natural that I should be the little devil and Helene the angel. An excellent arrangement— Didn't Helene look just like an angel in the flesh? So pink and white and delicate, with her blue eyes and folded hands. And she always wore—a pretty ribbon—round her neck— and smelt always of—rose-scented soap—"

A cold shiver passed through him. He felt it was degrading both to himself and the beloved to allow this half-tipsy girl to speak of her as if she were an equal.

"Stop!" he demanded hoarsely.

She only answered him with a dreamy smile. Wine and fatigue suddenly overpowered her. She lay stretched out, her head thrown back on the arm of the chair, and fought against sleep, like a Bacchante exhausted after a whirl of dissipation.

A great anger, that rose and fell within him like the sound of the storm outside, mastered him.

"This is what wine does," he thought, and yet drank more.

He wanted to wake her, to send her out, but he could not tear his eyes away from her face, and by degrees he became gentler again.

"She meant no harm," he thought, as he moved nearer to where she lay. "This is the last time she will sit here with me; to-morrow a new leaf will be turned. After to-morrow she shall find in me nothing but the master."

Then he remembered all he had wanted to ask her.

"Well, never mind," he said to himself, "it can't be helped. Why spoil her Christmas? Some other time will do."

The hurricane without seemed to have increased in fury. It roared through the keyholes, and battered the shutters. How brutally cruel it was to drive her out to sleep in a greenhouse on a night like this! But what was the use of being compassionate when it had to be done?

"Regina!" he shouted, and tapped her on the shoulder. At that moment there was a terrific thundering crash, that made the walls tremble as from a shock of earthquake. Regina screamed loud in her sleep and tried to grasp his hand, then sank back again into her old position. He went out to see what was the cause of the noise. Nothing had fallen in the vestibule, but on opening the door of the greenhouse snow drifted in his face just as if he had walked into the open air. All round was inky darkness. He went back to fetch his lantern. It shed its light on a scene of ruin that exceeded his worst expectations. Regina's little kingdom, from which she had ruled and regulated the household so unostentatiously, had seemingly been dispersed to the four winds of heaven. The roof was blown off, and had torn up part of the wall with it. Between the hearth and the door was a barricade of snow as tall as himself, riddled with bricks, beams, and splinters of glass.

What was to be done now? Where was Regina to sleep? Should he too let her lie like a dog on his threshold? No! rather would he turn out into the ruins himself, and seek a couch down in the cellar. It was imperative to act at once, and there was only one thing to be done. He drew Regina's bedding out of the snow, shook it thoroughly till not a flake remained hanging to it, and then dragged it into his room. Beneath the shadow of the Christmas tree in the corner by the stove he made up a bed on the boards.

Regina slept peacefully, her face illuminated by the light from the oil lamp. He came close to her, shook and called her by name; but nothing could wake her. At last he lifted her up, to carry her to the bed.

She gave a deep sigh, encircled his neck with her arms, and let her head sink on his shoulder.

His heart beat faster. The fair body in the first bloom of its superb young womanhood, gave him a sensation of fear and uneasiness as it unconsciously rested on him. He half carried, half trailed her across the room. Her warm breath fanned his face, her hair swept his throat.

226

The Cats' Bridge

As he let her sink on her mattress she raised her arms, with a gesture of longing, in the air, and pulled down the little fir tree. He drew it from under her, and then placed it as a screen and sentinel between himself and her. "To-morrow I'll rig up a partition," he thought. Then he undressed and went to bed.

The night-light burnt out, but there was no thought of sleep for him. The tempest still raged, and spent its fury on the locks and bolts. Boleslav heeded it not. While he listened to the sleeping woman's breath, his own fell on the night, in heavily drawn, anxious gasps.

The Cats' Bridge

CHAPTER XIII

"To the Nobly Born Baron Boleslav von Schranden.

"Your Lordship is requested to appear in person on January 3, at two o'clock in the afternoon, at Herr Merckel's official residence, and to bring the requisite papers relating to your Lordship's attachment, or non-attachment, to the Prussian First Reserve.

"(Signed) VON KROTKEIM,
"Royal Commissioner."

Boleslav found this communication in the draw-bridge letter-box on New Year's morning. The threatening nature of its contents did not at once strike him; he was only staggered at the authorities taking the trouble to investigate his case. He had resolved, on again adopting his father's name, to let the waters of oblivion close over Lieutenant Baumgart. He had discharged his duty to his country unconditionally; bolder and more self-sacrificing than thousands of others, he had gone to face death. Now that there was peace, and he had taken a great burden of inherited guilt on his shoulders, he had wished to avoid being involved in any way with official red-tapism.

The Cats' Bridge

Only gradually did he realize the new dangers that were gathering on his horizon. Pride in his past as a soldier afforded him the one prop and stay in his present ruined life, and he felt that slipping from under his feet. He stood defenseless in face of imminent peril. It would need only a little *malice prepense* to make him out a deserter from the flag, and the fact of his having borne the false name of Baumgart would go far to establish his guilt.

The son of Baron von Schranden had no reason to hope that justice would be tempered with mercy in his case. He would also have no reason to complain of harsh measures, if he were put under arrest on the spot, and brought before a court-martial of the standing branch of his regiment.

For a moment he entertained thoughts of flight, but afterward thrust the idea from him in scorn. He had too often valued his life cheaply now to think seriously of stealing into Poland to end his wretched career in safety.

But what would become of Regina?

At the thought of her, his heart smote him. She had no suspicion of the new troubles with which he was encompassed. Since Christmas night he had not addressed a single word to her that was not absolutely necessary, and even then his voice had been imperious and severe. The thought of her now seemed interwoven with a presentiment of coming calamity, which oppressed him like a nightmare.

At night he tossed about restlessly among his pillows. She never stirred in her corner. Apparently she fell asleep the moment she lay down. But her soft, quick, regular breathing was sometimes broken by a sigh. Perhaps, after all, she was not sleeping, but watching, listening, as he listened. . . .

And then the day dawned on which Boleslav's fate was to be decided. Toward morning he had fallen into an uneasy sleep, and was first awakened by the smoke that poured into the room from the vestibule, where he had erected a temporary fireplace, which would have to do as a makeshift till milder weather made the repairing of the glass roof practicable. It was a clear, frosty morning. The sunshine jeweled the hoar-frost on the twigs, and dark purple shadows crept along the dazzling sheets of snow.

He spent the morning in arranging his papers. All that was compromising to his father's memory should be destroyed, for were he put under arrest, as seemed likely, strangers' hands would meddle in this vortex. He held the sorted letters in his hand ready to burn in the stove, when he thought better of it. If he really were serious in his intentions of bearing his father's guilt, he ought to conceal or destroy nothing in order to lighten the burden. It was not worth while purchasing truth with falsehood. Rather die in disgrace than live in honor founded on lies and deceit.

When Regina brought him his midday meal he hesitated an instant as to whether he should tell her all or nothing. But he shrank from a touching scene, and decided on the latter course. A letter would serve the same purpose. So he wrote: "If I am not back at dusk, probably you will have difficulty in seeing me again. Inquire at the commissioner's office in Wartenstein. There they will tell you what has become of me. I advise you to leave Schranden at once. The draft I gave you will supply your wants. What else remains shall all be yours later. Good-by, and accept my thanks."

He left the note in a conspicuous place, so that, when she cleared away, she would find it. He was in a hard and embittered mood, and in no humor for a sentimental farewell.

But as he passed Regina in the vestibule where she was occupied with the fire, he felt a strong impulse to press her hand. For her sake, as much as for his own, he went out without giving her a word or a look. A group of staring louts, who appeared to be waiting for him, were loafing near the drawbridge. When they saw him coming, they ran off helter-skelter with loud exclamations, to the inn.

"My heralds," he said, and laughed.

The Cats' Bridge

Long before the stated hour the parlor of the Black Eagle could not hold all the customers that poured in, anxious to secure a foremost place for the proceedings. There was an overflow that extended as far as the churchyard square. Every one was eager to witness with his own eyes the final degradation of the last of the Barons of Schranden.

Three months had passed since the petition had been sent to the judicial authorities of the province, and even the most zealous patriots had begun to despair of its producing any results. Then at last had come the delightful intimation from the office of the Commissioner that a day had been appointed to wind up the case of the Crown *versus* Schranden, *alias* Baumgart, and the presence of the petitioners was urgently requested at the inquiry.

The Schrandeners had armed themselves in a way worthy of the occasion. For three days they had been busy polishing up their accoutrements. Those among the disbanded reservists who still possessed their uniform had donned it, and pikes and sabres were seen in the crowd. Possibly they might be called upon to help in an instantaneous administration of justice.

The Commissioner's sleigh had entered the village at one o'clock, and, as was customary, put up at the parsonage stable, where Master Merckel and his son stood ready to welcome the high functionary. There was no constable on the box, which greatly mystified the Schrandeners. But perhaps the services of one were not required when *they* could be depended on to despatch the criminal at the first signal.

Shortly before two, the Commissioner, accompanied by the old pastor, left the parsonage and entered the inn by a side door, where Master Merckel, senior, again was to the fore to receive him, while Felix slouched in the background, piqued at not being treated with what he considered sufficient respect by the civilian.

The Commissioner von Krotkeim was a tall, extremely slender man, whose hoary leonine head rose with great effect from his contracted, sloping shoulders. There was something awe-inspiring in its pose. He wore, in defiance of the fashion of the period, long whiskers, which flowed behind his ears, mingling with his thick iron-gray mane.

His part in the formation of defenses for the Fatherland had been an important and distinguished one. Two years before he had sat as a deputy for the knighthood in the famous Parliament to which Germany owed the foundation of the Reserve. He had hailed old General York with cheers, and helped to draw up the address to the King. Afterward he had hastened back to his native place to set the organization on foot, and had achieved results which made his district the

The Cats' Bridge

brilliant model that excited the admiring emulation of the whole country. Then arose those marauders attendant on success, vanity and egoism. What at first had been a labor of noble disinterestedness, gradually degenerated into a peg for self-advertisement and a means of memorializing his own fame. For the rest, and long before the treachery of the Cats' Bridge incident had been generally made known to the world, Master von Krotkeim had by repute been a bitter enemy of the house of Schranden. To hope any favor at his hands would therefore be oversanguine indeed. But Boleslav had abandoned hope of any kind as he entered the square in front of the church. He advanced composed, and almost indifferent, toward the crowd that formed a circle round the inn. He had, on his way, cast one shy glance at the parsonage, where in a window he fancied he had seen a fair face which withdrew into shadow directly he smiled up at it. He was received by a murmur of malignant tongues, but the crowd let him through, understanding enough to know that, without him, the game they were anticipating with such keen relish could not be played.

At the entrance to the best parlor, he stood face to face with the great man with the lion's mane, on either side of whom sat the old pastor and Master Merckel. Felix lounged in the window-sill, trying to assume an air of nonchalance. He now considered his former playmate too inferior an object on which even to bestow his hate. But the old landlord greeted Boleslav with a benign smile. Had he come there with the purpose of treating every one present to a bottle of the celebrated Muscat wine, the smile could not have been more smugly servile.

Lightning-flashes irradiated from beneath the prominent brows of the old pastor, and the Commissioner sat coolly contemplating his fingers, which were white and bony as a skeleton's. Boleslav felt his bosom swell proudly. "His hand against every man; every man's hand against him." It was the old story!

A voice from the crowd hiccoughed out some unflattering remark. The Schrandeners received it with laughter.

"It's the poor father, the unhappy father," old Merckel whispered to the Commissioner, with a melancholy elevation of his eyebrows.

"As you have summoned me here," exclaimed Boleslav, "I demand your protection from the insults of the mob!"

The representative of the crown drooped his eyelids and bowed.

"Silence, good people!" he commanded, stroking his clean-shaven chin, and then he added, "I shall have any person who makes a disturbance ejected."

The Cats' Bridge

He consulted a green portfolio that lay spread before him on the table. Behind him a little man in gray was energetically trying goose quills. Probably he was the reporter.

The examination began. With frigid politeness the Commissioner put the usual questions.

"Where have you resided hitherto?"

Boleslav enumerated several places.

"Your word is of course to be trusted, Baron, but have you proofs?"

"No."

"Up to what date does your answer hold good?"

"Till the spring of the year '13."

"After that?"

"I entered the army."

"Have you proofs to support that statement?"

"No."

"I regret to say that the name Von Schranden is not to be found in the army list."

"I enlisted under another."

"Under the name of Baumgart?"

"Yes."

"For what reason?"

There was silence. Boleslav bit his lips.

"Ha, ha!" came triumphantly from the window. The exclamation put Boleslav on his mettle.

"To have borne my real name would have involved me in difficulties."

"Why?"

The Cats' Bridge

"Because, through a rumor which I was power-less to contradict, there was a blot on that name."

"What rumor?"

It was clear this man intended to humiliate him to the dust before passing on him the inevitable sentence.

"You know it," he murmured faintly between his closed teeth.

The crown official bowed. Nevertheless I must ask for information on the subject."

"I decline to give it."

The mob sent up a shout of scornful laughter.

"Down with him! put him in chains!" roared the same hiccoughing voice that had made use of an abusive epithet earlier in the proceedings.

The Commissioner gracefully waved his long white hands.

"Has a note been made of that refusal?" he asked without turning round.

A small quavering pipe behind him, which greatly amused the Schrandeners, answered in the affirmative.

Then he continued with imperturbable polite-ness.

"May I ask you, then, to tell me to which com-pany you were attached?"

Boleslav did so, and also gave the names of his Heide comrades.

The official turned over the leaves of his portfolio with an air of boredom. The concerns of the volunteer rifles evidently had no interest for him.

"You were elected officer?"

"Yes."

"I do not doubt your word, Herr Baron, but have you proofs to back *this* statement?"

"No."

"A note must be made of that negative. And then you entered the First Reserve?"

"Yes."

"Your reason?"

Boleslav indicated, with a motion of his head, the companion of his boyhood. "Because I did not wish to meet that man."

Felix gave a scoffing laugh, and exclaimed, "Else the swindle would—" A sign from the Commissioner silenced him.

"Your regiment, if you please?"

Boleslav cited the colonel's name.

The Commissioner bowed low over the portfolio till his shock of hair almost concealed his faded shrunken face.

"So far that coincides with my information," he said, and then read: "There was a Lieutenant Baumgart, who at the time of the armistice entered the regiment. Besides him there were four other officers of this name in the army. The one in question, however, met his death between the 1st and 3d of March on the Marne."

The Cats' Bridge

"How did you learn that, Commissioner?"

"It is in the Gazette, Herr Baron. He is said to have been sent on a special mission, and shot by grenadiers in General Marmont's corps."

Boleslav felt his blood mount swiftly to his brow. The proudest and most arduous moments of his life rose vividly before him. "That is a mistake," he cried; "Lieutenant Baumgart fell into the hands of the enemy severely wounded, but escaped with his life."

"And it is your desire to be identified with that fallen emissary?"

"I believe I have clearly shown that it is my desire."

"Very well, that being so, you will of course be able to relate the incidents of the special mission."

"Certainly."

"Please proceed."

"The volunteers had been charged to get a message delivered to General von Kleist. Some days before a skirmish had taken place on the banks of a river, Therouanne by name, through which the General and his corps were cut off from communication with the main army. A reunion could not be effected owing to Marmont's and Mortier's troops, to which Napoleon himself was said to be marching, stopping the way. Field-Marshal Blücher suddenly resolved to retreat, in order, I believe, to pick up reenforcements, and therefore,

The Cats' Bridge

it was, under the circumstances, urgent to let General von Kleist know at once, in case he should find himself entirely isolated. It was necessary for the messenger to evade the enemy's outposts at night-time. Among those who volunteered to go on the mission, the choice fell on me. Major von Schaek led me to the Field-Marshal, who entrusted me with a letter—"

"One moment, please," interrupted the official, searching diligently among his papers; then he added casually, "And the letter of course contained the necessary command."

"No."

"What, then?"

"The letter was designed to deceive the enemy in case I should be shot from my horse on the way. The Field-Marshal desired me to give his command by word of mouth. I had to learn it by heart."

"How did it run?"

"As follows: 'If on the morrow the enemy attacks us on the right flank, General von Kleist is not to join in the engagement, but to seize the opportunity of gaining the command of the Marne from the south, so that he may bring himself in touch with me. On the way several bridges are to be destroyed."

The Commissioner nodded. "And then—Lieutenant?"

The Cats' Bridge

"I succeeded in delivering the message."

"You managed to evade the enemy and reach your goal?"

"I hope you have found proofs of it, Commissioner, in the history of the war—"

"Hum! When were you wounded?"

"On the way back."

"Why did you not remain where you were?"

"Because I had undertaken to bring the Field-Marshal an answer."

"You might have spared yourself this second act of daring."

"I might have spared myself the first also."

"You wanted to achieve fame?"

"I wanted among other things to escape the privilege of this cross-examination."

The royal official straightened himself and threw back his mane. "Permit me to draw your attention to the fact that you stand before the representative of your King, Baron von Schranden."

"Barefaced impudence!" muttered the voice at the window.

"I stand before my undoer," replied Boleslav, looking steading into the other man's eyes.

He fixed them on his papers again, with a suppressed smile. "I have now come to the last stage of my investigation," he continued. "It can not be denied that your statements bear a strong resemblance to the facts, and that your claim to be one and the same person as the Lieutenant Baumgart who served in the Silesian Reserve under Major von Wolzogen has gained in probability. Only this admission has to be weighed in the scale against the impossibility of an honorable officer, as the said Baumgart seems to have been, turning his back on the army in which he had won honors and wounds, and deserting its standard. He must have known a company of soldiers could not be dispersed like a flock of sparrows. And to think that the First Reserve"—his chest swelled and he tossed his mane—"the glorious First Reserve, that has always stood in the front rank of courage, love of order, and discipline, should have thus been hoodwinked! Baron von Schranden, I fervently hope that Lieutenant Baumgart was not guilty of this transgression, and am therefore bound to wish that he met his death."

Boleslav felt the crisis was approaching. He glanced round him and saw everywhere eyes flaming with hate and thirst for vengeance. Felix Merckel had laid his hand on the handle of his sabre, as if in another moment he would raise it. From the throngs behind him came a clash and din of arms. Malignant satisfaction beamed on the face of the old host of the Black Eagle. Only the pastor sat with his disheveled head bowed in his hands, staring despondently on the floor.

"It is not my fault," said Boleslav, "that the dead

man has been brought to life. He did his duty, I think. Why should he not have been allowed to rest in peace?"

The Commissioner shrugged his shoulders.

"A public indictment can not be ignored."

"An indictment!" cried Boleslav, his anger blazing up, and his eye met young Merckel's.

There he read, in unmistakable characters, the story of the shameless plot against him. He smiled in disgust.

"I see that I am answerable to a military tribunal," he said. "I was prepared for it. I beg you now to arrest me."

The mob pushed forward as if anxious to take him at his word without delay. Boleslav, who all this time had been standing on the threshold of the inner parlor, was hurled forward against the table, within a hair's breadth of the examining official, while the fists of his enemies touched his neck from behind.

"Patience, my dear friends," said that functionary, in an amicable tone. "The first who lays hands on him will himself be put in chains. One more question. If you were taken prisoner, as you maintain, how was it that later, when the disbanding followed, you were not registered and discharged in the regular order?"

"The French, in their hurried flight, left me lying on the field, as I was badly wounded. I was picked up by some peasants, in whose house I lay for months at death's door. When I was able to leave my rescuers, peace had been concluded, and there were no allies in the neighborhood."

"Your word of honor is of course sacred, Baron, but perhaps you can substantiate this with proof?"

"Only with my scars."

"Ah!— Make a note of that—" He pushed back his leonine locks from his brow, and seemed to be bracing himself for an impressive summing up—

"My friends! Indomitable defenders of your country, and inhabitants of Schranden! The founding of the First Reserve was the rising of a new sun, which has never ceased to cast new lustre on the fame of Prussia. Let us congratulate ourselves that we have been born in a time when such great things have been demanded of us, and that we have proved ourselves worthy of, and equal to the demand. Especially in this district, and foremost in this district the parish of Schranden. If we look round us, we see a very different spectacle in other quarters. Not everywhere did the King's appeal meet with such a warm and spontaneous echo.

"Oh, my friends, our hearts bleed when we hear of how, in the districts of Konitz and Stargard, for example, to escape serving, men took refuge in the woods, and lay full length among the wheat till they had to be baited like bulls. Thousands took flight across the frontier, and thus shirked the conscription altogether. And often what had been beautifully drilled companies overnight, by the morning were transformed into a shapeless mass of panic-stricken deserters. But not in the district that I have had the pleasure of mobilizing.

"In less than two weeks, friends and comrades, the Reserve of the Wartenstein district was ready drilled and armed from top to toe. The levies were double in strength what the government had required of us, and eighty per cent consisted of volunteers. From the parish of Schranden came only volunteers."

The crowd set up loud hurrahs, and the pastor nodded and smiled in grim satisfaction. He knew whose work that had been.

"I must admit," continued the speaker, with a chilling sidelong glance at Boleslav, "that the parish of Schranden has one hideous stain on its reputation"—(several loud imprecations were audible) —"a stain which in spite of all its deeds of bravery will never be dissociated from it" (renewed curses) ; "but if it is the King's pleasure to overlook it, and only to see the brighter side, his graciousness is due to those who, in defending his realm, have rendered him such able services, whose leader I am happy and proud to call myself. The King's favor—("Why does he harp thus on the King's favor," thought Boleslav, "when he might wind up the case and be done with it")—"has been abundantly lavished on us, and we are almost overpowered with his blessings. Yet let all who reap the fruits of the harvest remember they owe it to the men of the Reserve, and not least to their organizer, who sowed for them the seeds of undying fame."

Again he began to turn over the leaves of his portfolio, then he went on: "Take your caps off, intrepid inhabitants of Schranden. Attention, my brave men! Gentlemen, if you please, rise. Whoever keeps his cap on at back there will be ejected. I am commissioned to read over to you an order of the Cabinet of supreme import. It is as follows: 'Should it prove true that the Baron von Schranden, of Castle Schranden, and Lieutenant Baumgart of the 15th Regiment of the Silesian First Reserve, be one and the same person, and that, as was naturally supposed of so fearless an officer, he had no real intentions of deserting, I appoint him to a captaincy in my First Reserve, and entrust him with the command of the company in his division. I also bestow on him, in recognition of his extraordinary valor and distinguished service, the iron cross of the first class. The Royal Commissioner for the district will invest him with these honors in the presence of his accusers.—FRIEDRICH WILHELM REX.' "

The proclamation was received in profound si-

The Cats' Bridge

lence. The patriotic Schrandeners stood glowering at each other in consternation. Felix Merckel had sunk back on the window-seat. His fingers clutched convulsively at the cross that shone between the black froggings on his coat. Boleslav felt a buzzing sensation in his head. He was obliged to cling to the door for support, for he feared he might swoon. Not joy, only infinite bitterness, welled up within him. He bit his lips hard to keep back his tears.

The official drew a small black case from the depths of his pocket, and presented it to Boleslav with an exaggeratedly obsequious bow. The cover sprang back. The black smoothly polished scrap of iron, on its background of blue velvet, seemed surrounded by a halo of shimmering light. Boleslav grasped it with one hand in growing excitement, while he offered his other to the Commissioner. The latter retreated a step or two, closely regarding his long, white, skinny hands, as if the act of handing over the case had done them some injury. Then he deliberately hid them behind his back.

"Commissioner, I offered you my hand," cried Boleslav threateningly, flushing darkly at this new insult.

"According to his Majesty's wishes I have discharged my duty. My instructions did not include a shake of the hand."

The Cats' Bridge

At this moment a cross, like the one Boleslav had just received, flew through the air and alighted at his feet. Felix Merckel had torn it from his breast. Swelling with righteous indignation, he swaggered up to the official, whom he now felt sure he had no reason to be afraid of, and cried:

"There it may lie. I don't want it now. Any decent soldier would be ashamed to wear it when such as *he is* decorated with it."

A cry of mingled pain and fury escaped Boleslav's lips, and with raised fists he turned fiercely on his enemy.

Felix Merckel unsheathed his sabre, as if with the intention of hewing down the unarmed man. But the old landlord threw his corpulent form between them. The Commissioner confined himself to waving his hands soothingly; and the pastor vigilantly kept watch on his Schrandeners. He knew his flock, and read murder in their glance.

"Back there! keep back!" he shouted to the tumultuous throng in a voice of brass. With outstretched arms he sprang into the doorway, where already a line of pikes appeared, ready to fell the victim from behind.

Boleslav looked round and saw with a shudder how near he stood to death.

The pastor, clinging to the roof of the doorway, endeavored to stem the murderous tide. Would that frail and venerable frame be able to repulse

The Cats' Bridge

this onslaught of unmuzzled wolves? Would it not be swept away on the crest of this bloodthirsty wave? A weak shield to rely on, indeed! Yet his was the only authority not swamped by the tumult. The royal functionary's protesting hands waved impotently above the seething heads, like limp towels; the gentle flute-like tones in which he declared the ringleaders of the disturbance should be turned out and bludgeoned were totally ignored. His parasite, the little portfolio bearer, had taken the precaution to creep under the table.

A voice within Boleslav cried, "What! You will let this old man protect you? Can not you protect yourself?" And a wild resolve consumed him. This seemed a moment given him to balance his account with fate—a moment of all others in which cowardice was to be avoided. He caught hold of the old pastor in a grip of iron and drew him aside.

"This is my place, reverend sir," he said, and planted himself in the doorway.

He stretched out his arms above him, as the old man had done, and offered his breast as a target for the pointed weapons. His eye penetrated unflinchingly into the heart of the struggling and ramping mob before him. He felt the foam from their mouths bespatter him, and their hot, foul breath fan his face.

"Here I stand!" he cried. "I have left my pistols at home; so you can make short work of me. Any of you who have the courage."

But no one had the courage, for his back was not turned to them now. Sabres were lowered, pikes dropped.

"I see—you don't wish to murder me after all," he said, holding them with his eyes. "You are going to behave like men, and not like wild beasts. Very well, then, I will speak to you as to reasonable men. Move backward and keep quiet."

The crowd wavered; the next moment he had the threshold to himself.

"And now—speak! Tell me what you want with me!"

There was no answer, no sound in the room except the labored breathing of excited lungs.

"You hate me. You would like to take my life. Tell me why? Here in the presence of a representative of the King whom we all serve and fear, in the presence of a representative of the God in whom I believe and you too—tell me what I have done? I submit myself to their judgment. Now is your opportunity of charging me."

But the silence continued. Only one spluttering voice arose for a moment and died away in a gurgle, as if it were being stifled by force.

"You are dumb. You can not say what my offense has been—and you, gentlemen! Won't you come to the assistance of these poor, speechless people? There on the ground lies a cross, the mark of honor our nation cherishes more highly than any other, which some one threw away, because through my possessing one like it, he considered it contaminated. Some one else declined to shake hands with me just now, a common act of courtesy which no man of honor refuses another unless he be a blackguard. It does not matter, if in this instance judges and accusers unite in a common cause. Accuse me of what you like, condemn me! I am prepared."

Another long pause. The representative of the King twisted his whiskers in embarrassment.

"And you, reverend sir—it is hardly fitting that I should call the instructor of my youth to account —but some months ago you showed me the door in your own house. Could you not be spokesman now for your parishioners?"

The old man's jaws worked, his lips moved, but no sound issued from them. He appeared to have exhausted his strength, but the wild, fiery glance he darted from beneath his bushy brows boded no good to Boleslav.

With a laugh he went on. "Then I must be my own accuser." He felt intoxicated with his own courage. "Your hand against every man, and every man's hand against you," cried jubilantly within him. "You think you ought to visit the sins of the fathers on me; empty the vials of your

wrath on my head because you can not reach the
dead. Very well. I am his heir. I take his guilt
upon me, and do not refuse to do penance, when
right and justice demand it of me. But why were
no steps taken against the dead man himself?
Why was he not tried? Why not dragged to the
scaffold when he deserved it? Commissioner, I
ask you, as the embodiment of the law, why did the
State remain silent and suffer these gallant men
who smarted under wrong to take revenge into
their own hands? And such a revenge! So childish, so cruel, that one would have thought it could
only have occurred to the primitive brain of bloodthirsty savages. Revenge for a deed which at this
hour I neither admit nor deny, because it lies
shrouded in mystery. Which of you can say how
it happened, or whether it happened at all? And
in spite of this uncertainty, you have damned and
defamed him and his race, deprived them of honor
and justice. Is that fair play? Now I ask you to
put us on our trial, me and the dead man, and—"
He paused, shocked at the thought that he had
nearly let fall Regina's name.

The pastor's eagle eye flashed ominously. Then
collecting himself, he continued: "Inquire, speak
out, unravel the mystery, clear up the matter, and
then judge and pass sentence. But at the same time
sit in judgment and pass sentence on that other
crime, the crime that has wrecked my property,

and leaves me only uninhabitable ruins to live in, a crime that cries aloud to Heaven for vengeance. On the subject of other outrages and indignities I will be silent—threats of murder to me and mine; the blocking of the churchyard entrance to my father's funeral procession—all that shall pass. But the fire, *that* I swear shall be avenged! If till to-day justice has been blind to my wrongs, its eyes shall be wrenched open. I will not rest day or night till I have dragged the skulking authors of that cowardly, atrocious deed into the light of day, and may God have mercy on those who attempt to screen or defend them."

Again the mob showed signs of uneasiness. Its foremost ranks pressed back on the others, as if to fly from the vengeance of the wrathful man who had addressed them in words of such burning indignation. Again from the neighborhood of the window came hoarse, stuttering laughter that was choked off as before.

The occupants of the best parlor made an effort to appear as if they had not been listening to Boleslav. The Commissioner, who was really painfully affected, busied himself with more zeal than ever in looking through his papers. Old Merckel had picked up the discarded cross, and was trying to persuade his son, who resisted sulkily, to wear it again. The little man in gray had come out from under the table, and was employing himself in

The Cats' Bridge

carefully rubbing dust off his knees. Only the old
pastor was on the alert. He had propped his stick
against the table; the thin white hair that floated
round his bald skull quivered. He stood looking,
with his vulture profile, and small eyes flashing
beneath his sharply projecting brows, like a bird
of prey waiting to pounce on its booty.

Had Boleslav caught sight of him at that moment, he might have hesitated to make a fresh
challenge. But he wanted to score all along the
line and complete his victory.

"In order that there may be a clear understanding between us," he cried, "that all may see who
has right on his side and who wrong, I ask, which
of you has a charge to prefer against me? To
whom have I done an injury? How have I
sinned?"

Then the voice of the old pastor was raised behind him. "Is Hackelberg, the carpenter, here?"

Boleslav winced. That voice so close to his ear
sounded intimidating and uncanny, and prophetic
of coming evil. There was a scuffling and swaying
in the crowd. The ragged figure of the village
drunkard, by means of shoves and kicks, was pro-
pelled forward into the front row. He struggled
and beat the air with his hands, and when forced
on to the threshold of the inner parlor, tried to
duck beneath the legs of the men on either side of
him.

254

The Cats' Bridge

"There is nothing to be afraid of, Hackelberg," said the pastor. "I will see that you are not hurt."

Reassured, he drew himself up, and scanned the gentlemen he had been brought before with a suspicious, glassy eye.

"What creature is this?" inquired the Commissioner, scandalized. "Why is he not put under restraint?"

"Because his condition is owing more to his misfortune than his fault," the pastor answered.

Master Merckel thought it his duty to whisper an explanation to his superior.

"He is the poor father so much to be pitied," he said, with a mock pathetic air, "whose sad story I related to your lordship."

At the same time he watched uneasily some Schrandeners, who seemed to be waiting for a signal to take the drunkard into custody.

"Have you nothing to say, Hackelberg?" asked the pastor.

"What should I have to say, Pastor?" he lisped, beginning to cringe again, and drawing the lappets of his tattered coat over his naked breast.

"Have you no accusation to make?"

"Let me go," he growled. "I haven't—"

"Not even against *him?*" and he pointed to Boleslav.

A glimmer of intelligence came into the dull, glazed eyes. He understood his cue. Old Merckel

255

nodded at him encouragingly, and he began to play his favorite rôle. Floods of tears that the besotted inebriate can always command so easily, poured over his cheeks. He rubbed his wet face with his black hands, till it resembled some hideous mask.

"Poor fellow! poor outraged father!" crooned Master Merckel, senior, wiping his own eyes.

"What is the meaning of this absurd farce?" asked Boleslav, with a scornful laugh. But his face had become visibly paler.

"Here we don't enact farces, but sit in judgment," answered the pastor.

Boleslav shrugged his shoulders. "I am pleased to hear it," he said, and there was a tremor in his voice.

The Schrandeners craned their necks to get a better view of the edifying scene, of which they now expected to be spectators. In the momentary calm that ensued, distant whoops and yells were heard from the crowds who filled the square, having stormed the inn in vain, and with the noise there seemed to mingle a woman's voice crying for succor.

What if it were Regina? But it was not possible that it could be she; and the idea vanished as quickly as it had flashed into his brain.

"My child, my poor wretched child!" howled the carpenter, who now found himself in more familiar waters.

The Cats' Bridge

"What have they done to your child, man?" asked the royal official, who was not going to tolerate the conduct of affairs being taken out of his hands.

"My child was seduced—he ruined her—my fatherly heart is—lacerated— I am a poor beggar— Only one coffin—"

"I fancy I have heard you harp on this string before," the Commissioner interrupted him sharply, "at the time when I examined your daughter about the Cats' Bridge disaster. If you haven't learned anything a little newer than that in five years, you'd better hold your tongue. It seems," he said, turning with a smile to the pastor, "as if this ruffian were bent on playing Virginius."

The little man in gray laughed shrilly at this facetious sally on the part of his chief, and then was overcome with confusion at his own temerity. But the old pastor was less disposed to appreciate this turn of urbane humor.

"I will speak for you, Hackelberg," he said. "My words must be taken seriously. I will speak for you and for all of us in the name of our Heavenly Father, whose commandments were not made to be flouted and set at naught by aristocrats. Baron von Schranden, just now you challenged me to speak. Will you listen to what I am going to say?"

He assented impatiently. For the second time

The Cats' Bridge

he fancied he heard that cry of distress rise above the hubbub outside.

"You have entered into the inheritance of your father?"

"Can there be any doubt in the matter?"

"God knows! None."

"What do you mean by that?"

"I mean you have only too quickly appropriated that which was his unlawful possession."

"Your reverence—" But he could not go on. He felt a choking sensation in his throat, and a stony horror creep over him.

"Where is your spirit?" he asked himself; "your boasted defiance?"

"You found a woman, Baron, on your estate who had been your father's mistress. You found her degraded, defiled, dragged through the mire of wickedness and vice. Year-long slavery had robbed her of the respect of every living creature. She had been treated as a mere animal by animals. This wretched woman belonged to my parish and to me. I reared her in the way she should go. It was my hand that sprinkled the baptismal water on her brow; my hand that held the chalice to her lips at the Holy Sacrament; and I promised and vowed before God, and in presence of my flock, to watch over this young soul; doubly orphaned, because he who generated her was not responsible for his actions."

The Cats' Bridge

"Ah, my poor orphaned child!" murmured the carpenter. "Only two, only one other coffin—"

"I am answerable for her to God and the parish. I could not command your father to give her up, for, as I told you, I had handed him over to a heavenly tribunal; but *you*, who have courted this inquiry, I command to give her up, and, what is more, in the present hour of reckoning, I exhort you to render account of what you have done for her soul."

A red mist floated before Boleslav's eyes, and in this mist the figure of the venerable priest seemed to grow till it became almost god-like. He could only stammer forth:

"What should I—?" And the old man took up the thread of his speech again:

"To-day you have been honored before all men by our King; but, Boleslav von Schranden, look to it that God holds you in equal esteem. What should you have done, you ask? This impure, abandoned creature ought to have been more awful, more sacred to you than any other earthly being. What have you done to atone for the guilt your father heaped on her? Have you freed her from the bondage into which she had sunk, loosed her from the chain of her sin? Have you pointed her soul upward to God, the All-gracious and All-forgiving? Or have you dragged her down deeper and deeper into the hell that your own flesh and

259

blood created for her? Above all, in what fashion have you been living with her? It is said that, amid the devastation of your island, there is only one habitable room. Have you never lost sight of the fact that by all laws, human and divine, your father's property in this instance was forbidden for you? Have you taught her to repent and pray, or have you filled her poor undisciplined senses with fresh poison? And have you preserved your own blood intact from sinful desires and lust? Or have you let your passions, like greedy beasts waiting whom they may devour, keep watch on her, ready to spring in an hour of weakness, thus adding fresh shame—?"

"Cease!" cried Boleslav. "This is too much!"

Truly scorpions sprang out of the mouth of this mild Christian priest, who knew how to reveal and lash secret sins of the imagination, which till this hour Boleslav never suspected had existed in his.

But now he saw it all. Everything was clear. Now he knew what it was had sent his blood tearing impetuously through his veins in the long night vigils, and had made him hold his breath, and listen to hear whether that other breath did not come faster or slower, showing that she, too, was sleepless and on guard. It was sinful desire for her body—the body that had been dishonored and abused, yet in spite of all remained so triumphantly beautiful.

The Cats' Bridge

Thank God! ah, thank God! that the sin was still confined to his mind. There was yet time to lock it behind bolts and bars to prevent its stealing forth over the fatal threshold. So far he could claim the right to be his own judge, to stand before the private judgment-seat of his own conscience.

He looked round him, and his face was distraught and ghastly pale. He saw triumph flame up again in the eyes that watched him.

"What right have you to impute this crime to me?" he said to the pastor.

"I did not impute it—I merely asked you," the old man interposed quickly. "You have become too pale, Master Baron, for us not to observe your discomfiture."

"Condemned out of his own mouth, unhappy man," murmured Master Merckel, senior, with a sigh.

The Schrandeners, in the renewed hope of being allowed to spring at his throat, set up a fearful howl, and pressed forward once more.

Then above all the din there was distinctly heard from the yard a shriek of anguish that caused Boleslav's marrow to freeze in his bones. There could be no mistake now. That *was* Regina!

"Regina!" he cried, and rushed to the window that opened on the yard. There the mad chase was in full cry. A crew of furious disheveled women were dashing over hedges, ditches, wagons, barrels, and frozen dunghills, followed by boys armed with clubs. The air was thick with flying stones.

"Help! help!" shrieked Regina's voice. But she herself was not visible.

But as he wrenched open the back door she flew like a wounded bird into the dark corridor, followed closely by her would-be assassins whooping and panting.

He pulled her with a powerful movement of his arm into the room, and shut the door on the furies in pursuit.

She sank on the floor at his feet and pressed her face against the hem of his coat.

Her hands relaxed their cramped grasp on two splintered pieces of wood—all that was left of her tub, the shield with which she had been in the habit of warding off assaults. Her hair was loose, her dress torn, the pretty fur-trimming that she had been so proud of, hanging about her in tatters.

"A charming pair of lovers," said Master Merckel, rubbing his hands in keen enjoyment of the scene, while the Schrandeners displayed a strong disposition to continue the work begun outside by their womankind. The very sight of Regina was sufficient to excite to an uncontrollable degree their predilection for "throwing something." With a yell of delight they looked round them in search of missiles—and already two earthenware mugs had been hurled into the gentry's parlor, one of which struck the carpenter on the shoulder. This instinct for smiting was now stronger in them than the thirst for a life.

The Commissioner wrung his bony hands in despair. All his courtesy and distinction of manner was lost on this pack of devils.

"Master Commissioner," said Boleslav, pointing to the woman cowering almost insensible at his feet, "I beg you to make a note of this pandemonium. If you do not feel inclined to interfere, I take the liberty to warn you that you may have to appear in your own august person as a witness in a court of law against these gallant people."

Certainly the representative of royalty seemed hardly aware of the pitiable figure he was cutting. His splendid mane now hung in shaggy disorder about his face, which had assumed a peevish expression.

"Merckel," he rasped, "you are mayor. I'll have you superseded, unless you can maintain order. Order! do you hear, good people. Order! This is breaking the public peace. You deserve imprisonment—in fact, you *shall* be sent to prison. Taken with arms in your hand means three years, not a day less than three years, good people. To-morrow I shall send military police."

It must have been his good angel that put this

threat into his head, for no other could have had the same effect in bringing the rebels to their senses. Since the war no military police had been stationed in Schranden, which was a piece of good fortune not to be scouted at, for its inhabitants feared them more than they feared the king.

Master Merckel, who began to tremble for his office, was now assiduous in his efforts to restore peace. His son leaned back with folded arms in the corner of the window-seat, affecting to be highly amused at the proceedings.

But the old pastor's gaze never wavered from the pair, and seemed to be searching the innermost recesses of their hearts.

"Stand up, Regina," said Boleslav to the kneeling girl. "They shall not hurt you. I will defend you."

But she remained huddled at his feet, still quaking with fear.

"It's not true, master, that they are going to take you away?" she sobbed. "If it is, I will starve myself and freeze to death."

"No, it's not true; but get up, Regina."

"Master; ah, my dear, dear master!" and she pressed her forehead against his knee.

"Boleslav von Schranden, do you deny it now?"

"Deny what?" he asked. "That this poor unhappy girl whom you have denounced and ostracized regards me as her rescuer and savior, because

The Cats' Bridge

I am the first who for years has spoken a kind word to her? Or would you have me deny that this same unhappy girl has endeared herself to me, because she is the only human being on God's earth who has clung to me in my hour of need, when every one else has forsaken me? I should be an ungrateful ruffian if I did not value her after all she has done for me. I never asked her to share my solitude among the ruins. It is not so comfortable or lively up there, and my charity to her has consisted only in my allowing her to sacrifice herself for me. I have not been able to supply her with pleasures. There has been no unlawful intimacy between us. If she prefers to be my body-slave to being stoned and harried to death, that is no concern of any one's in the world, least of all of you Schrandeners, and of that despicable drunkard who bartered away his own flesh and blood."

Gently prompted by old Merckel, the carpenter recommenced playing the rôle of the injured father.

"Oh, my daughter! my poor, misguided daughter!" he groaned.

"Do your duty," urged the landlord; "claim her."

"Come, my child; come back to your broken-hearted, deserted father. He has taken to drink through grief—driven to it. He will only make two more coffins; one for himself and one for—"

The Cats' Bridge

He stretched out his dirty hand to her, which, shuddering, she violently repulsed.

"Do not distress yourself further," said Boleslav. "She belongs to me as I belong to her."

"Nevertheless, I demand her from you this day, Boleslav von Schranden," said the old pastor, placing his hand on Regina's head. She cowered, but let it lie there.

"That you may be able to stone her better?"

"I promise you that no harm shall come to her. I will confide her to the care of one of my spiritual brethren, who will see to her wants for this side of the grave and the other. If you oppose her redemption, you will only be knitting the chain of your sin the closer."

Boleslav was silent. A thousand thoughts rushed through his brain. This old man's word was to be relied on; he was no cheat. And what lawful claim had he to this woman lying helpless at his feet? How could he make it worth her while to perpetually risk her life for him?

Then the Commissioner, who had partially recovered from his panic, put in his word. "Is the young person of age?" he asked.

The pastor calculated a moment, and replied in the affirmative.

"The paternal decree therefore can not be enforced against her wishes, otherwise she might be sent to a penitentiary, where—"

The Cats' Bridge

The rest of his speech was cut short by a burst of ironical laughter from Boleslav.

"She may decide for herself. Does that satisfy you, Master Baron?"

"I shall not influence her one way or the other," he muttered, and he felt the form at his feet vibrate. He bent over her. "Regina, do you hear what the pastor promises to do for you? You know your future is monetarily provided for. Will you leave the rest, and go with him?"

Then she lifted her glowing face streaming with tears to his, and sobbed out, "Please, master, don't make fun of me."

"You wish to stay with me?"

"Ah, master, you know I wish it! Why do you ask?"

"Stand up then, and we will go."

The pastor barred their way. He had become ashy pale, and his vulture gaze pierced Boleslav through and through. He laid his hand solemnly on his shoulder as he had done the day he had demonstrated to him his father's guilt.

"My son," he said, "you too I received into holy baptism, and taught you to lisp God's name, and opened your eyes to the marvels of His creation. You were to me as my own child, and more, because you were the son of my terrestrial lord and master. I have to answer for you too before the throne of God. You have not been able to clear

The Cats' Bridge

yourself of the suspicion that rests upon you, and if I read your soul aright—don't cast down your eyes—I think I am not mistaken. Therefore, I again command you to give up this woman. I command and exhort you to do so in the name of your father, the name of the parish, the name of our Master in Heaven who is the Father of all orphans and irresponsible children who sin unconsciously. Give her up—and you shall be acquitted as blameless, and go your way in peace."

Regina had raised herself, and now clung to his arm, trembling from head to foot.

"Come!" Boleslav said. "It is to be hoped they will let us pass," and he made a motion as if he were going to push by the old man. But he planted himself again in their way, and holding his arms aloft, said:

"Then you are worthy of your father. And as I once cursed him, I curse you to-day, you and this woman together. You shall be like Cain, whom the Lord banished from His sight— You shall be a fugitive and an outcast on the earth, and your home shall lie in ruins for evermore. There you shall abide with this woman— Now go! Make room for them there! and who lifts a hand against either of them or lays a finger on them shall be cursed, as they are cursed."

Boleslav uttered a sound that broke discordantly on the solemn silence:

The Cats' Bridge

"Come!" he said, and took Regina's hand in his; "let the old man curse, it seems to be his trade;" but he felt a cold shiver run through him.

He saw a lane open which reached to the door, in the densely packed tap-room. Hand in hand he and Regina walked down it.

No one laughed, no one sneered, no one stirred. A superstitious awe seemed to have struck the onlookers dumb. The breath of the winter evening met their faces with an icy tooth. Had some one spread the news of what had happened within, among the crowd that waited outside, or had they divined it by instinct? Here too was profound silence; here too a path was made for them, which they followed, bending their footsteps riverward with bowed heads.

The Cats' Bridge

CHAPTER XIV

THE glow in the evening sky had faded. A
violet vapor hung about the bare tracery of the
tree-tops, and showers of sparkling crystals rained
from the branches.

Boleslav ground the snow under his heel. His
breath curled in front of him in slender columns.
The keen frosty air was balm to his fevered face.
He had sent Regina on before, and was trying to
regain calmness and presence of mind in solitary
wandering, for his brain boiled like a witch's
caldron.

The curse stood out intangibly in his rumina-
tions; it was like the bogy that little children people the darkness with. He saw it everywhere; it
haunted him. How well his father's old enemy
had availed himself of the opportunity of doing
what probably he had long connived at, putting
the son under the same ban as the father.

But it was a terrible reflection to think he might
have deserved that curse. As it was, he had not
merited it; a thousand times no! What the venerable priest in his dark suspicion had alluded to
as an accomplished brutal fact, had really only

swept his soul with phantom wings. Now that his conscience was awakened to the danger of the situation, the danger itself was over. After all, he ought to be indebted to the pastor for showing him the yawning precipice that lay at his unwary feet.

"Think no more of it," he said to himself; "I am the master, she the servant, and I should be an accursed—"

He stopped. Was he not already accursed? Then he laughed at his foolish fears. It was childish to care. Bah! he was too susceptible. At all events, this day should be the beginning of a new epoch in his relations with the outer world. The possession of the iron cross was a proof that he was not dishonored or outside the pale of law and justice. With it he might, if he had the courage, outwit the knavish tricks of his personal enemies, and appeal to the assistance of the courts. If the judge of the district had chosen to condone the fire by ignoring it, he might in his turn light a fire that would send forth such a blaze that the very holes where the incendiaries skulked would be illuminated. But it would involve dragging his father's dealings also into the fierce light of day. Could he dare to disturb the peace of the dead, like a body-snatcher, and blazon forth the shame of his house in the face of all the world?

His mouth became distorted with the defiance that inwardly consumed him. He felt for the moment as if deliberate self-destruction were a mere joke. Why should he hold back; stop at anything? Was he not under a curse? A bitter laugh rose in his throat. He could not forget that curse!

Then he went into the house. Regina was laying the table for supper. She had mended her jacket, and smoothed out her hair with water. Her face was as calm as if nothing in the least out of the way had happened; only a scratch on her throat testified to the hours of peril she had lately lived through.

With affected severity he asked, "What induced you, Regina, to be so silly as to come near the inn?"

She measured him with a shy glance. "I beg your pardon," she said, with a graceful bend of her neck. "I found your letter, and I saw everything swimming green and yellow before my eyes, it made me feel so queer. I hardly knew what I was about. I thought perhaps I could help to set you free."

"Stupid child!" he said, and laughed; but a feeling rose within him that had to be forcibly repressed.

"Bring the wine," he ordered, as he sat down to the table.

"Which kind, master?"

"The best. It is high festival and holiday to-day!"

The Cats' Bridge

She looked at him in surprise, and went.

"Fetch a glass for yourself," he said, as she uncorked the gray cobwebby bottle.

"Oh, please, I'd rather not. It's too strong."

"Nonsense! you will get used to it."

He poured out the wine. The dark-gold fluid foamed sparkling into the slender-stemmed emerald rummers, which, perishable as they were, had been saved from the ruins.

"Clink!" he said.

The glasses as they came in contact produced music like muffled bells.

"The curse of a priest has to-day coupled me with her," he thought, and his eyes sought hers and probed their depths. "How extraordinary! how monstrous!" This woman was to be part of his existence, the old man had said. This woman —why, oh, why this one?"

"A curse is a sanction," he meditated further. "Something that never happened, and never would have happened, through him has been substantiated and vouched for before Heaven as if it were an established fact."

And again his thoughts began to encroach stealthily on that forbidden ground, in whose insurmountable barriers the preacher's words themselves had quarried access. "You are master," he repeated the formula over and over to himself, "she the servant"; and then he added:

273

The Cats' Bridge

"What is more, she is your slave, and so let it be."

One course of action seemed clear enough at the moment, and that was that progress must be made immediately with his work of retaliation. He bade Regina remove the dishes and bring another bottle of wine. Then he fetched his writing materials and motioned her to sit down in the place she had occupied on Christmas evening. With shy delight she obeyed, for since that night she had spent her evenings till bedtime alone in the vestibule.

"I'm going to ask you, Regina," he began, "to answer very briefly, and to the point, several questions!"

She started, then whispered, "Yes, master."

"Drink, and that will make you more talkative."

She struggled to do as he desired, but to-day the effect the wine had upon her was to make her more nervous and reserved, instead of less so.

"To go back to the night in which you led the French across the Cats' Bridge. Was there any one on the premises who knew of the expedition?"

"No, master."

"How did they get wind of it in the village then?"

She cast down her eyes. "I believe through me," she stammered.

"To whom did you confide the information?"

The Cats' Bridge

"To my father."

"How, and when?"

"He used to come to the Castle secretly from time to time to get money from me, and if I hadn't any to give him he pinched and beat me."

"Why did you not call out for help?"

"Because it was at night; and if he had been found there they would have flogged him."

"Go on."

"And so he came soon after—after the expedition, I mean—and asked me to do all sorts of things. I was to get money from the noble master—or to turn out his pockets when no one was looking; and to be left in peace, I fetched the bag the French general had given me. And when he saw the moonlight shine on the coin that was in it, he was half mad—"

She paused abruptly.

"Well?"

"Must I say it?"

"Of course you must."

"But he *is* my father."

"You are to do as I command you."

She drew a deep sigh and went on. "And he caught hold of me by the throat with one hand, and beat me with the other, and hissed in my ear: 'Unless you confess how you came by all that money, I'll squeeze the life out of you—' And when I could hardly breathe, I—"

The Cats' Bridge

He laughed harshly to himself. *His* father and *her* father—both had resorted to the same chivalrous measures.

Regina thought the laugh was at her expense.

"Oh, master," she went on with an imploring upward glance, "I was so dreadfully stupid then. Even a fortnight later, when they cross-examined me, they could have strangled me before they would have got anything out of me. But then—I suppose it was because he was my father—"

"Oh, yes, I understand. You told tales out of school to your father. Well, what else?"

"The very same night my conscience pricked me, and in the morning when I took the noble master his coffee—he would always have me take it—I told him all."

"And what did he say?"

"He turned as white as chalk, but said nothing at first. He took down a gun from the wall and pointed it at me; I folded my hands and closed my eyes, and then I heard him utter an oath, and then he put the gun over his shoulder and rushed out. I thought to myself, he's gone to put an end to father! And I watched him run toward the draw-bridge with his two bloodhounds, and then I, as quick as lightning, hurried through the park, across the Cats' Bridge to the village, to let father know his life was in danger. Had he been at home I couldn't have saved him. But he was in the

The Cats' Bridge

Black Eagle, and had blabbed everything the night before, and was now blind drunk. The master won't fetch him out of the Black Eagle, I thought—and besides it was too late, for the mayor and every one knew, and they all made a great hullabaloo when they saw me, and caught hold of me, and tried to force me to speak; but I bit my tongue till it bled, and kept silent. Then they let me go, and I ran to meet the Baron, and threw myself at his feet, saying: 'Spare his life, for it will do no good to take it. All the world knows now'— He gave me a kick that made me faint, but he left father alone. And then a fortnight after a constable came for me, and took me to the Black Eagle. There, in the wine-room, were assembled five or six gentlemen; the Commissioner, who was there to-day, among them. And they shut the door behind me, and began to cross-question me. I felt as if I could do nothing but cry, and then I grew calmer, and pretended that father had dreamt it all in one of his drunken fits. But they showed me the bag he had taken from me—and so—I was obliged to say—that the money—was—the—reward—that I—" She broke off, and hid her face that was suffused with a dark crimson flush of shame, in her hands.

"Proceed with your story," he commanded, grinding his teeth.

"They didn't believe me, but they saw it was

no good trying to get the truth out of me, and asked me no more questions. And then they held a consultation in low voices (but I have good ears, and understood all they were saying), as to whether they should lock me up till I found my tongue, and arrest the noble master, and so on, and then they came to the conclusion that to blaze it abroad would cause too great a scandal in the district, and be a dishonor to the whole of Prussia, and as there was no direct proof, the affair might be left in the dark. I have forgotten the exact words, but it was something like that."

"And then they let you go?"

"Yes. Master Merckel said I was to take myself off, or my presence might breed a pestilence in the house."

A silence ensued: then hastily gulping down three more glasses of the old wine, he said:

"Now, then, for the night of the fire!"

She jumped up from her chair and stared at him, her eyes starting with horror.

"What! I'm to tell you about the fire?"

"All you can recollect."

"All!— Not all?"

"All."

"Master—I can't." The words rattled in her throat like a death-agony.

"You mean you refuse?" He too had risen, and stood looking at her with dilated eyes.

The Cats' Bridge

She folded her hands on her breast. "I have always been obedient to your every wish. I have never been unwilling or grumbled. I'll go on doing all you order me to do. If you say, 'Go out and be stoned to death,' I'll go. But just this one thing, I beseech you from the bottom of my heart, don't ask me?"

He regarded her in wrathful amazement. So accustomed had be become to her unconditional obedience, that this explosion in her of a spark of resistance was incomprehensible to him. Was his power over her, that he had imagined unlimited, thus suddenly to end? Surely this woman had of her own accord made herself his body-slave? She had sold herself body and soul to his house, and therefore it was unpardonable presumption in her to assert unexpectedly that she had a will of her own.

The blood mounted hotly to his head, and his eyes flashed. "You shall!—I say you *shall!*"

She retreated and shrank against the wall. From the dark background her eyes shone out at him like a persecuted wildcat's. "I won't," she muttered.

All the inherited brutality of the feudal master awoke in him. The wine, too, was doing its work. He sprang on her, and caught her by the throat.

The buttons of her jacket burst beneath his violent attack, and her bare bosom gleamed forth. He transfixed her with the intensity of his gaze.

"Shall I throttle her, or shall I kiss her?" he asked himself.

Then in her deadly terror she made a counter-attack. Her hands were fastened in his shoulders like iron rivets. It needed a gathering up of all his strength to withstand their muscular pressure.

A noiseless struggle began. It lasted a minute, and yet seemed to be no nearer its end. Embittered and desperate at first as a wrestle for life and death, it became eventually a sort of game. The combatants apparently had lost sight of what it was they were struggling for. His eyes, bloodshot and wild, sought hers. Her bosom, wet with perspiration, pressed hard against his. Their breathing mingled. Tightly locked in each other's arms they staggered and swayed to and fro. He pressed her in the back of her knee, but she did not yield. For one second in their delirious grappling they gazed dreamily into each other's eyes. Then she vibrated from head to foot, and in the midst of the conflict laid her cheek caressingly on the arm that was raised against her. He saw the action, he saw how her eyes hung on his face with melting solicitude—saw the beautiful disheveled head droop like a broken flower.

"If you are cursed, why should it be for nothing?" And as the thought flashed through him, he bent over her with a sigh, and kissed her on the mouth.

She groaned aloud, clung heavily to him, and buried her teeth in his lips. Then, overcome, with limbs suddenly collapsed, she slipped from his arms on to the floor, and lay with the back of her head flat on the bare boards.

He stared down at her half-stunned. She would have looked as if she were dead, had it not been for the heaving bosom, that seemed to fight for air. Blood trickled from his lip, and unconsciously he wiped it away with his tongue.

"What next?" he asked himself.

The longer he gazed at the prostrate form the intenser became his anxiety, till it almost amounted to insanity; anxiety for what must come.

"Away! out of the house! Away before she moves!" an inward voice commanded. He tore down his coat from the wall, crushed a fur cap over his brow, and flew out into the bitter cold night, as if chased by the Devil.

But he could not escape—could not run away from *her;* wherever he went she was beside him. A tornado raged in his breast, and lashed the blood to froth in his veins.

He was fleeing from his young manhood's senses, and they were in hot pursuit.

He dashed through the woods at full speed.

The Cats' Bridge

The frosty air did not cool him, nor the darkness restore his serenity.

Was there no salvation? None?

He thought of the parsonage. A jeering laugh rose to his lips. Helene had shrunk from him when he had approached her with clean hands and a pure heart. What would she do to-day if he came into her presence bearing a curse and an insupportable burden of guilt upon him?

And yet that one spot of earth was sacred to memories of all that had been purest, most peaceful and happy in his blighted life. Ought such a refuge of light to be denied to him, even if a thousand curses had descended upon his head from the outer darkness?

Almost against his will his footsteps took the road to the village. It was reposing peacefully. Only from the windows of the Black Eagle a ruddy glow was cast on the white expanse of snow. The clock in the church tower struck one. He must have been tramping about for five hours, and it seemed like five minutes. Faint moonbeams shone on the sleigh-ruts, which looked like long white ribbons unrolled on the ground, and the mass of icicles hanging from the church roof spread a delicate silver filigree on the dark, time-stained walls.

He passed the church and came to the parsonage garden. There was a light in one of the gable windows. His heart seemed to bound into his mouth. He swung himself over the hedge, and strode through the deep snow to the summer-house, which stood at a distance of twenty paces from the gable. In its shadow he took up his position.

A white curtain was drawn across the illuminated casement. On the surface of the chintz a delicate tracery of leaves and stalks was reflected from flower-pots inside. There was her virgin paradise; there she ruled as modestly and sweetly as the Madonna in her rose-garden.

And again the picture in the cathedral rose before his mental eyes, as it always did when he tried to realize the presence of the beloved. Oh! for one second in which to feast his bodily eye on that dear, forgotten face, so that what time and guilt had deadened in him might revive and live anew!

For a moment the outline of a girl's figure darkened the illuminated window-pane. A corner of the curtain was lifted.

Instinctively he stretched out his arms. The curtain dropped quickly, and a moment afterward the light within was extinguished.

He waited, hardly daring to draw a breath, for a sign from the darkened spot. But none came. All was motionless and still.

"It is madness to think of it!" he said to himself. "Probably she didn't recognize you. She only saw a man's figure that gave her a fright. Make haste!

The Cats' Bridge

For the whole house will be roused and turned out
to hunt the supposed thief."

So he retraced his steps. In turning into the
street he was conscious that his blood was flowing more calmly, and his pulses not throbbing so
fiercely. Being in her neighborhood even for a
few minutes had soothed him.

"Where now?" Anywhere in the world, but not
home. At the bare thought of that outstretched
figure on the floor, his veins began to pulsate again
with violence. Oh, she was a fiend, and he hated
her!

He took a side path, not knowing where it led.
It was divided from the castle island by stables
and carters' huts, and ended in an open field. On
the opposite side, he saw the indigo belt of woods
that encircled the flat white plains. The woods
drew him toward them again like a magnet. There
he would hide, in their majestic depths where the
peace of winter reigned and slept its mysterious
dreamless slumber.

He trod the pathless field covered with hills and
dales of snow which swept away before him like
the billows of a boundless ocean of liquid light.
His feet crunched through the frozen crust till he
sank to his knees, and then it needed all his powers
to step forward once more. But with strenuous
effort he plowed his way, still taking flight from
his own thoughts. There was something almost

The Cats' Bridge

comforting in this objectless striving. His lungs fought for breath; moisture poured from every pore of his body as he plunged and stumbled on. Here and there the crust was strong enough to bear him, and then he felt as if he had been endowed with wings and floated over the ground, till another crash laid him low, groveling on his hands and knees.

Now the wall of woods rose higher and darker before him;—he was only a hundred steps from his goal, when his eye was arrested by something in the shape of a hillock extending a distance of about fifty or sixty feet in the direction of the wood. Coming nearer, he saw it was too regular in form for a hillock, and its corners too sharply defined. A few feet off there was a second mound of the same description, and to the left again, a third. They must be gravel heaps, he thought, that had been dug up in the autumn and left to be removed till after the thaw set in. Why should the peasants not get gravel from his property when there was no one to prevent them?

But what did those crosses mean, that stood out so solemnly and eerily in the night, at the foot of each mound? At first he had not noticed them against the dark background of the woods. They were three in number. Roughly hewn out of fir trunks, they were so firmly planted in the earth that they did not move a hairbreadth when he shook them. They bore no inscription, and if they had he would not have been able to read it. Inscrutable as memorials of forgotten misfortune, they stood ranged there in the dim moonlight like rugged sentinels.

And then the mystery was solved. He saw what they were. With a loud cry he dropped his face in his hands. He had stumbled on the graves of the men who had fallen on that accursed night in the year '07. Here lay the bones of his father's victims. What evil chance had led him here to-night? Or was it chance? Had not a thousand invisible arms beckoned him cajolingly and irresistibly along this maniacal route, and let him fight his way through snow and ice, till he was ready to faint from exhaustion? It seemed as though fate had kept in reserve the most excruciating lash of her scourge till this hour of his bitterest humiliation; so that he should no longer be in doubt as to there being any salvation in store for him, and to demonstrate once for all that he was doomed to sink forever under the weight of shame and despair.

"But it is well that I came," he said, conversing with himself; "where better can I convince myself that the old pastor's curse was not unjust—and that what was not a sin has become one?"

His eyes wandered over the row of flattened graves, and now there seemed no end to them— How many were buried there? If they had been

The Cats' Bridge

closely packed, a hundred or more might rest in each grave—or perhaps even double that number. And they had all been brave soldiers who had left their homes gaily, in light-hearted devotion to fight for King and Fatherland— Through foulest treachery they had been butchered here in cold blood, under cover of night.

He clung to one of the crosses, and held his face so tightly against the rough wood that splints dug into his flesh.

"Arraign him before the whole world!" something cried within him—"him and *her*—and then go with her to perdition."

He gazed at the distant prospect, and sought the outline of the ruins against the horizon. But nothing was visible except the tall trees that crowned the park, which were only dimly discernible. A little behind to the right of them lay the Cats' Bridge.

He could fancy her emerging from those trees with the troop of remorselessly cruel Frenchmen following her, bent on their work of blood. How terrible must the regular echo of their marching feet have sounded in her ears. Deeper and deeper into the wood they must have gone, till they reached that ravine which ran parallel with the thicket, almost in a half-circle. She had never told him the road she had taken, but he saw exactly how it had all happened. Everything was as plain as if

The Cats' Bridge

he had been there himself and seen it with his own eyes.

He stretched out his arm, and with a trembling finger traced the path against the horizon.

And afterward when they let her go, and she had made her way home alone, with the wages of her sin in her pocket—how the cracking of bullets, the beating of drums, the clouds of gunpowder, the death-shrieks of the massacred, must have followed her, galloping at her heels like an army of furies!

How she had gone on living with those awful sounds ringing in her head, those ghastly pictures floating before her eyes, he could not understand. If he had been in her place he would have sought instant deliverance in the first halter or pond that came handy.

But not she! Visions were no terror to her. Her conscience, instead of tormenting itself, was apparently scarcely conscious of its guilt. She had only the feelings of an animal or a demon. He shuddered. And it was to her, *her*, that he had been on the brink of succumbing!

Then in his sore distress he flung himself across the grave, face downward in the snow, folded his hands and stammered forth an incoherent prayer, while tears gushed from his eyes.

The intense cold of his exposed position stung his face, and drove him to stand up again. He patrolled the row of graves, unable to evolve a single rational thought. He felt as if he were caught in a brazen net, that was drawing its meshes tighter and tighter around him.

"God in Heaven," he cried aloud, "visit not the sins of the fathers on me! Let the dead sleep— *I* have not murdered them. Let something happen, a miracle, a sign that I may be shown that Thou wilt not have me perish in this anguish of despair." He cast his eye round him as if looking for help.

But coldly and unsympathetically the moonlit, lead-colored sky looked down on him. There was no sign, no miracle.

He laughed. "You are going mad," he murmured inwardly.

Terrible exhaustion overwhelmed him. He reeled, and his feet gave way beneath him. The next moment he was sitting in the cavity which the weight of his prostrate figure had made in the snow. He drew up the collar of his coat, and nearly frozen, brooded on, half sleeping, half waking.

When he rose with cramped limbs, happy to have escaped falling asleep and being frozen to death, one thin purple streak had appeared in the eastern sky. An ague, hot and cold at the same time, like the beginning of fever, shook his frame.

Now there was nothing for it but to go home.

The Cats' Bridge

But where was he to find the strength necessary to obliterate forever from his mind what had happened in the night that was over at last? His tongue instinctively felt for his lip— The impress of her kiss burned there still.

And there had been no sign from Heaven, no miracle. One course only remained that might save him from the worst, and that was death.

Death! The thought came to him like a ray of light in the darkness, yet his brain was too weary, his soul too dispirited for him to grasp it, and it died out as quickly as it had come.

In his own footprints he walked back to the village. No one was stirring out of doors, but here and there a chimney smoked, and a cock from his perch crowed a greeting to the new-born day.

As he took the path down to the river, he thought he saw the fleeting shadow of a woman's figure hurrying from the drawbridge. Perhaps it was Regina, who after long waiting and watching had now come to meet him.

But no! Regina was not so slim and dainty. Who in all the village could want to come to the drawbridge at this unearthly hour? His heart beat fast. He had been seen. A soft, squealing sound fell on the air, and the next instant the figure had vanished down a bypath. He did not think of following her. It might possibly be a dairymaid who had been taking a morning dip, and was shy of meeting him; but on coming to the drawbridge he saw footmarks on the freshly fallen hoarfrost, and these came to an end at the pillar to which the letter-box was fixed.

Who could be his nocturnal correspondent? It was ridiculous, yet a flood of hope suffused his soul.

He snatched the little key, that he always carried about with him, from his pocket. The box opened —a letter fell out.

He broke the seal with shaking fingers. Helene's signature! Had God heard his petition? Had He after all sent him fresh strength for the struggle, and deliverance?

The dawn gave him sufficient light to read by, but the lines danced before his eyes. Only here and there he drank in a broken sentence or a single word: "Wait patiently." "The hour when I summon you to come to me." "Longing." "Childhood's days." "Happy."

And one thing that was not written there at all he could read distinctly. The sign that he had prayed for by the grave of the warriors had fallen from Heaven. The miracle had happened!

Renewed confidence in himself possessed him. He was not forsaken; he need not yet despair of his better self. This pure, bright angel, the good genius of his youth, was still faithful, still believed in him. Her trust should not be abused. Rather die than, through despising himself, bring her to feeling shame at her faith in him.

He turned his face toward the purple morning glow, and, raising his hand solemnly, uttered the following words:

"God, who art a great and just Judge, and visitest the sins of the fathers on the children to the third and fourth generation, I hereby swear to take my life with my own hand rather than let the curse of Thy priest gain ascendency over me. Amen."

Then he walked toward the house as if freed from an intolerable burden.

"Now the Devil is exorcised!" he said as he entered the vestibule, heaving a deep sigh of relief; nevertheless, the hand that lifted the latch still trembled feverishly.

He surveyed the room with one quick shy glance.

In the rosy light of dawn he saw her crouching, dressed on her bed, her hands clasped over her knees. Her jacket was open; her hair hung about her face in tangled masses. Her dress was exactly as it had been when he left her the evening before.

She raised her head slowly, and gazed at him as if in a dream with soft melting eyes.

He shrank before that gaze.

"Haven't you been to bed?" he asked in as harsh a tone as he could command.

The Cats' Bridge

She continued to look at him with the same blissfully rigid expression, and said nothing.

"Didn't you hear?" he asked again imperiously.

She did not start as she used to do when he spoke thus; but a scarcely perceptible vibration passed through her frame, as if the sound of his voice filled her with ecstasy. She smiled a little.

"Hear what?" she asked.

"My question as to why you hadn't been to bed."

"I waited up for you, master."

"I did not order you to wait for me."

"Nor did you forbid me."

He clung to the back of a chair.

"Why are you afraid of her?" he asked himself. "You have just sworn that danger exists no longer."

Then to get rid of her he told her to go and prepare him something hot for breakfast.

She rose deliberately, stretching her stiff limbs. A dreamy languor seemed to pervade her whole being. Since last night she was completely transformed.

Directly he had shut the door after her, he tore the letter from his pocket, and read it to reassure himself of his happiness. It ran:

"DEAR FRIEND OF MY YOUTH—I hear from papa that you have been highly honored by our wise and noble King—that he has made you captain of your division, and given you the Iron Cross. I congratulate you heart-

The Cats' Bridge

ily, and am rejoiced at your good fortune. What else passed papa wouldn't tell me, but he was very excited about it, and in a great rage when he mentioned you. Ah! if only you could have managed to win his affection and the good-will of the parishioners! Then I shouldn't have to be so careful, and could see and speak to you often— Dear Boleslav, I implore you never to think of coming into the garden again.

"You know papa—what he is; and if he found out— ah! I believe he would kill me! Wait patiently, my dear friend! The Bible says, you know, patience shall be rewarded. So have patience till the hour when I shall summon you to come to me; then I will tell you all the news. How full of longing I am to see you! Oh, those lovely days of childhood! What has become of them? How happy I was then! Your   HELENE.

"*Postscript*—Never come to the garden again. I will appoint another place of meeting. Not in the garden."

Strange, that what a few minutes before had filled him with delight now seemed flat and colorless, and disappointed him. Doubtless the half-wild creature was to blame, whose close proximity confused his judgment. A kind of delirium of bliss seemed to have taken possession of her. And how she had smiled! how strangely she had stared into space!

She came back into the room, and moved about it like a somnambulist.

The Cats' Bridge

"Regina!"

She half closed her lids, and said, "Yes."

"What's the matter with you?"

She smilingly shook her head. "Nothing," she answered, and again that look came into her eyes; they seemed to swim in dreamful contemplation of some infinite felicity.

He felt his throat contract. Clearly there was still reason to be afraid of himself.

Then he resolved to speak and listen to her no more, but to live in his work. He immersed himself in his papers again, sorted and laid aside important documents, filed, registered, and made copies of them. It seemed to him that he must get everything in order in anticipation of some pending catastrophe.

So the day went by, and the evening. Regina crouched in the darkest and remotest corner she could find and remained motionless. He dared not cast even a glance in her direction. The blood hammered in his temples, yellow circles danced before his eyes, every nerve in his body was on edge from overfatigue.

On the stroke of ten she rose, murmured goodnight, and disappeared behind her curtain. He neither answered nor looked up.

At eleven he put out the lights and went to bed too.

"Why does your heart beat like this?" he

The Cats' Bridge

thought. "Remember your oath." But the superstitious, indefinable dread of coming disaster haunted him like a ghost in the darkness.

He got up again, and stole with bare feet across the room to the case of weapons, that was dimly illumined by the newly risen moon. He caught up one of his pistols, which he always kept loaded to be forearmed against unforeseen events. It had been his faithful friend and protector in many a bloody fray. To-day it should protect him from himself. With its trigger cocked, he laid it on the small table by his bedside.

"It's doubtful whether you sleep a wink now," he said, as he nestled his head on the pillows. Yet scarcely three seconds later he lost consciousness, and slumber lapped his tired limbs.

.   .   .   .

A curious dream recalled him from profoundest sleep into a half-dozing wakefulness. He fancied he saw two bright eyes like a panther's glittering at him out of the darkness. They were only a few inches from his face, and seemed to be fixed on it with fiery earnestness, as if with the intention of bringing him under the spell of their enchantment.

His breath came slower, almost stopped, then he felt another breath well over him in full soft waves.

The Cats' Bridge

It was no dream after all, for his eyes were wide open. The moon cast a patch of light on the counterpane of his bed, and still those other lights glowed on, devouring him with their fire. The outline of a face was visible. A woman's white figure bent over him.

A thrill of mingled pleasure and alarm ran through his body.

"Regina," he murmured.

Then she sank on her knees by the bed and covered his hands with kisses and tears. In the enervation that had crept over him he would have stroked the black tresses which streamed across the pillow, only he lacked the strength to extricate his hands from hers.

Then— "Your oath, think of your oath!" a voice cried within him.

In dismay, he started up. Not yet fully awake, he reeled forward, and tearing his hands out of her grasp, fumbled for the pistol.

"You, or her."

There was a report. Regina, with a cry of pain, fell with her forehead against the edge of the bed, and at the same moment a great rumbling and crackling was heard from the opposite wall. The portrait of his beautiful grandmother had crashed to the ground.

He stared wildly round him, only just arriving at complete consciousness.

The Cats' Bridge

"Are you wounded?" he asked, laying his hand gently on the dark head.

"I—don't—know, master," and then she glided across the floor to her mattress.

He dressed himself and kindled a light. It now all appeared a confused nightmare.

Ah! but if she died, if he had killed her?

When he drew aside the curtain, he beheld her cowering and shivering in her corner, holding up the counterpane in her teeth. It was smeared with blood.

"For God's sake—show me. Where were you hit?" he cried.

She let the counterpane drop as far as her breast, and silently offered her naked shoulder for his inspection. Blood was streaming from it.

But the first glance satisfied him, who had seen many a bullet wound, that it was a mere surface shot. It would heal of itself in a few days.

"Thank God! Thank God!"

She stared up at him absently with wide eyes.

"It is nothing," he stammered. "A scratch—nothing more."

She appeared not to hear what he said.

"Pull yourself together like a man. Not a word, not a look, must betray your real feelings."

With this self-exhortation he withdrew, and wearily put down the light on the table.

The Cats' Bridge

What now? Where should he go? To stay meant ruin and damnation.

This very hour he must go away. Away! Somewhere, *anywhere,* so long as a barrier of his fellow-creatures separated him from her for evermore. And in breathless haste he began to gather together papers that proved his father's guilt, as if they were the most precious possessions in the world.

The Cats' Bridge

CHAPTER XV

MORE than three months had passed away since Boleslav von Schranden had turned his back on the inheritance of his fathers.

In the meantime spring had come. Moss, starred with anemones, grew among the short-bladed grass; the ditches were full of a luxuriant growth of bindweed and nettles; and at every breeze the boughs rained a shower of crumbling catkins. The plow left a trail of smooth, black furrows on the bosom of the awakening earth, and seed-cloths were already being put out to air.

It was the first spring for many and many a long year that had begun in peace, and of which there were hopes of its ending in peace.

Europe's evil genius was vanquished. Like Prometheus he lay chained to his barren seagirt rock; and so the sword was hung up to rust, and the plowshare and harrow resumed their sway.

Of what had taken place on the shores of the Mediterranean in the month of March, the inhabitants of quiet country towns and out of the way moorland villages had as yet no suspicion. Not a breath had reached them of that interrupted quad-

The Cats' Bridge

rille at Prince Metternich's ball, of the fury and consternation of sovereigns and potentates; they knew nothing of foam-bespattered proscriptions issued against the escaped rebel, of rearming and rumors of war.

The lark's caroling in the sky seemed a jocund invitation to resume labor in the fields; the womb of the earth opened with yearning for the crops from which it had fasted so long.

One day toward the end of April, a curious band was seen on the king's highroad approaching the county town of Wartenstein, which excited the wondering interest of all whom they passed by the way.

It was not easy to decide at once whether they were soldiers or workmen. Most of them were armed, but side by side with the gun on their shoulders was a spade, and from the red bundles slung across their backs peeped whetstones and scythe-blades. Ten or twelve of them were mounted, but behind came as baggage a stream of rough wagons, numbering about twenty axle wheels, loaded with bursting sacks of corn and implements of every description. Altogether the company came to about a hundred and fifty, marching in half military fashion, double file. It consisted of muscular youths, for the most part fair and of ruddy complexions, with thickset figures. Their faces were broad and bony, not German, and still less Polish, in type. They spoke a language unknown in the neighborhood, and sang songs of which no one knew the tune. Notwithstanding, their leader was German, and so was the discipline which had trained their limbs and given to their movements a certain dignity of bearing.

At the head of the procession rode one to whom they looked up with awe and affection, and whose brief and not unfriendly words of command they obeyed with almost childlike zeal. It was Boleslav, who came with this little army to reconquer his own territory.

He had recruited it far away in the Lithuanian East, on the remotest border of the province, whither neither good nor evil reports of the name of Schranden had ever penetrated. During his five years' previous intercourse with this people, he had become intimately acquainted with their habits and customs, and took care to choose his pioneers from those who had been in the war, and become accustomed to the rigors of a soldier's life, but who were still unfamiliar enough with the German tongue to have their minds poisoned by the Schrandeners' gossip.

Now he had every hope that the fate of his father, who had failed to find either serf or laborer to bind himself to work for him, would not be his. And should the Schrandeners offer fight to these workpeople, as they had done to the Polish serfs whom his father had been obliged to call to his assistance, so much the worse for the Schrandeners; they would only be sent home with bloody noses.

In proud self-reliance he looked coming events in the face. He would willingly have returned home earlier, only, to prosecute his enterprise on the scale it demanded, he was forced to wait till the time in which he could claim his aunt's legacy, and so have the necessary means at his disposal.

He had lived through hard times since that January night, when, to flee from temptation, he had dashed out into the snow-clad, moon-illumined landscape, followed by the cries of the unhappy woman who could not understand what ailed him.

In Königsberg, where he had gone direct from home, he had meditated obtaining, through boldly seeking a trial, that justice long denied to his house. But though the iron cross of valor on his breast compelled the doors that had been shut on his father to open to him, the polite shrug of the shoulders with which the judges promised to see what could be done, and then coolly referred him to one court of appeal after another, taught him that the passionate self-sacrifice he had dreamed of would be here ill-timed and out of place.

So he again packed up his father's correspondence, which of his own free will he had desired to make public in order to clear up every shadow of mystery, and felt he must keep it till a more favorable opportunity offered itself. Besides, he had destroyed too much that might have had a vindicating effect, and to court the risk of his own condemnation might after all be acting unfairly to his father's memory.

Contact with the outer world cooled and damped his ardor in a singular way; and the feverish tension of his emotions gradually relaxed, giving place to a more normal state of mind. He was confronted with reasoning instead of anathemas, courteous words instead of threats—and this worked a soothing and beneficial influence on his nature. He projected plans, and prepared himself with composure and deliberation for what the future might have in store for him.

At the same time the magic fascination the wild girl had exercised on him was becoming dimmer in his recollection. Every new face, every new thought, alienated him further from her. Gradually he ceased to reproach himself for having acted with merciless cruelty toward her, and the mastery she had acquired over his senses was now incomprehensible to him. Nevertheless, often when he sat alone at dusk in his private room at the hostelry, he saw those eyes again flashing soft fire, and felt her presence thrill through his veins. But of course this was only a freak which illusive

The Cats' Bridge

reverie played him, and which lamplight and work soon dispelled.

He had written to her once or twice in order to set her mind at rest on the subject of his sudden departure, or rather flight—had asked for an answer, and promised a speedy return.

Once he had had news of her—a letter written in bold characters and correctly expressed. After all these years of bondage, the lessons she had learned in the old pastor's school still evidently stood her in good stead.

In prospect of his near approach to his home, he drew the sheet from his pocket, and read sitting in the saddle the lines, which, in spite of himself, he almost knew by heart:

"My dear Master—Don't be anxious on my account. No one will do anything to me. They do not know down in the village that you are gone away, and they are frightened of the wolf-traps, for no one has told them that we cleared them away. Every night I see to the pistols and guns in case they should come; but they won't come. As for the wound, I have quite forgotten it. The grocer at Bockeldorf gave me some English sticking-plaster, and when it peeled off, it was entirely healed. The thaw and floods are now over, thank God. For several days I was obliged to go with very little food, because the water was too high on the meadows for me to wade through, and I would rather have died than go

305

The Cats' Bridge

down to Herr Merckel. Ah! dear master, I am so glad that you are coming home soon; for I seem to have nothing to live for when I have not you to wait upon. I climb up on the Cats' Bridge very often and wait for you there, so that when you come you shall not find it drawn up. Please don't come in the night, nor on Thursday before seven, because then I shall be going to Bockeldorf. The snow is all gone now, and the grass is beginning to get quite green. Yesterday I heard the swallows twittering in the nest they have built in the eaves; but I haven't seen them yet. Now and then I suffer from stitch in my side, and giddiness, and I have not much appetite. I believe it comes from being so much alone, which I can not bear. But I don't know why I should tell you all this. Perhaps it is because you were always so kind to me. I can't help always remembering your great kindness to me. Your Lordship's humble servant, REGINA HACKELBERG."

This letter had filled him with pleasure and satisfaction, for it showed on the one hand that she had very reasonably bowed to the inevitable, and that there was no cause for his anxiety; and on the other, that she still faithfully clung and belonged to him heart and soul. And glad as he might be to feel his blood purged of the unwholesome excitement with which she had inspired it, he could not help being pleased at this proof of her remaining ever his true and willing servant.

306

The Cats' Bridge

His belief in Helene's sacred influence on his destiny had, he imagined, received a new impetus, since her note had saved him in an hour of imminent danger. He wore it gratefully as a talisman on his heart, even if he did not read it so often, and with such delight, as he read Regina's.

Soon after his arrival in the capital, an intense yearning had drawn him to the Cathedral, where he had sought out the old altar-piece, which contained her living image. He experienced a bitter disappointment. The Madonna amidst her lilies and roses appeared absolutely ridiculous. She looked to him now as if she had been baked out of *Marzipan,* and the flowers, with their stiff stalks and drooping heads, appeared as unnatural and insipid as their doll custodian.

And this was what he had carried about with him for years, as the image of his beloved! Certainly it was high time she appeared in her own person before his bodily eyes, otherwise he would be in danger of loving a mere phantom.

And now, in this the hour of home-coming, it was not she at all with whom he looked forward to a joyous meeting; his senses saw only the picture of a girl waiting and watching for him whose fresh and unbounded loveliness was no myth.

It was early morning, and the sun was shining. He had made his last halt, the night before, at a hamlet not far from Wartenstein, as he proposed to pass rapidly through the town, to avoid being gaped at, and exciting idle curiosity. Once there he was within three miles and a quarter of home, and hoped to enter his native village at the hour for vespers, for his stalwart followers were used to rapid marching. As he rode up to the moss-grown ramparts, eight sounded from the belfries of Wartenstein, and he counted on being able to quit the town quite early, and so escape awkward questions.

Thus, he was little prepared for the surprises awaiting him within its gates. The sentinel, instead of stopping him and demanding his passport, shouted up to a window in the gateway tower:

"Ring the bells! ring the bells! The first detachment is here!"

Then he saluted with his pike, while a merry peal clashed from the watch-towers of Wartenstein to announce Boleslav's arrival.

"What can be the meaning of it?" he asked himself, shaking his head; and his astonishment increased, when on riding through the streets he found them thronged with crowds of men, women, and children, who waved their caps and handkerchiefs, and welcomed him with resounding cheers.

His Lithuanians, who had been accustomed on their triumphal marches to being received everywhere with open arms, took the present ovation as a matter of course, and responded to the hurrahs with lusty lungs.

But to Boleslav it was plain that there was some misunderstanding, which in the next few minutes would be explained.

As he entered the market-place, which, like the streets, was filled with an enthusiastic crowd, the Commissioner, at the head of an impressive procession, consisting of the Burgomaster, Corporation, and other magnates of the town, advanced to meet him. He laid his delicate bony hand on his breast, and cleared his throat with a rasp, preparatory to speaking.

When he recognized Boleslav, who had quickly sprung from his horse, he drew back in embarrassment. Nevertheless he began:

"I congratulate you, Baron von Schranden, on your being the first who has hastened here with your troops—"

"Not so fast, Commissioner," Boleslav interrupted. "There is an error somewhere. These people are workmen, whom I have recruited in Lithuania for domestic use. I am on my way with them to Schranden."

An amused smirk passed through the ranks of the town magnates. They enjoyed seeing the Commissioner make a fool of himself, even if they themselves were made to look foolish in the process.

The Cats' Bridge

"And you really haven't heard yet?" he stammered out, concealing his annoyance.

"I have come straight from the remotest corner of Prussia."

"You haven't heard that Napoleon has escaped from Elba, and that the King has again appealed to his gallant Prussian subjects to arm?"

Boleslav felt a rush of mingled horror and joy flood his heart.

So once more the world's history had absorbed the solution of his career in its own, and he would be saved further self-doubt and suspense with regard to it. His vast schemes, the work to which he was to consecrate his life, lay shattered at his feet scarcely begun, and now ended perhaps forever. But away with all regrets and fears. Did not the Fatherland, *his* Fatherland, call him?

"Thank you," he said, while he endeavored to still his wildly beating heart. "I feel honored at your thinking so well of me and my contingent of Schrandeners. We will prove ourselves worthy of your high opinion, and in four-and-twenty hours be in readiness."

The Commissioner held out his hand. Boleslav retreated a step or two, and was in the act of repaying the other in his own coin for the insult he had not long ago subjected him to.

Then he reflected. The Fatherland calls you,

and what is your petty hate or love weighed in the balance? And he seized the bony hand, which its owner, offended, had already withdrawn, and shook it heartily.

Then he learned further particulars. The evening before the King's proclamation, dated April 7, had reached Wartenstein. All night the administration had been hard at work getting the decrees ready for local heads of departments, and arranging to send out special mounted messengers to distribute them.

"Will one be sent to Schranden?" asked Boleslav.

"Certainly," was the answer.

"Then may I add a military order?"

"Yes, if you wish."

He tore a sheet of paper from his pocket-book and hastily scribbled the following lines:

"At five o'clock in the afternoon all troops liable to service are to muster in the churchyard square, bringing with them accoutrements and canteens. The hour for marching will then be stated.

"Von Schranden,
"Captain, First Reserve.
"To the local administrator."

"And what will become of Regina?" was a question that rose warningly within him.

The Cats' Bridge

But he would not listen to it. He was almost delirious. The fever for action possessed him.

He called his workpeople together, explained to them that he no longer needed their services, and bade each to return as quickly as possible to his native place, from there to join his respective company. He paid them off, and took leave of them with a shake of the hand and a blessing.

The stalwart youths, who had lost their hearts to him, kissed the hem of his coat, and went their way with tears in their eyes. Then he found a place of safety for the wagons, whose freight alone represented no small capital, made arrangements for the sale of the seed and provender, and left the horses at the disposal of a dealer.

Only the one on whose back he rode did he keep for his own use.

It was half-past two before he had transacted his business, and was free to start on his homeward road.

He had seen hanging up for sale in a tailor's shop an undress state-uniform, which, as the officers of the Reserve were forbidden any gorgeous display of ornament, and it happened to fit him exactly, he purchased promptly, first having the elaborately braided collar replaced by a plain scarlet strip.

Thus fitted out, he was ready to confront his Schrandeners, whom he now saw delivered into his

The Cats' Bridge

hand in a rather different manner from the one he had anticipated.

. . . .

While Boleslav was riding home, Lieutenant Merckel was pacing up and down the back parlor of the Black Eagle in furious excitement.

"I won't, no, I won't submit to being under the command of that scoundrel," he roared at his father, who, to soothe him, had the best wine in his cellar (the best was sour enough) set on the table, and never wearied of refilling the raving youth's glass.

"Felix," he supplicated, "be sensible. If the King has ordered it so, and the authorities demand—"

"But what if my honor demands the contrary, father?" cried his son, angrily twirling the ends of his mustache. "I am an officer, father; I have some sense of honor, and my sense of honor bids me die by putting a bullet through my body with my own hand rather than follow and serve under that son of a traitor."

"But if the King—" repeated the old man in desperation.

"The King! what does he know about it? He has been taken in, deceived, kept in the dark. But I, _I_ will open his eyes. I will say to him, 'Here, your Majesty, are thirty brave soldiers, and an honorable, upright officer, who would rather—' "

The Cats' Bridge

"Drink, my boy," entreated the old man, and wiped the sweat of anxiety from his brow; "this wine cost me, to begin with, a thaler the bottle. Nowhere else in the world could you get anything to compare with it."

"The devil take your swipes!" exclaimed the dutiful son, smashing the bottle with his sabre-hilt. "I don't intend to sacrifice my honor for any Judas reward. My honor is not to be bribed into silence. My honor dictates that I should tear the hound's heart out of his breast. And I'll do it. The Fatherland must be rid of such a scandalous reproach once for all. This plague-spot among Prussia's officers must and shall be branded out. I'll see that it is. So sure as I am a brave soldier I will do it, even if I die for honor's sake— Good-by for the present, father; I must go now and bid my little sweetheart farewell." And rounding his lips for a defiant whistle, the half-inebriated young man swaggered out, his sabre-blade clanking the ground at every step.

Boleslav, as he entered the village shortly after four, found the street full of women and old people, who ran from under the horse's hoofs, maintaining a glum silence, and then followed like evil spirits in his wake. He felt for the pistols in his side pockets, and loosened the scabbard of his sabre; then he fully expected a skirmish of some sort. "Even if they have no other officer with a

The Cats' Bridge

soldier's coat on, they may be planning to attack me from the front this time," he reflected, and his breast expanded proudly at the thought.

The crowd was denser in the churchyard square, and he was obliged to rein in his horse to give it time to get out of his way. Here and there a smothered laugh or a half-whispered imprecation fell on his ear. Otherwise total silence was the order of the day. Close to the church, some twenty paces from its flight of stone steps, he saw the troops drawn up in double line, about fifteen or sixteen squadrons in strength.

Lieutenant Merckel was prancing up and down, giving first one and then another—as it seemed—a word of encouragement. His face was aflame, his gait uncertain; once or twice his cavalry sabre got entangled with his legs and nearly tripped him up.

Boleslav cast one rapid, searching glance at the parsonage. Its windows were closely curtained, and in the garden too there was no sign of life.

He drew a deep breath, and rode into the heart of the crowd, which closed behind him.

Once again he stood single-handed, face to face with the Schrandener wolves, but this time he was master.

The sense of iron calm and perfect coolness, which he had always experienced at moments of life and death issues, did not forsake him now.

The Cats' Bridge

"I am waiting for your salute, Herr Lieutenant," he cried in a threatening tone.

He was answered by a drunken, jeering laugh.

So they intended to mutiny! His suspicions had not been ill founded.

He tore his sabre from the scabbard. "Halt!" he commanded.

There was a murmur of dissent. Two or three stepped out of the ranks, and Lieutenant Merckel, with an abusive epithet, drew his sabre and rushed at Boleslav.

This was a moment in which hesitation would have been fatal. A flash of steel, a whiz, and Lieutenant Merckel sank howling on the sandy earth.

The men broke ranks, as if they would spring on him: but surprise and terror petrified them.

"Halt!" The command came forth for the second time in a voice of thunder; and no one dared move an eyelash.

Boleslav drew a pistol from the saddle-pocket, and, holding it with the trigger cocked in his left hand, he let the reins slip into his armed right.

"Men of the Reserve!" he shouted in a voice that reverberated through the square, "you know that during the last six hours you are bound in obedience by a war-decree, and that the slightest attempt at insubordination will cost you your lives. What has taken place up to this moment I will overlook, but whoever does not instantly comply

with my commands without grumbling will find
that I shall not scruple to send a bullet through
his brain on the spot."

Felix Merckel, who was bleeding copiously from
a wound in his head, regained consciousness, and
tried to raise himself. But the blood that streamed
over his face blinded him.

"Take away his sabre and bind him!" were
Boleslav's instructions.

The men exchanged glances; they had nothing
to bind him with.

To hesitate again would be to lose the day; so
with a quick resolve he sprang off his horse, tore
the bridle from its bit, and handed the thongs to
the man on the left wing.

"Set to work, and two others help."

Reluctantly, and with evil sidelong glances, they
obeyed. The prostrate man hit out with hands and
feet, and endeavored to wipe the blood out of his
eyes with his sleeve, but his struggles were in vain;
the reins bound his wrists, and the foam-spattered
curb served as a gag.

Meanwhile the spirited black charger had
broken away, and was rearing among the terrified rabble.

Boleslav saw, as he looked behind him, that the
church door stood open for a farewell service, and
that the key was in the lock.

"Put him in the church," he commanded; and

at the same moment the old landlord of the inn appeared on the scene, whimpering and wringing his hands.

"Felix!" he yelled, "what are they doing to you? Don't give in; cry for help. Help him, dear people. I order you to help him. I am your mayor. I insist—I command you."

"It is my place to issue commands here," exclaimed Boleslav loftily.

Then the old man changed his tactics, and, by cringing, tried to soften the disciplinarian's heart.

"Herr Captain, have compassion on a wretched father. I have known you since you were a little boy, who sat on my knee, and I always, always was fond of you. Isn't it true, you people? Wouldn't any of us have willingly given our lives for his young lordship?"

Had his corpulency permitted, he would have thrown himself at Boleslav's feet. On seeing his son hustled away, he ran after him in despair, and made a futile attempt to hold him back by the coat-tails. But the door was promptly closed on him.

"Give me the key!" shouted Boleslav.

The old man hurled himself on the steps, and pounded the oak panels of the door with his fists.

The key was delivered up by Boleslav's three men.

"Your name?"

The Cats' Bridge

"Michael Grossjohann!" the Schrandener answered curtly.

"And yours?" turning to the two others.

"Franz Malky."

"Emil Rosner."

He entered the names in his pocketbook.

"You three will keep watch on the prisoner through the night, and are answerable for him with your heads."

Old Merckel, finding the church door did not yield to his furious onslaughts, came to his senses, and squinting askance at Boleslav, sneaked off in the direction of the parsonage. The latter thought he knew what he wanted there.

"Three more of you," he continued, "will guard the vestry door, the key of which I have not got in my possession, and take care that no one goes in and out except the barber, who is to bandage the prisoner's wound."

Three voices quivering with suppressed anger assured him his orders should be obeyed.

"Now then, to business!" he exclaimed. "According to the lists the village of Schranden is capable of supplying troops to the number ——." And the mobilization began.

The Cats' Bridge

CHAPTER XVI

Two hours later Boleslav quitted the gaping crowd, who glowered at him with a sort of stony superstitious awe, as if he were a magician, and as he crossed the open common he felt as if he had just left a cage of wild beasts, the duty of taming which had fallen to his share. The danger seemed safely over for the present. "Having mastered them to-day, they won't dare to mutiny to-morrow," he thought, and reveled in the joyous sensation of having won a victory.

Now he had only to take leave of Regina, and his troubles would be at an end. The world was all before him once more; an unknown future seemed to be enticing him onward with bugle-peals and battle-cries.

"Regina! now for Regina!" welled up in him with such jubilation, from the depths of his soul, that he was frightened at himself. He took a turn through the wood before approaching the Cats' Bridge, to brace and harden his nerves for this last and most arduous encounter.

The sun pierced the topmost boughs of the trees. Over the tender young green of the mead-

The Cats' Bridge

ows floated a shadowy haze, and an odor of fermenting slime rose from the damp ditches. Only the fir wood looked as dark and mysterious as in winter, with scarcely a light-green spike peeping anywhere from its black, bare branches.

He threw himself at full length on the mossy ground and watched the sunbeams glint through the purple haze that hung over the surrounding thicket.

Once again he reviewed the daring enterprise of the last few hours, and the thickly curtained windows of the parsonage recurred to his memory. How careful she had been to keep herself out of his sight and reach, and how well she had succeeded! Surely she must know what had brought him into the village—must know that to-morrow he would quit it, perhaps never to return.

Had she no longing to see him just once before his departure, and to wish him Godspeed? The hour she had told him to wait patiently for, was it not time it came to-day? What availed the letter he wore close to his heart, if the hand that penned it was refused to him? Her image was now quite effaced from his heart; it could no longer lead him to battle, unless the impression was renewed.

"If she loves me, she will send for me. If she

doesn't send for me, she must be lost to me for-ever."

Having arrived at this conclusion he left the wood and bent his footsteps in the direction of the river. The park, in its new spring dress of light-est green, smiled him a welcome. A shimmer-ing crown of silver rested on the tall poplars, and the dark masses of ivy glistened on their slender trunks.

How beautiful was this home, that had been a source of such infinite pain and sorrow! How his whole being yearned for that impoverished dwell-ing where he had lodged like a criminal! Was this longing owing to the woman who had volun-tarily shared his loneliness and wretchedness, and who had tried to make her own misery the foun-dation of a new happiness for him?

But he had no reason to fear what was to come. He felt that since the Fatherland had summoned him, he was safe from all weak and vicious in-stincts. Even long before this he believed he had completely freed himself from her influence. Their relations now were merely those of master and servant.

One more night, and the priest's curse would be remembered only as an old man's idle babble. Yet what would become of her? She must look after herself. He had provided for her future. No one could say he was bound to do more. And to-day

The Cats' Bridge

he would renew his bounty twofold or threefold, so that she would stand in the position of a wealthy widow. When thousands of women and children would perish of hunger in broken-hearted distress, without any one heeding their fate, why should he concern himself so much about deserting this one strange girl and leaving her in solitude?

He steeled and hardened his heart, for it had begun to beat faster—

And as he mounted the steep ascent to the Cats' Bridge, he caught sight of the familiar figure among the bushes above, illumined by the setting sun.

"Regina," he called. But she did not move.

"Come and meet me, Regina!"

Then with elevated shoulders she slowly glided nearer, the fingers of her left hand outspread, and pressed against her breast.

He looked at her, and was horrified. "My God!" he exclaimed, "how changed you are!"

Her appearance was wild and distraught in the extreme. Her clothes were torn, her hair, which under the frequent use of the comb had begun to fall into such splendid glossy waves, once more hung over her forehead and cheeks in a shaggy, unkempt mass. Her eyes shone with feverish, almost uncanny lustre from dark-blue cavities, and she dared not raise them to his.

"She is pining away," something cried in him.

The Cats' Bridge

"She will die, because of you." He took hold of her hand and it lay limply in his palm.

"Regina, do speak. Aren't you glad that I've come back?"

She ducked her head, as she had been in the habit of doing when she instinctively expected blows instead of kind words.

He stroked her rough, dry hair. "Poor thing!" he said. "You must have had a dreadfully dull time of it, with not a human soul to speak to—"

She shrank from his touch and still maintained her silence.

"Why did you not write and tell me that you found it so terribly lonely?"

She shook her head, and then said timidly, "It wasn't the loneliness."

"What was it then?"

She looked at him nervously and again said nothing.

"Well, what was it?"

"I—I thought—you weren't coming back."

"But, you foolish girl, didn't I write and say I was?"

"Yes, you wrote and said, 'I am coming perhaps in about ten days,' and I went to the Cats' Bridge, and there I waited day and night—day and night —but you didn't come. And then three weeks afterward you wrote again, 'I shall come home perhaps in about ten days.' And you never came, and then I thought you were only putting me off with promises—so as not to break it to me suddenly that you weren't coming back at all. And I thought you repented being good to me, because I didn't deserve it, and because I—" She broke off and buried her face for a moment in her hands.

"But your letter was so sensible."

"Yes, master," she faltered. "Would it have done for *me* to write differently?"

He bit his lip, and stared before him into the lacework of the young green foliage. Did she suspect what would befall her in a few hours?

"But now all is right again, isn't it?" he asked unsteadily.

With a cry she sank on the ground, and clinging to his knees exclaimed, "Yes, oh yes! When you are here everything is right, everything is different. If you were to go away again, what should I do?"

No, she suspected nothing. The heaviest, most crushing blow of all was in store for her. He felt as if there were a thunderbolt concealed in his sleeve, which the next time he stirred would descend and shatter her to fragments. But he had still time to dispose of as he pleased. A few hours to devote to this poor creature, in which to revive and make her happy again before signing her death-warrant, and in which she would unconsciously gather up strength for the ordeal.

"Stand up, Regina," he said gently. "Let us enjoy ourselves, and not think of the future."

Then they walked side by side through the dusky garden, the neatly kept paths of which were strewn with white gravel, and skirted, like glittering rivulets, the smooth turf. The shrubs exhaled an indescribable fragrance, the breath of spring mingled with the scent of dying things, and in the tree-tops that waved above their heads they heard the subdued whispering twitter of home-coming birds.

"How beautifully everything has come out here since I went away!" he exclaimed.

"Yes," she answered. "It has never been so beautiful as it is now."

"It has become so all at once?" he asked, smiling. He looked at her sidewise and noticed the hollows in her cheeks. But an exquisite color was already tinging them.

She has begun to live again, he thought to himself, and it seemed as if the next few hours were to be the last vouchsafed to him too of a vanishing happiness.

"In spite of everything, you have worked hard," he said, striving to retain his tone of condescending patronage, and he pointed to the neat borders in which auriculas and primroses were planted.

The Cats' Bridge

She gave a proud little laugh. "I thought to myself you should find everything in order if you *did* come back."

"But you have neglected yourself, Regina. How is that?"

She turned her face away, blushing hotly.

"Shall I tell you the truth, master?" she stammered.

"Of course," he said.

"I thought—I—was—going to die—and so—it wouldn't matter."

He was silent. It was as if she poured forth an ocean of infinite love with every word, and that its waves rolled over him.

The lawn on the farther side of the castle, sloping gently down to the park, now opened before his gaze. There stood the weather-beaten socket of the Goddess Diana's pedestal. Regina had collected the pieces and put them together again, but the torso had been beyond her strength to lift, and it lay in the grass, while the head, with its blank white eyes, looked down on it. A few steps farther on, a dark four-cornered path stood out in relief from the emerald turf. That was the spot where he had first seen her busily employed in digging a grave for her seducer, whom every one else refused to bury.

Then they walked on toward the undergrowth that surrounded the cottage like a thick hedge.

The Cats' Bridge

"I have mended the glass roof," she said.

"Ah! indeed!"

Their eyes met for a moment, and then they both quickly looked in front of them again. There was an aspect of peaceful welcome about the little house. Its window panes had caught a ray of the departing sunlight, while all else lay buried in deepest shadow.

A sense of contentment at being at home, and of gladness that this was his home, overcame him, and for a moment allayed his gnawing restlessness.

"Go," he said, "and cook me something for supper; I am hungry and exhausted after a long ride."

He remembered his horse for the first time, and wondered where it had galloped to. Then the next instant he forgot it again.

"And make yourself neat," he continued. "I should like you to look your best when you come to table."

They separated in the vestibule. He went into the sitting-room, and she to her kitchen. He threw himself with a deep sigh on the sofa, that creaked beneath his weight. Everything seemed the same as on the night he had left it, except that the curtain had been taken away from the corner by the stove, and the couch removed; the portrait of his grandmother, too, had disappeared. The shot

The Cats' Bridge

which had grazed Regina's neck had proved its final destruction, and reduced it to ribbons.

One of the windows was open. The strange perfume of fermenting earth, which to-day he could not get out of his nostrils, flooded the apartment. But here it might possibly come from a lime heap, which had been shoveled up at the gable end of the house.

From minute to minute his unrest increased. Why shorten for him and her the all too scanty time? He could tolerate solitude no longer, and got up with the intention of going into the kitchen, but when on the threshold he saw her cowering on the hearth with naked shoulders, mending her jacket by the firelight, he retreated, shocked. But in a few seconds she came herself to open the door to him, fully dressed.

"Is there anything I can do for you, master?" she asked respectfully.

"Show me where you have repaired the roof," he replied, not being able to think of anything else to say. He praised her work, without looking at it. Then he took up a position on the hearth and stared at the tongues of flame in the grate. By this time it was nearly dark, and the firelight flickered on the rush walls.

"I'll help you to cook," he said.

"Oh, master! You are laughing at me," she answered. But her face lighted up with pleasure.

The Cats' Bridge

"What am I to have for supper?"

"There isn't much in the house. Eggs and fried ham—a fresh salad—and that's all."

"I shall thank God if I—" he stopped abruptly. He had nearly betrayed the secret of which as yet she had no suspicion, and she should not, must not, suspect anything. Till the dawn of to-morrow her felicity should last.

"Very well, make haste," he laughed, while his throat contracted in anxious suspense, "else I shall expire of hunger."

"The water must boil first."

"All right, we'll wait, then." He squatted on one of the wooden boxes. "And, Regina," he went on, "come here; do you know I am not satisfied with your appearance even now? Your hair—"

"I've not had time to comb it yet."

"Comb it now at once, then."

She flashed at him a look of shy entreaty.

"While you are here, master?" she asked hesitatingly.

"Why not? Have you become prudish all in a minute?"

"It wasn't that—"

"Then don't stand on ceremony."

She went into the far corner of the apartment, where her bed stood, and with a quick movement loosened the floating wealth of tresses till they hung below her hips. In the middle of her combing, aware that his eyes were fixed on her in admiration, she suddenly spread out her arms, as if overcome with shame and joy, and threw herself on her knees by the bed, burying her face in the pillows.

He waited silently till she got up. When her hair was done she went to the hearth and busied herself among the pots and kettles, without looking at him.

"Tell me, Regina, what have you been doing with yourself all this time?"

She shook her head. "Bockeldorf was the same as ever; besides the grocer and his wife, I never saw a single soul. During the floods I didn't go once down to the village. As I told you in my letter, I had to starve for a time, but I didn't mind. And then, during the last few weeks, some letters have come, from Wartenstein, and Königsberg too—and to-day one—from—"

"Ah, never mind! I'll look at them later, when you've brought some light.'"

What concern had he with the outer world to-day, when he had burned the bridges that connected him with his past, and nothing remained of all he had suffered and lived through?

Then when the supper table was spread, and the lamp shone at him from Regina's hand, he crossed over with her to the sitting-room.

The Cats' Bridge

"You have not laid a place for yourself," he remarked.

"May I, master?"

"Of course you may."

And so once more they sat opposite each other in the soft lamp-light, as they had so often done on winter evenings, when the snow was driven against the window panes, and gales shook the roof and rattled in the beams. Now gray moths flapped gently to and fro, bringing with them into the room whiffs of the balmy outer air, and the rising moon, which was full for the first time since Easter, shimmered through the young foliage.

He pushed his plate away. Not a morsel could he eat. The precaution of leaving the wine in the cellar had done no good, for the excitement he had wished to shun was, notwithstanding, creeping over him. He took a stolen glance at Regina, and trembled. Her eyes rested on him in such a transport of happiness that she seemed oblivious of everything in heaven and earth, except the fact that he was sitting near her. Every trace of sorrow and distress had vanished from her face as if by magic. Its curves had taken a new roundness, a new freshness bloomed in her cheeks. But what struck him as most lovely in her was the languorous, yielding tenderness of her whole being, as if she had loosened herself from the trammels of earth and floated in space.

332

The Cats' Bridge

"Regina," he whispered. His heart seemed throbbing violently in his throat. A voice of warning rose within him, saying, "Take care. Be on your guard—this is the last time she will lead you into temptation."

"The last time!" came a melancholy echo.

"Yes; she will die—perish of heart-sickness and unsatisfied longing. Take her in your arms and then kill her; that will save her all further misery," was the next thought that rushed through his brain. "But it would be literal madness to do such a thing," he added to himself, shuddering.

And again their eyes met and sank in each other's depths. Their souls knew of no resistance, even though their bodies still sought despairingly for weapons of defense.

"Save yourself!" cried that warning voice again. "Think of the curse! Keep yourself pure and unspotted for the Fatherland!"

He tried to think of words to speak that would break the spell of blissful enchantment; but none would occur to him. Then he rose and walked to the open window to bathe his hot brow in the cool night air. "Speak—act—end this silence," he exhorted himself. He thought of the letters she had spoken of.

"Give me the letters," he said. His voice sounded harsh.

She fetched a packet, which she laid by his plate.

The Cats' Bridge

He opened the first letter he came to, and stared vacantly at the unfolded sheet. Would it not be better to allude now to the unavoidable? Why spare her the illusion to a parting which was inevitable? But he put the idea from him in horror. "Till midnight she shall be happy. Take her in your arms, and then—"

"The nobly-born Baron Boleslav von Schranden is hereby informed that his appeal for an inquiry into the causes and events which eventually led to the destruction by fire of Castle Schranden, on the 6th of March, 1809, is receiving attention, and that a day has been appointed for—"

With a discordant laugh he tossed the communication to one side, and fumbled for the next letter. His eye fell on Helene's handwriting. A feeling almost of aversion shot through him. What did she want now? Why disturb him at this the eleventh hour?

"My dearest Boleslav—I can't let you go to the war again without once seeing and speaking to you. I beg and implore you to meet me this evening at nine o'clock, near the churchyard side-gate, where I will wait for you.
"Your Helene."

"Why not before," he murmured, "when there was plenty of time to spare?" Then suddenly it flashed across him that again in an hour of danger

334

his guardian angel had put forth her rescuing hand to him, and that it would be criminal folly on his part to disregard the sign, and not respond to the summons.

"You must—you must," he said to himself, "or you won't be worth the cannon ball that at this moment is being cast for you in France."

Was it not a special dispensation of divine grace that the daughter should intervene at such a perilous crisis as this to transform the father's curse into a blessing? He looked at the clock. It wanted only a few minutes to the hour mentioned. He dragged himself on to his feet.

"I must go down to the village," he said. "There is some one who wants to see me." And though he avoided meeting her eyes, her pathetic beseeching glance penetrated to his innermost soul.

"I shall soon be back," he stammered.

She folded her hands, and placed herself silently before him.

"What is it?" he asked.

She could hardly articulate her words.

"Master! I am so frightened—I feel as if something dreadful was going to happen!"

"Since when have you been given to presentiments?" he said, trying to joke.

"I don't know—but I feel so strange, master! —something in my throat—as if— Oh! I know

The Cats' Bridge

it's stupid of me, but I pray you—not to go
—not to-night—"

He pushed her gently to one side. The hand
that she stretched out to hold him back fell helplessly.

"Please—please don't go, master!"

He set his teeth and went—went to his guardian
angel.

336

The Cats' Bridge

CHAPTER XVII

THE Schrandeners, as many as could leave their homes and property, were meanwhile gathered together at the Black Eagle, engaged in a farewell orgie.

Old Merckel served them himself. He stood behind the bar, refilling unceasingly the empty glasses, with the melancholy smile, which to-day there was every reason to believe was not put on.

"Drink, dear friends," he exhorted; "don't let the unhappy event in my family prevent you! What does it matter even if he is shot? He will die a noble death for his honor and his Father-land!"

He wiped the sweat from his shiny forehead, while his little eyes wandered in uneasy anticipation from one face to the other.

"Go and take a glass, Amalie," he said, turning to the barmaid, "over to those on guard. I won't bear them malice for helping to bring him to his ruin!"

The Schrandeners, deeply touched at the expression of so much high-minded sentiment, gazed into their tankards in moody anger. They would have been ashamed of rushing to the inn and displaying such avidity for a carousal in the face of their landlord's private misfortune, had they not felt they could not better show their sympathy than by taking advantage of the old man's generous impulses.

So they poured beer and schnapps down their throats in positive streams, and emulated each other as to who could drink the fastest.

The barmaid, as fat and cunning as her master, slipped out with a tray containing a dozen foaming tankards, after she had received a few whispered instructions from him, accompanied by a knowing nod and wink.

"And if you should see old Hackelberg about," he called after her, "ask him in—ask him in. He has suffered too at the hands of the scoundrel. He ought not to be missing on this sad occasion."

"Brave soldiers," he continued, wiping his eyes, "drink! drink! You must try to forget that this day your honor has been forfeited. Yes, indeed, your case is lamentable—even more lamentable than that of my poor son, to whom it will at least be granted to meet death for honor's sake. But you! faugh, for shame! What will be your feelings to-morrow morning, when you have to march away under the leadership of that son of a traitor,

The Cats' Bridge

the villain whom our revered pastor has cursed?
It'll be 'Braun, clean my boots!' and 'Bickler, hold
my stirrup!' and that sort of thing."

The two men mentioned thus by name started
up with an oath.

"And all you others, however much he may
oppress and bully you, you must submit because
he is your commander; and if you dare to mutiny,
you'll only be shot down like vermin for your
pains. Such, my poor dear friends, is your pitiable
lot! Therefore I say drink, and bid farewell to
your military honor. To-morrow the very dogs
will hesitate to take a crust of bread from your
hands!"

A half-stifled murmur ran through the room,
more ominous than a howl of rage.

Then the carpenter Hackelberg, who had been
loafing about in the neighborhood of the inn, reeled
into the common parlor, half-drunk as usual.

He was received in silence. But old Merckel
advanced solemnly to meet him, seized him by the
hand, and led him to a seat of honor.

"You, too, are an unhappy father," he said to
him in a voice quivering with emotion. "Your
heart, like mine, has been broken by the ruin of
your child. You, as well as myself and us all, has
the tyrant up yonder on his conscience. So sit
down, you miserable man, and take a drop of something with us!"

The Cats' Bridge

The drunkard, who was used to being fisticuffed and held up to derision, even by those who bore him no ill-will, scarcely knew what to make of this highly flattering reception. He glanced suspiciously round him with his fishy eyes, and appeared to be considering earnestly whether he should begin to brag or to weep. Meanwhile he drank all he could lay hands on.

"Look at this deplorable victim of baronial lust," Herr Merckel continued. "A man who is deprived of the possibility of revenge must lose his self-respect as he has, and degenerate into a sloven. Day and night he broods inwardly on the wrong that has been done him. But even the trodden-on worm turns at last, and who can blame us if we wish with all our hearts that the miscreant should not live to see another day?"

"Strike him dead!" spluttered the carpenter, suddenly waxing furious, but there was only a faint echo in response, for to the men who were now soldiers under orders for active service the glibly made suggestion seemed no longer a trifle.

Herr Merckel assumed an air of holy horror. "For shame, dear people! we must not listen to such treason. I, being your mayor, can not countenance it. To strike him down in broad daylight would be an unwarrantable act of violence, and I wonder you dare entertain such an idea for a moment. But who can stem the torrent of right-

The Cats' Bridge

eous wrath that vents itself in imprecations and anathemas? And so it is my most earnest desire that our arch-enemy and tyrant may die in his bed to-night, or disappear and never be seen again, or that his body may be found to-morrow morning in the river Maraune. Then it would at least be clearly proved that there is still a God above to judge and condemn sinners. Amen."

"Amen," growled his listeners, and folded their horny hands.

"But, alas! it won't come to pass. We shall live to see the miscreant fatten and prosper, and grow gray in this vale of tears. To-morrow he will ride up triumphantly and drag out my Felix like a lamb to the slaughter. And others who have demurred by a word or look will be sacrificed too. Indeed I shall be very much surprised if any of you escape with your lives. It is his intention, I firmly believe, to extirpate every Schrandener from off the face of the earth. Like a herd of cattle that has been purchased for the shambles, he'll drive you forth to-morrow morning, leaving your widows and orphans behind to weep and bewail your fate."

An ejaculation of fury arose, so loud and violent that even the inciter of it recoiled in alarm.

"Quietly, dear people, quietly! No lawbreaking. Although, truly, there is no informer among us, we would sooner bite our tongues out than betray each other. Hackelberg knows that. Thereby hangs a tale, eh, old friend? But who knows that our Herr Captain may not himself be hanging about outside, spying through the windows."

Five or six heads turned, and were pressed against the panes.

"You think he wouldn't spy on us? Oh, I can assure you he is not the one to stop short at any low trick. I know what you'd like to say, and I can't blame you for it—that if you catch him sneaking around at night-time, woe betide him!"

"We'll kill him!" fumed the topers.

"Don't be forever screaming that, children; it offends my ears. So much can be achieved quietly. Thus, bang! Some one has fired. Bang again— another report. Simply a poacher in the forest. It swarms with deer, eh, Hackelberg?" He laughed, and clicked his tongue.

"You mustn't sit dozing there, my man. One would think you had no more blood in your veins than a jelly-fish. Have you forgotten how the late Baron had you flogged till your skin hung in ribbons? By thunder, how you danced and bellowed! It was a charming spectacle."

Hackelberg writhed and grunted over his glass.

"At that time you were a sportsman, a terror to

your master, and your bullet never missed its mark. Drink away, man! It's difficult to believe now that you were ever a good shot."

"I am still," lisped the carpenter.

"Ha, ha!—pardon my laughing, old fellow. To begin with, you don't even know what you've done with your gun."

"But—I do."

"And besides, your hand has become too slack, and your honor has evaporated, and your courage with it.'"

The carpenter laughed. An evil light gleamed in the corners of his eyes.

"What? You would maintain that you have a spark of honor left in your composition when you submit without a murmur to your daughter being brought to shame? And what's more, you can bear to see her and her seducer at large. Didn't she, your own flesh and blood, scorn you and slap away your proffered hand? Ungrateful, disrespectful wench that she is!"

The carpenter staggered to his feet.

"No one follow me," he roared, and shook his fist.

"Where are you going?"

"That's no business of any one's."

The Schrandeners, even in their wrath, could not resist making fun of the drunkard, but Merckel signed to them to let him go in peace.

The Cats' Bridge

"He is going to scratch up his gun from the dung heap," he exclaimed. "Still, what good will it do?" he added with a sigh, while his eyes wandered uneasily to the door. "He'll take care not to deliver himself into our hands at night. To-morrow, at dawn of day, he'll come, when none of you can defend yourself, and hand you over to your executioners, along with my son Felix, and none of you will see Schranden again. So drink your last, children—take leave of old Father Merckel— Ah! there comes Amalie," he said, interrupting himself, and the lackadaisical expression of his face changed to one of cheerful expectancy.

The door was thrown open, and Amalie burst in greatly excited. She whispered something hurriedly in his ear.

He beamed, and folded his fat hands as if in prayer.

"Children," he cried, "there is yet a judge in Heaven. The Baron is in the village."

The Schrandeners rose from their seats yelling with delight.

"Where is he? Who has seen him?"

"Tell them, Amalie!" he urged the barmaid, and sank back exhausted, like a person who is satisfied that his day's work is done.

And Amalie told them. She had waited till the men on guard had finished their beer, and had

The Cats' Bridge

taken a little stroll in the moonlight to get a breath of fresh air. Then she had seen a man coming across the fields from the Cats' Bridge. He was going in the direction of the churchyard, and wore an officer's coat with scarlet collar and gold buttons.

"Was he armed?" inquired a cautious son of Schranden.

Yes; she had seen his sabre flash in the moonlight.

This information afforded food for reflection.

"He has gone to inspect the guard," suggested some one, scratching his head.

Master Merckel laughed ironically.

"Since how long has it been customary to review sentinels in the churchyard?" he exclaimed. "I tell you what he has gone there for. He wishes to pay his dear, chaste Herr Papa a visit—to swear on his grave that he will avenge him, so soon as you are delivered into his hands as soldiers. Congratulate yourselves on the expedition."

At this juncture an ally cropped up on whom he had ceased to count. The old carpenter rushed in at the door, flourishing in his right hand an old fowling-piece, on which hung straw and manure. He seemed in a perfect transport of fury, beating his breast and capering about like one possessed.

"Who said I had no sense of honor," he

The Cats' Bridge

screamed; "and that I allowed my child to be ruined? Where's the hussy who has brought shame and disgrace on my gray hairs? I won't make her a coffin. No; I'll shoot her down—I'll shoot them both."

"Come along to the churchyard," cried out a voice from among the villagers, who felt their courage rising.

The old landlord winced. "No, not to the churchyard," he exhorted them. "In the first place, the ground is sacred; and in the second, you might miss him there. If you really wish to settle matters quietly with him once for all—I'm not supposed to know what you have against him, and don't wish to know—well, my advice to you is to go to the Cats' Bridge. Just there, you know, the bank is wooded—not thickly, certainly, but thick enough for you to hide behind."

"But suppose he returned by way of the village and the drawbridge?" put in the cautious trooper again.

Master Merckel knew better. "Not he!" he laughed. "The Cats' Bridge is handier."

"Let's be off, then, to the Cats' Bridge," yelled the carpenter, bumping the butt end of his gun against the chairs and tables. There was a general stampede. Master Merckel crammed bottles of brandy into as many pockets as he could catch hold of, as his customers hurried out.

The Cats' Bridge

"Take it, friends," he cried, "and welcome! Defend your honor—defend your honor!"

Then, when the last had gone, he mopped his perspiring brow, and folding his hands, exclaimed with an uneasy sigh:

"Ah, Amalie, if only they don't offer him violence!"

The Cats' Bridge

CHAPTER XVIII

ON reaching the highroad Boleslav saw the figure of a girl come out from the shadow of the churchyard yews, and advance to meet him with hesitating footsteps.

The moment to which he had looked forward with tender yearning for eight years had come at last, yet his heart beat no quicker. "You ought to be pleased; congratulate yourself," he said inwardly. "She loves you! She saved you—has freed you from Regina." And something echoed sadly within him, "From Regina!"

The contour of the too slender figure was sharply defined against the moonlit background. The shoulders looked angular, and her hips fell in straight, ungraceful lines from the high-waisted bodice.

He jumped over the ditch, and held out both his hands to her. With a prudish simper she placed hers behind her back.

"Don't be so impetuous," she lisped.

He was amazed. The action chilled him, and almost excited his contempt; but he was ashamed of the emotion, and tried to suppress it.

The Cats' Bridge

"You have kept me waiting a long time, Regina."

The face she turned on him was illuminated by the moon, and he saw plainly how insignificant and commonplace she had become. She tossed her head scornfully.

"My name is Helene," she said. "I am sorry you have forgotten it"; and, pouting, she turned her back.

He winced. "Pardon," he stammered; "it was a slip of the tongue."

This was certainly an unfortunate beginning. She made another grimace, but seemed disposed to accept his apology.

"Don't let us stay here," she begged. "I'm afraid."

"What of?"

"Of the churchyard—if you *will* know."

Again he had to struggle against a feeling of contempt. In all she said and did he found himself involuntarily comparing her with Regina, and the comparison was immeasurably to her disadvantage.

"You know how timid I am," she said, as they retraced their steps. "It was rash of me to have chosen this place for an appointment; indeed it was exceedingly rash to come at all—and if it weren't—"

Instead of finishing her sentence she cast at him

an affected sidelong glance. Then, as he offered
to help her over the ditch she gave a little scream
and said, "No, no!"

His half-defined sensation of disappointment
now gave place to blank astonishment. She gazed
round her nervously.

"We can't stay here either," she whispered. "If
I were caught here alone with a gentleman, I believe I should die of shame."

"Where do you wish to go, then?"

"You must decide."

"Very well. Come into the wood."

She clasped her hands together with an agitated
old-maidish gesture.

"What are you thinking of?" she exclaimed.
"At night—with a gentleman!"

He rubbed his eyes. Was it really possible,
what he heard and saw? Could this be Helene,
the guardian angel to whom he had looked up, as
to a being belonging to another world?

But perhaps it was he who was to blame. Perhaps the language of innocence and virtue was no
longer intelligible to him because of the fair savage who had perverted his tastes, and filled his
imagination with impure pictures.

"Then let us walk quietly along the highroad,"
he said.

"But if some one comes?"

"We can see that no one *is* coming."

The Cats' Bridge

"Yet some one might—"

He was at a loss for an answer. A silence ensued, and then he said, "Won't you take my arm?"

"Oh, I don't know whether I ought," replied the love of his youth.

And again they walked on in silence. It almost seemed as if they had nothing at all to say to each other.

"Regina is waiting!" a voice cried within him.

"How silent you are!" Helene lisped, playfully pinching his elbow with two of the finger-tips that lay on his arm. "You wicked man! Haven't you a little bit of liking left for me?"

He felt he had no right to say "No." She had been true to him, had trusted his word for eight long years; he dared not prove himself unworthy now of her faith in him. When he had reassured her with a stammered "Of course, of course," she sighed, a deep-drawn, languishing sigh.

"I hear such dreadful things about you," she said, "that I don't know what to believe. Tell me it's not true."

"What?" he asked wearily.

"Ah, a girl can't discuss such matters. Immoral things, I mean. In old days you were a good, noble fellow, and I can't believe it's true that you've altered so completely."

She drew a little closer to him. In doing so, she dropped her blue silk reticule. As he stooped

The Cats' Bridge

—with her—to pick it up, the peak of his cap brushed her face.

"Oh, take care!" she simpered, drawing back hastily.

"A thousand pardons!" he answered, in a tone of rigid politeness, and bit his lips.

"Well, you don't answer my question," she continued. "Perhaps it is true, then, what people say! I should be sorry to think that poor unhappy me had been so deceived in you. But papa always thought you would come to a bad end." She said this with such a ludicrous little air of superiority, that he could not help smiling.

She seemed to discern that she was appearing absurd in his eyes, and went on in a deeply injured tone, "Ah, it's very well to laugh at a poor girl, whose intentions toward you are so kind, and who would give anything to prevent your ruin."

"Please, do not trouble yourself on my account," he replied.

"Now you are making yourself out worse than you are," she interposed. "I know you have a noble nature at bottom. And if fate parts us forever, I shall always, always keep a warm place for you in my heart. Oh, what bitter tears have I shed for you many a time! And I've prayed every night to God to keep the dear friend of my youth from sin, and from wicked revengeful thoughts, and to give him a good conscience."

The Cats' Bridge

"I am afraid the behavior of the Schrandeners is not exactly calculated to cure a man of revengeful thoughts," he replied.

She turned up her sharp little nose. "The Schrandeners are an uncouth lot," she remarked. "And one can't have much to do with them. I would much rather stay altogether with my aunt in Wartenstein. There at least one associates with respectable, well-mannered townspeople, who lift their hats to a lady when they meet her in the street. Not a single Schrandener, with the exception of Herr Merckel, and Felix, of course, dreams of doing such a thing. Felix," she added with a sigh, "has the manners of a gentleman and an officer." Then as if something had suddenly recalled the events of the afternoon to her mind, she screamed, wrung her hands, and said: "Oh, Boleslav, Boleslav!"

"What is it, Helene?"

"Boleslav, how could you be so wicked! Poor, poor Felix! I did not see it myself, for I was in the back-garden drawing radishes, but they told me afterward how you slashed at his head with your drawn sabre, till it poured with blood." She shuddered and shook with suppressed sobs. Then she wrenched her hand out of his arm and skipped to the opposite side of the road. "Go! I won't have anything more to do with you," she cried. "You acted in a harsh and cruel manner—"

The Cats' Bridge

"But you don't understand, dear Helene," he protested.

"And he was your schoolfellow and playmate, and used to play hide-and-seek with us both in the garden. He often climbed over the hedge for you to get your ball when you had tossed it too far, and he used to give you guinea-pigs. Have you forgotten everything? You ought to remember the dear old times."

"Because of the guinea-pigs, eh?"

"Oh—and to think that you have shut him up in the cold dark church! Papa is of opinion that you had no business to do it; he says he will report your conduct at headquarters, and that probably you will get the worst of it."

She resembled her father so little, he thought, that his words of thunder when repeated by her lips sounded like the most insipid chatter. And it was on this cackling little hen that he had let hang the great question of to be or not be!

She had now come back to his side, and with a mincing gesture pushed her hand again through his arm.

"They say that you intend carrying him off to-morrow as a prisoner, to be tried by a court-martial, and that he will be shot dead for certain. But it must be a lie. It is, isn't it? You couldn't do such a thing; I wouldn't believe it of you. You are not so bad as all that."

The Cats' Bridge

He suppressed an exclamation of impatience.

"Say you won't?" she besought, wiping her eyes. "If *I* ask you, dear Boleslav, to let him go free, you will grant me the favor—I know you will."

She spoke calmly, as if the request she made were merely a casual one. But there was secret anxiety in the eyes that glanced at his suspiciously.

"Dear, dear Boleslav!" she continued more urgently, her arm trembling violently, "if you care for me the very least little bit, don't let us part before you have promised me this. I will cherish your memory always in my heart, if Fate is cruel enough to separate us forever, and will at least never cease to pray for you and bless you."

"I am sorry, Helene," he said, moved to speaking more warmly by her now evident distress, "if I must seem hard and inexorable to you. But it is all of no good. Your wish can not possibly be fulfilled."

She had not in the least expected this answer, and regarded him for a second with a cold, angry expression. Then suddenly she burst out weeping, and sank against the trunk of a tree for support, with her thin hands before her face.

At the same moment the report of a gun was heard in the distance, the echo of which slowly rolled through the woodlands.

Helene gave a frightened cry, and, throwing up her hands, sobbed out:

The Cats' Bridge

"Now they have shot him for certain, because you, inhuman monster, have commanded it! Oh dear! have you *no* mercy?"

Listening in the direction from which the gunshot had come, he did his best to soothe her.

That the shot had anything to do with Felix Merckel was, of course, out of the question.

It had undoubtedly been fired in the wood, on the farther side of the castle, probably by a poacher on the track of a wild red deer.

But she sobbed more violently than ever:

"It's all very well—but you—you—intend dragging him out to his death—you know you do."

Her increasing agitation began to bewilder Boleslav. He assured her he would do everything in his power to ameliorate Felix's sentence. He himself would testify to his being hopelessly intoxicated at the time. His old rancor against himself, his wounded vanity, all should be cited in extenuation of his offense, and might influence his judges to mildness.

But she was not satisfied, and at last dropped on her knees in the clay soil, and cried aloud:

"Be merciful! be noble! Save him!"

"For God's sake, stand up!"

"No, I shall not. In the dust I'll kneel to you and implore your mercy."

"But don't you see that I shall be imputing to

The Cats' Bridge

myself a murderous design if I represent him as innocent?"

"Never mind," she sobbed. "If you really love me, you won't object to making this little sacrifice for my sake."

Then it began to dawn on him that it was not for the pleasure of seeing him she had summoned him to her side, but, in accordance with a preconceived plan, to make use of his love for her on behalf of another. And of such stuff as this the woman was made, of whom for long years he had considered himself unworthy! This was the radiant angel who had represented his ideal of purity and goodness, whose name he had held too sacred to mention in the same breath as Regina's!

And Regina, the dishonored, the outcast! What worlds she seemed now above this sly virtue!

A wild laugh burst from him.

"Why did you not tell me at once that you were in love with some one else?"

She started. "This is a slander!" she cried. "I am an honest, innocent girl!"

"Well, I presume you are betrothed?"

She began to cry again, though even in her grief she did not forget to carefully brush the mud from her skirts.

"Oh, Boleslav," she wailed, "it's all your fault. Why did you keep me waiting for you so long? And why have you given people so much cause to

357

gossip about you? And then you know, there was papa! His consent could never have been won! What was I, poor girl, to do?"

"Please say no more. It really doesn't matter!" he broke in cheerily.

"You aren't angry with me, then?"

"Oh, no! not in the least!"

In silence he accompanied Helene back to the village, took a friendly farewell of her, and promised to do all he could to save her betrothed.

She thanked him, made a formal little courtesy, and they parted.

And so ended the great love of his life.

As he watched the shadow of her meagre little figure disappear behind the houses, his whole soul cried out for Regina in uncontrollable, boundless jubilation. Now the road was free—free for sinful, exultant love.

But what was sin, when virtue had collapsed so deplorably? How could there be any evil, when what was good appeared so absurd and contemptible?

"Take her in your arms—crush her to your breast—even to-morrow shall not cheat you of her. She shall follow you to the camp, from battle to battle—let her wear men's clothes like that Leonore Prohaska, the heroine whom all Germany admires and honors!"

"Regina! Regina!" he caroled anew, stretching

The Cats' Bridge

out his arms exultingly, in anticipation. He bounded over the moonlit meadows, and higher and darker every minute rose the wooded bank of the river before him.

She would be standing on the Cats' Bridge looking out for him, as she had always done.

"Regina!" he shouted over the river. But no answer came. Deep silence all around. There was only a faint rustle among the young leaves of the willows that sounded like slumberous breathing through half-closed lips; and a gentle splashing came up from the invisible river. Its waters were low, and broke on the sharp pebbles. He climbed the steep steps.

"Regina!" he called again. Still silence. Then he saw that in the centre of the plank, the rickety hand-rail had given way: rotten splinters hung on either side. Horror-stricken, he looked down at the river.

On its silver surface floated a woman's corpse.

The Cats' Bridge

CHAPTER XIX

WHEN the Schrandeners left the Black Eagle they dispersed to their homes, with the intention of arming themselves to the best of their ability.

Half of them did not appear again. The others —about twenty in number—careered in detachments behind the limping carpenter, round the castle island in the direction of the Cats' Bridge. Once united under the shelter of the bushes, they believed they would be unseen and unfollowed. They sneaked in silence through the damp grass; only the old drunkard insisted on keeping up an incessant chatter and mumbling. He conversed excitedly with his gun as if it had been a human being—shook and exhorted it not to fail him. From time to time he held the butt-end to his cheek in an aiming position, and when his range of vision became confused by the sight of his own dancing fingers, or imaginary bats and fireflies, he would take a long pull at his bottle to clear it.

On reaching the Cats' Bridge, which darkly spanned the river, its rivets glittering in the moonlight, the Schrandeners divided, some going to one side of it and the rest keeping to the other. As

The Cats' Bridge

noiselessly as their half-drunken condition would permit, they slid down the decline in order to screen themselves behind the alders. Those who had firearms, led by the old carpenter, stationed themselves on the edge of the sand-bank, so that they might bring their victim down from the plank bridge, should he by any chance escape the meditated attack from below of pikes, scythes, and flails.

For the space of five minutes there was scarcely a sound audible, beyond the crackling and swishing among the twigs caused by some one stretching out a hand for his bottle of schnapps. Death-like stillness reigned too on the island.

Then the carpenter, whose eyes were momentarily sharpened by brandy, and who was on the alert like a tiger crouching for a spring, discerned a figure emerge and walk slowly and softly on to the Cats' Bridge. It must have been cowering in the boscage above, on the opposite bank, for several minutes.

As the figure came out of the shadow into the full light of the moon, he recognized his daughter. Clearly she had discovered the assassins, and was now on her way to warn the Baron of his peril.

"Go back, you vermin!" he cried, all a sportsman's fury at being deprived of his certain prey taking possession of him and clouding his erratic brain.

The Cats' Bridge

She ducked her head, but glided forward, holding on to the hand-rail.

"Back, or I'll shoot!"

With one frantic leap she tried to propel herself forward, but a shot was fired at the same instant, and she sank noiselessly against the rotten balustrade. It snapped in two, and a dark, lifeless mass fell from the heights of the Cats' Bridge into the river. The water rose and fell in sparkling cascades. In the shallow bottom the stones rolled and ground against each other.

Then slowly the whirling, swaying body rose to the surface of the ripples, till the face gazed upward and was brilliantly illumined by the moon.

A profound stillness reigned on the bank.

Motionless, and with bated breath, every one stared down on the dead, upturned face, with its wide-open eyes, which seemed full of warning and rebuke. A corner of her skirt had caught on a gnarled stump of a tree, which projected into the river; thus she was anchored, and prevented from drifting down with the stream.

Softly and cautiously, as if playing with it, the current moved the body to and fro, and no one, however much he might wish to avoid it, could help seeing the head as it floated on the water.

The silence lasted a full ten minutes, and then one of the Schrandeners, who had helped to incarnate the evil conscience of the village, shyly with

The Cats' Bridge

bent head slunk away, making the bushes crackle and rustle as he went. A second followed; a third, a fourth—until at last the scene of the catastrophe was deserted.

The carpenter, who had been contemplating his daughter's dead face, grumbling, and talking to himself the while, found himself alone.

Suddenly he roared out hoarsely, "Fire! fire! fire!" and hurled his gun at the corpse. It went splashing to the bottom of the river, and he staggered after the others as fast as his legs would carry him.

Nothing stirred now near the Cats' Bridge. Boleslav was safe!

.   .   .   .

Some time elapsed before he was able to take in what he saw. He stared in stupefaction, first at the floating corpse, then at the broken balustrade.

"You should have had it repaired long ago," he thought, and toyed dazedly with the fragments.

Then, as if waking from a dream, he went back to the bank, and climbed down the ravine, where he found broken branches lying about, and freshly-made footmarks. A vague suspicion of what had happened dawned on him, and then quickly died out; the hope that there might yet be time to restore her to life absorbing his mind, to the exclusion of every other emotion.

The Cats' Bridge

He crawled cautiously along the tree-stump as near the body as he could get, and drew it ashore with the hilt of his sabre— Now she lay on the shining sand, and a hundred little rivulets ran from every part of her. He took his sabre-blade and cut her wet jacket off her, and became aware of the blood that had dyed her chemise crimson. As he ripped this away, too, he discovered the fount from which the stream flowed in a wound beneath her left breast.

Now he knew what that gunshot had meant. And when the first wild impulse for vengeance, which seemed to scream in his ear, "Go and burn their houses to the ground, and hew them down till you yourself are hewn down!" had subsided and consumed its own rage, he flung himself on the corpse, and broke into passionate weeping. He lay thus for a long time, then slowly rose, and, bearing her on his shoulders, carried her through the footprints of her murderers up the steep incline over the Cats' Bridge to the island. She was no light burden, and three times he sank on to his knees, gasping under her weight.

Near the shrubbery that surrounded the cottage he was obliged to put her down, for he feared he should swoon from his exertions. She lay on the same spot where he had found her, motionless and bleeding, after his father's funeral.

Now as then the moonbeams played on the still

pale face; only now she would not revive, could never be recalled to life.

"They have succeeded at last!" he cried, breaking into a loud, bitter laugh.

A sharp spasm of pain shot through the back of his head; he felt as if he must go raving mad if those fixed, glazed eyes continued to look up at him much longer.

But his anxiety to get the corpse interred before he went away brought him to his senses. The Schrandeners were capable of laying the murdered girl beneath the earth somewhere in the heart of the forest; thereby removing all evidence of their crime, and crippling the hands of justice.

The one person he felt could be relied on to do what was right in the matter was the old pastor. Much as he might have denounced and slandered her hitherto, he, at all events, would not be a party to this last foul outrage. Boleslav therefore resolved to rouse him from his bed, and to bring him to the spot, so that later when he himself was God knew where, a witness might not be wanting.

The belfry clock struck eleven as he reached the village street. The sentinels were parading noiselessly up and down in front of the church door, otherwise the whole world was apparently wrapped in profound slumber.

But from one of the cottages he passed, loud blows, oaths, and scolding cries fell upon his ear.

The Cats' Bridge

He looked over the hedge, and saw the green coffin which was the carpenter Hackelberg's trade-mark, looming uncannily from its stand.

The drunkard's imbecile formula occurred to him. "His wish is likely to be fulfilled," he thought; "he has now the chance of making a coffin for his daughter;" and in a bitterly ironical mood he determined to communicate to the old man, if he were still in possession of his faculties, his child's terrible end, and to demand the fulfilment of his promise.

He entered the gloomy passage. From a room on the right proceeded the gurgling cries of the thick, drunken voice which excited his involuntary disgust. Mingled with it was a spasmodic hissing and whizzing that he could not explain, till he had lifted the latch and witnessed a spectacle so horrible and revolting that, rich as the day had been for him in horrors, he recoiled before it faint and shuddering.

The old carpenter, his clothes half torn off, bleeding from the throat and arms, the moonlight bringing into prominence the hideous filthiness of the room, plunged about as if seized with an attack of St. Vitus's dance. Every limb quivered violently, and he foamed at the mouth. His eyes rolled in a maniacal frenzy, and the muscles of his face twitched convulsively. A huge plane hung from his right hand, the handle of which, formed

The Cats' Bridge

in the shape of a ring, had grazed his knuckles, and which he vainly endeavored to steady with his palsied fingers. Whenever he came to a wooden surface, whether on the table, the walls, or the planks that covered the floor, he tried to plane it, and this caused the hissing sound which always ended abruptly with a rasping jerk.

"It'll soon be ready now!" he cried. "One more blow"—ssh—"and the shaping's done"—ssh—ssh— "Damn the bats!—why can't they leave a man alone?"—ssh—ssh— "Forward— Listen! Fire! fire! The castle's on fire! Fire! fire! Keep out of the way, you baggage—if you tell any one you've seen me—with the tinder and the bundle of flax"—ssh—ssh— "I won't finish your coffin"— ss—ssh— "Get out of my sight, you snake." He lunged against Boleslav, who, with a presentiment of what ghastly disclosures were to be made to him, had planted himself in his way. The drunkard appeared to be laboring under the delusion that Boleslav was his daughter. "Go back— off the Cats' Bridge—the Baron shall get his deserts to-day—back—or—" He laid the plane against his cheek, and took aim; then, as if confronted by another vision, he yelled once more at the top of his voice, trembling with fright, "Fire! fire!" and made an attempt to creep under the table, planing the tattered tails of his coat as he went. "Fire! fire! Get away—I didn't do it! My daugh-

The Cats' Bridge

ter is a liar— The flames are spreading. Fire! fire! Look at the flames!"

With the flames he seemed to reach the zenith of his delirium, and then gradually descended again to the bats, which he made a feint of chasing away with his arms and legs, and then resumed planing the legs of the table.

"Nearly ready, dear sir"—ssh—ssh— "Just a couple more boards"—ss—ssh— "My daughter's debauched— There can be no mistake"—ss—ssh —"finely polished"—ss— "Now there she lies, and will howl no more"—ssh— "What, not gone yet? Your father'll drive you out"—ss—ssh— "The Baron will get a shot lodged in his ribs to-day"— ssh— "We want extra hands. Hurrah, men!— Hurrah, Merckel!"—ss— "Come off the plank —down from the bridge, you beast. Have you any more French behind you? If you don't go at once—"

Here he made for Boleslav. He looked in the moonlight, with his tottering legs, his palsied head, and his flapping arms, like some ghastly phantasmal monster, whose limbs were pieced together by a hundred movable joints. Just as he was reaching his goal, the flames began to pursue him once more, and to escape from them he crept, with a piercing shriek this time, beneath a stack of wood, where, with dense swarms of bats, the fearful cycle of his delusions recommenced.

The Cats' Bridge

Boleslav, shaken to the foundations of his being by the awful truth the old man had revealed in his delirious ravings, felt he could no longer bear to gaze on such a hideous scene.

He fled from the house as if the imaginary flames which so terrified the maniac were pursuing him too, and he did not pause till he had left the village behind him, and found himself encompassed by the shadows of the ruins.

The Cats' Bridge

CHAPTER XX

THE church clock had struck the midnight hour by the time Boleslav got back to the spot where he had left Regina's soulless body.

A protecting darkness now veiled the white face, for the moon had passed behind a bank of clouds, yet even from the darkness the great lustreless eyes gazed appealingly up at him as if asking a question to which there was no answer here or hereafter.

He threw himself on his knees beside her, and saying good-by to the two stars whose light had gone out, he tenderly closed their lids. She now looked as if she were asleep, and he breathed more freely. He felt something almost approaching a painful satisfaction as he watched by her. "You belong to me, only to me," he said. "No one else shall have any part or lot in you, in death as in life."

What he had resolved to do, in a spirit of defiance, as he left the murderer's house, in his present calmer mood still seemed the most commendable course to take. Past events appeared to him now like a brazen chain of guilt, to which for years one link after the other had been added. And into this chain had been forged, till it was made a component part of it, an unlawful love. For the sake of this love which was sinful as hell and pure as heaven, that which only the silence of the night had witnessed should in the silence of the night be buried—buried with this corpse.

What retribution could be rendered by the poor tribunal of man, in a case in which fate had so clearly interfered and pronounced sentence? Would it not be profaning the dead body to drag it into the glare of publicity, and so expose it to the sniveling curiosity of the vulgar herd?

Should he permit the priest who had cursed her in her lifetime to consign her to the grave with a perfunctory blessing? And would not this involve her being laid in a coffin manufactured by her father's bloodguilty hands, followed by his accomplices as mourners, hooting and throwing stones?

Ah no; it should not be! She should be the prey, now she was dead, of no Schrandener wolves. He alone, for whom she had lived, for whom she had gone to meet her death, must prepare her last resting-place. He would hide her in the lap of mother earth, and smooth the turf so carefully above her that no body-snatcher would ever discover and profane the holy spot. He lifted the corpse in his arms and carried it to the grass-plot. The moon had risen high in the heavens and shrouded the landscape in a veil of silver. From the dewy glistening grass rose the fragments of the old Diana statue in dazzling whiteness. Here he bore her and let her sink on the turf, her neck supported by the cracked pedestal, so that with her face turned toward the moon, she looked as if she had fallen asleep in a sitting position. Then he sought a burial-place. His eye fell on the black, four-cornered patch which Regina had intended for his father's grave. How vividly she came back to him, as she had looked then, in the full splendor of her sunburnt strength and beauty, driving the heavy spade into the ground with her naked foot, as if it had been a ramrod. If he had not then interrupted her in her work, he would to-day have been spared his.

The service of love she had wished to render his father it was now his duty to do for her. What could be simpler than to go on digging deeper the grave that she had begun that day, little dreaming it would be her own?

He fetched a spade from the kitchen, where the fire she had kindled was still smoldering, and began with all his strength to throw up the sod. From time to time he paused and glanced at her. She seemed well content to sit there in the bright moonlight, and quietly contemplate his labors. Now and then, when the shadow of a cloud flickered on her face, he half fancied she moved, and was going to rise to her feet.

The Cats' Bridge

Then that tormenting skepticism that all experience in the presence of their beloved dead overwhelmed him. He called her name and rushed to her side. Her hand rested on Diana's head, which lay close to her in the grass. He dared not touch her, and stole back to his work, his face buried in his hands.

The grave began to grow deep, and he feared that soon he might not be able to climb on to the edge again. He went to get the flower-stand out of the greenhouse, on the shelves of which she had ranged the plates and dishes in such beautiful order.

"No one shall eat off them again!" he said, and dashed the earthenware crockery on the floor, where it broke to atoms. He placed the stand against the inside of the grave, to serve as a ladder, and then continued throwing out the soil as before.

By the time the clock in the village had boomed out the second hour of the morning, his melancholy task was finished. He had no coffin for her, but to prevent her lying on the black moist earth, he fetched from his bed, which she had always taken pains to keep so daintily clean and tidy, a quilt, and two feather pillows, and lined the grave with them.

And now the time for parting had come. He raised her in his arms, and bore her to the edge of

the pit; then sitting down on the mound of turf
to take breath, he lifted her head on to his knees.
Never before had he been able to look at her so
leisurely, for he had never dared trust himself to
let his eyes rest on her for long. Now he studied
lovingly every feature of the dead face, caressed
the stiff cheeks, and wrung the water from her
heavy curls. A cold shiver passed through his
frame. He had held the wet body, with its drip-
ping skirts, so long in his arms, that his own clothes
were damp from the contact.

"Farewell," he murmured, and kissed her on
the forehead. He was going to kiss her on the
lips, but drew back quickly.

"You disdained them in life," he said to himself, "so in death they may not belong to you."

And then he edged the corpse nearer the grave,
and jumped down on to the top step of the stand.
Slowly and cautiously he lifted her in, stretched
her on the quilt, and cushioned her head on the
soft pillows.

Once more he wanted to kiss her, but was afraid
to leave the stand that bridged her feet; so he con-
tented himself with stroking her hands, which he
could reach from where he sat; then he clambered
out of the grave, drawing the stand after him with
the top of the spade-handle. But afterward he
found he had forgotten to draw a corner of the
quilt over her face, to prevent the soil from falling

on it. "Flowers," he thought, "will do as well"; and he went in search of them. Under the trees in the park grew great masses of anemones and bluebells, and there were violets and primroses, that she herself had cultivated, in the garden.

He gathered all he could see in the uncertain light. The anemones and primroses had closed their calyxes in sleep, but the violets looked up at him with their confiding blue eyes, as if inviting him to pluck them.

With his hands full he returned to the grave, and, as he looked down into it, stood spellbound at what he saw. It was indeed a picture of almost magic loveliness. The moon had passed its height, and, shining at the foot of the grave, illuminated it on the east side, so that the head, reposing in its deep resting-place, was thrown out clearly in relief, while the blood-stained body was hidden in darkest shadow.

The still, white face seemed to smile up at him, as if lapped in blissful dreams.

He threw the flowers aside, and, crouching down in the loose earth he had thrown up, stared and stared down on her, holding a solemn and silent wake.

Thoughts chased each other through his brain in a confused whirl, until gradually he came to a calmer and more rational frame of mind.

He reflected on how she had gone through life

The Cats' Bridge

despised and guilt-laden, and yet unrepentant, appearing to be satisfied with her past rather than regretting it.

Once, in an hour of dire perplexity, he had asked himself whether it was the dull indifference of the brute or the wiles of a devil that made her will so strong and her conscience so lax, and he had not known what to answer.

To-day, when it was too late, her true nature was revealed to him.

No, she had not been a brute or a devil, but simply a grand and complete human being. One of those perfect, fully developed individuals such as Nature created before a herding social system, with its paralyzing ordinances, bungled her handiwork, when every youthful creature was allowed to bloom unhindered into the fulness of its power, and to remain, in good and in evil, part and parcel of the natural life.

And as he pondered thus, it seemed to him that the mists which obscure the source of human existence from human knowledge had dispersed a little, and that he had been granted a deeper glimpse than most men into the fathomless gulf of the Unknown. What is generally called good and bad drifted about anchorless on the cloudy surface, but below lay dreaming in majestic strength, the Natural.

"And those whom Nature favors," he said aloud

The Cats' Bridge

to himself, "she lets take root in her mysterious depths, so that they spring boldly into the light, with vision undimmed and conscience untrammeled by the befogging illusions of morality and worldly wisdom."

Such a highly favored, completely endowed human creature was this abused and abandoned woman.

"And I for whom she lived and died, have I deserved such a sacrifice?" he meditated further. "Was I worthy of the trust and confidence she so unhesitatingly placed in me?"

With ruthless severity he sat in judgment on himself, and he came out of the ordeal anything but unscathed.

"Of course I belong to the other type," he thought, "to the people who are torn all their life long between right and wrong, and who lose their way in the fog. We regard the tribute Nature demands of us as impurity and vice, and yet the restraint of moral laws often appears to us hollow and far-fetched. Thus we vacillate perpetually between defiance and fear of them. We crave for the good opinion of the world, in which we don't believe, and tremble in face of its condemnation, which we despise and condemn in our hearts. Once I thought it would be an indelible disgrace to bury my father in this unconsecrated ground; now I should be glad if I had done so. Once I tried to forget my bitterness in the ambition of restoring my ancestral inheritance to its pristine glory; now I am delighted at the thought of shaking its dust from my feet. Then I held the Schrandeners to be mere barbarous savages; but to-day I awake to the fact that my own race has made them what they are. *Then* I thought this woman too degraded to take bread from her hand; to-day I am weeping by her grave. All my heart was centred on the extinguished flame of youth's first foolish fancy; I insisted on making the arbitress of my destiny a simpering, prudish minx, for whom I really had long ceased to care—and I repulsed in horror the most splendid and satisfying of natural loves. But truly this natural love represented deadly sin, and tempted me to contaminate my blood.

"Yet when the worst came to the worst, and the life that flowed in my veins had burst from the control of all laws, human and divine, could I not have made atonement by paying the penalty of death?"

And then the question occurred to him, whether the body he talked so lightly of surrendering at his own caprice belonged exclusively to him? What if it were the Fatherland's inviolable possession? Certainly, then, he was not privileged to desecrate it.

"It is well that in an hour of chaos like this,

The Cats' Bridge

when good and evil, right and wrong, honor and dishonor, seem to be swaying about in hopeless confusion, and when the old God of our childhood with his Heaven seems to have vanished away—it is well for swooning men to have one prop left to lean on, one firm rock to cling to, on which even to be shipwrecked were a delightful relief. Such a prop, such a stay, have I in my country."

Thus spake the son of his country's betrayer, and fervently folded his hands.

The moon had shifted its radiance away from the grave, and the dead face it had illumined now lay in shadow. It was scarcely possible to distinguish it from the surrounding earth.

"The time has come," he said, and looked round him.

In the east glimmered the first rosy streak of dawn. A bluish haze suffused the landscape, and above him in the branches began the dreamy twitter of awakening birds. He was in the act of throwing the flowers into the grave, when suddenly he changed his mind, and with a frown cast them aside.

"What need of such fastidious effeminacy?" he asked himself rebukingly. "Dust has no reason to fear meeting dust."

Then he seized the spade, and shutting his eyes, began with zest to shovel the dark earth over the beloved body. A quarter of an hour later the grave was full. He laid the turf carefully in its original place, and took care to remove the remnants of superfluous soil and scattered flowers, so that when the sun rose no one could have found the place where Regina slept forever.

As he searched for a stone to commemorate the sacred spot, his eyes fell on the head of the ruined statue, which smiled at him in stony vacancy. He lifted it, and planted it in the turf.

"Diana, the chaste," he murmured, "shall serve her as a tombstone. The sister by whom she will keep eternal watch is not unworthy of her."

And again he flung himself on the grass and became lost in meditation. On the stroke of six he rose, and made preparations to depart.

"They will be fools indeed," he muttered to himself, "if they don't make an end of me to-day."

He filled his pistols with new cartridges, and sharpened his sabre, for he was determined his life should be dearly purchased.

But when he crossed the drawbridge to the village, he was greeted by familiar and friendly faces. They belonged to Heide's sons, who were making their way to the Schranden military station. They pressed round him and offered him their hands.

"We are come," said Karl Engelbert, "to put ourselves under your command, for we wish to make amends for our conduct to you in the past."

The Cats' Bridge

"I thank you with my whole heart," he replied. "All is forgiven and forgotten."

Then he walked up to Schranden's gallant troopers, who, pale and with chattering teeth, cowered near the church door, like criminals awaiting execution.

His comrades pointed out to each other in dismay the blood-stains on his clothes, but not one dared ask him to explain how they came there.

"Bring out the prisoner, and get a wagon for him," he ordered. Felix Merckel was led out, but Boleslav did not deign to give him a glance.

When farewells had been said, and all was in readiness for the march, the old pastor made his way through the crowd. His face was haggard and his hands shook.

He hastened to Boleslav's side and whispered in his ear: "I hear that Regina met her death last night—I am willing to give her Christian burial."

"Many thanks, your reverence," answered Boleslav, "but I have already buried her with Pagan rites," and he turned away.

A Schrandener, who, to ingratiate himself, had probably spent part of the night in capturing Boleslav's horse, now came forward holding it, with a servile grin.

He swung into the saddle, and his sabre flew out of the scabbard. His voice rang out clear and threatening above the heads of the crowd as he gave the word of command.

"Left! Quick march! Right, left, right!"

The village was soon behind them; the woods loomed nearer.

He did not look back.

.   .   .   .   .   .

Of the subsequent career of Boleslav von Schranden, very little is known. It was considered inadvisable by the military authorities to gazette him again to his old regiment, owing to the mutiny that had taken place under his command.

While the East Prussian Reserve remained behind in the ancient provinces, he obtained the much-coveted permission to go direct to the seat of war.

It is supposed that he fell at Ligny.